Shane forced himself to remain coolly cordial.

Tina Henderson was probably just passing through and hadn't been able to resist the temptation to show the locals how well she was doing.

Meeting her eyes, he knew she saw the suspicion in him. For a taut second, they engaged in a visual duel.

And suddenly Shane was reminded of the past, when she'd looked at him with that same defiance, a slight smile at the corners of her mouth, as if daring him....

He had dared.

He'd kissed that mouth.

He'd tasted the honey.

And he'd never forgotten the feel of those soft, pouty lips under his. She'd resisted at first, then her mouth had trembled...and parted...and responded...just for an instant....

Dear Reader,

Welcome to Silhouette Special Edition...welcome to romance.

That telltale sign of falling leaves signals that autumn has arrived and so have heartwarming books to take you into the season.

Two exciting series from veteran authors continue in the month of September. Christine Rimmer's THE JONES GANG returns with *A Home for the Hunter*. And the Rogue River is once again the exciting setting for Laurie Paige's WILD RIVER series in *A River To Cross*.

This month, our THAT SPECIAL WOMAN! is Anna Louise Perkins, a courageous woman who rises to the challenge of bringing love and happiness to the man of her dreams. You'll meet her in award-winning author Sherryl Woods's *The Parson's Waiting*.

Also in September, don't miss *Rancher's Heaven* from Robin Elliott, *Miracle Child* by Kayla Daniels and *Family Connections*, a debut book in Silhouette Special Edition by author Judith Yates.

I hope you enjoy this book, and all of the stories to come!

Sincerely,

Tara Gavin
Senior Editor

Please address questions and book requests to:
Silhouette Reader Service
U.S.: 3010 Walden Ave., P.O. Box 1325, Buffalo, NY 14269
Canadian: P.O. Box 609, Fort Erie, Ont. L2A 5X3

LAURIE PAIGE
A RIVER TO CROSS

Silhouette®

SPECIAL EDITION®

Published by Silhouette Books
America's Publisher of Contemporary Romance

SILHOUETTE BOOKS

ISBN 0-373-09910-X

A RIVER TO CROSS

LAURIE PAIGE

writes: "Sometimes an idea catches the imagination and won't let go. That happened eight years ago when I read about a pair of eagles in a nature magazine. I knew it right then that I'd write the 'eagle' story someday. Each time I'd come up with a hero and heroine, I'd wonder, 'Is this the eagle story?' It wasn't until I visited the Rogue River that it all came together—the eagle theme, the story ideas (like a lightning storm my husband and I witnessed there, several stories hit me at once) and the characters. Every part of the river was grist for a story—ranches, logging operations, pear orchards, resorts, towns and fishing villages. It was going to take more than one book to tell them all. And so the Wild River series began...."

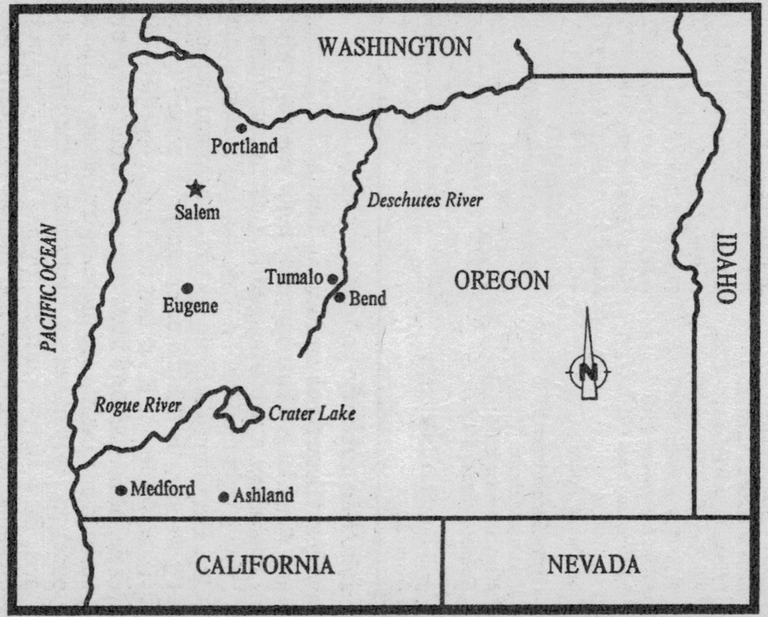

WASHINGTON
Portland
Salem
Deschutes River
PACIFIC OCEAN
Tumalo
Bend
Eugene
OREGON
IDAHO
N
Rogue River
Crater Lake
Medford
Ashland
CALIFORNIA
NEVADA

Chapter One

"If you'll sign here...." The lawyer slid a sheet of paper and a pen across the polished surface of the desk. "It basically says you picked up the key from us."

Tina Henderson read the form over carefully. She'd learned long ago not to take things—or people—at face value. When she finished, she wrote her name, Bettina J. Henderson, at the bottom, laid the pen on the desk and picked up the key.

Her heart suddenly kicked into overdrive, beating so hard it nearly shook her whole body. Until that moment, she'd thought she was confident about returning to the Rogue Valley area of southern Oregon. She wasn't. Doubts crowded in and she felt...scared.

She stared at the key. Would it open the door to a new life for her? Or would it lead to new hurt in the town that had rejected her and her mother so long ago?

"You'll join me and my wife for lunch, won't you?" Jack Norton asked. "Adrianna would never forgive me if I let a famous international TV reporter get away without her getting a chance to ask you all about it."

Tina forced her gaze from the key, which felt hot in her hand, and nodded at the attorney. He was in his early thirties. His manner was brisk and his smile generous. He'd been a great help, handling the details of the inheritance during the past months.

Tina Henderson, Heiress! That should make the headlines of the *Riverton Daily News*.

"Good," he said. "I made reservations at the ski lodge. It's a little out of your way, but I thought you might enjoy seeing the countryside. Then I can drop you off—"

"Thanks, but I have a car." She smiled in satisfaction. Having her own transportation was important. "I'll follow you."

She placed the house key in her purse, then slipped her arms into her warm coat when Jack held it for her. In the outer room she said goodbye to the secretary, who had called her many times at the office in Rome during the months it had taken to settle the estate of Anne Snyder, her godmother.

Outside, she unlocked the door of the shiny blue station wagon she'd bought shortly after returning to the States. Its four-wheel drive would make it easier to get out and about in the mountainous country.

March 28, she thought, turning on the wipers to clear the windshield of the snow that had been falling steadily since she'd arrived. What had happened to spring?

Some welcome home.

Again her heart went into a flurry of beats. She clenched the steering wheel, frightened by things she couldn't put a name to.

Quickly, she brought herself under control. She was twenty-nine years old, for heaven's sake, not eighteen. No one could scare her into leaving the way Shane Macklin had long ago.

She sighed, then smiled ruefully. The Macklins were a law unto themselves. They ruled the town and the county. Shane was the sheriff now. He could run things with the sanctity of the law behind him.

He'd better not tell her to get out of town this time. She knew her rights. She'd tell him where to get off. She laughed at her bravado and ignored the sinking feeling in her middle.

The attorney pulled out of the parking lot. She put the car into gear and followed him. Out on the interstate, she stayed several car lengths behind his black sedan. Their sedate pace gave her an opportunity to study the country around her.

The land was ruggedly beautiful. Medford was only 1300 feet above sea level. At 7533, Mount Ashland, thirty miles distant, was the highest point west of the Cascades. Ski trails meandered through the fir and pine forests on the high slopes. Ironically, she'd learned to ski in France, not Oregon.

It had been a long time since she'd been back to the town—eleven years, to be exact—and twenty years since she'd actually lived there. Without the inheritance, would she have returned?

No. She answered the question truthfully in her own mind. The memories of her visits and of the year she and her mother had lived there after her grandfather's death still hurt.

Lorrie's love child.

She'd overheard her grandmother and grandfather talking about her and her mother more than once. They'd talked in hushed, bitter tones about her father, wondering who he was. She herself had wanted to know the identity of the man who'd been her biological father, but her mother had refused to talk about the past.

Tina sighed. She, too, would put the past behind her. Her grandparents had died long ago. Her mother, who'd once left town in disgrace, had married a wonderful man, a college philosophy teacher who'd adopted Tina and treated her as his own.

At the present, she had a job to do—write a book, based on her coverage of events for CNN, on the effects of war on women and children. She had many chilling, unhappy stories to tell. Maybe the world would wake up before it was too late.

A sheriff's car passed her. Her breath caught in her throat. She glimpsed the driver. It wasn't Shane Macklin.

She relaxed her grip on the steering wheel and pulled the cold air into her lungs. She'd have to face him sometime. She knew that. She just wasn't quite ready to do so on her first day back.

The parking lot at the ski resort was pretty full for a Monday in March. People from the valley up for a day of skiing, Shane Macklin decided, pulling into an empty slot. When he stepped out of the warm patrol truck, the wind hit him full in the face, blowing fiercely down the mountain, bringing more snow.

Just what they needed, he thought with a frown of worry and irritation. There would be a dozen accidents on the county roads and main highway before midnight. He'd already ordered a full crew out on extra duty. That would blow the budget even more.

So what else was new?

The winter had been unusual, with hardly a day without fresh snow falling, even in the valley, which was supposed to have mild winters. Mild, ha! So far, it had been colder than a witch's nose in the Klondike. He smiled as he used his family's version of the saying. His mother had been stern about vulgarisms.

He settled his hat more firmly on his head and leaned into the wind. He had a luncheon meeting with the ski-resort owner about some break-ins on the property. They suspected some squatters on public land. He'd probably have to run them off.

The thought of telling people to leave made him uncomfortable. Years ago, he'd done that to someone. He recalled the unreadable emotion that had flitted through her eyes. Then she'd smiled at him. "Make me," she'd challenged.

At the time, he'd been furious. Looking back, he felt other things. Regret, for one. Over the years, he'd tried to figure that out. After all, he'd been acting in the best interests of his family. He'd had to do something about her.

But those eyes…gray and stormy like clouds. She'd been defiant, foolhardy, as she faced him. And valiant. Even now, he felt a niggling admiration for her spunk.

He shook his head. He'd used the oldest, low-downest trick a man could use on a woman—the threat of physical harm.

The kiss, meant to punish and frighten, had backfired. He'd never forgotten it. He didn't know if it had been the rage or her, but no other kiss had ever stirred him like that one.

He grimaced in disgust. His action had been that of a bully, and she'd repaid him in kind by biting him. He still carried the scars of that ill-advised episode. Anyway, the kiss had worked. She'd left town and hadn't been seen in those parts again. He had no reason to feel guilty about that little gold digger.

Enough of the past. He had other problems. The hassles never let up, it seemed. Maybe he was just getting old. He'd be thirty-six on his next birthday. If a male's life expectancy was seventy-two, he'd have lived half of his at that point.

Now *that* was a depressing thought. He grinned at his own morbid thinking.

After stamping the snow from his boots, he entered the lodge and went upstairs to the restaurant. He paused on the threshold of the attractive room.

The view from the plate-glass windows was magnificent—mountains and conifers, creeks and boulders, all covered over with ice and snow... a fairyland to behold. He liked nothing better than strapping on skis and heading out cross-country over the frozen meadows and streams.

The grandeur. The quiet. The solitude.

God, he missed the solitude. Not much of that in his life anymore. He wondered when things had gotten so complicated.

Since his brother's marriage, for one. And since his brother's separation from his wife, for another. Maybe he'd better try and talk some sense into the two of them. Again.

"Hey, Shane, over here." The voice of his friend, Rafe Barrett, broke into his thoughts.

He hung his coat and hat on a hook and hurried to the table. "Sorry to be late. Another wreck on the interstate." He chose a seat giving him a direct view of the room and its occupants rather than the scene outside.

"You'd think people would slow down a tad in a blizzard," Rafe said, shaking his head at the foibles of mankind.

"But they don't," Shane finished.

"Well, I hate to bring more bad news, but we had another case of vandalism over the weekend."

"Windows?"

"Yes. In the cabins this time. Two windows in adjacent A-frames. It's strange. My security chief couldn't detect any attempt at a break-in. In one cabin, the door could have easily been opened from the broken window."

"What's the time frame?"

"Broad daylight. The couples renting the cabins returned from the ski slopes by four in the afternoon in each case."

Shane got out his notebook and wrote down the date and location. "Okay, give me the names of everyone involved," he told his friend. "How much damage was there?"

"Two windows. Less than a hundred dollars."

Shane frowned. This was the third window-breaking case in two weeks, all with no entry. Definitely a pattern there.

When the information was recorded, Rafe signaled the waitress. "I ordered lunch for us. My treat," he said.

"I don't know. That might be construed as bribing an officer of the law."

"That would be the day," Rafe scoffed. "Your integrity is matched only by your stubbornness."

Shane ignored the backhanded compliment. "So what other items are on your agenda?"

They discussed the problems of the resort in particular and county politics in general while waiting for their meal.

A couple arrived for a late lunch. Shane automatically looked them over.

He recognized Jack Norton, a lawyer out of Medford. The man's companion wasn't his wife, though. This woman had dark hair, so dark Shane couldn't decide if it was brown or black. It was thick, almost straight, then curled under at her shoulders.

A client, he deduced.

She had her back to him while Jack helped her out of her coat. The lawyer hung the garment on the hook next to the one Shane had used. The sleeve of her coat—an expensive-looking fleece—brushed intimately against the black leather of his jacket.

He felt an instinctive tightening in his gut as she turned toward him. Time crawled in slow motion while he waited to see her face, but he already knew who she was.

When she looked directly at him, his lungs quit working. Out of the jumbled thoughts that buzzed through his mind like a planing saw in a logging mill, he realized one thing—he'd never forgotten those eyes. They were the color of storm clouds.

For a second, Tina was overcome by an awful need to run...just run, anywhere, away from Shane Macklin and the cutting stare he bestowed on her. It didn't take a great intellect to know that he was surprised to see her, nor to deduce his next reaction, which was one of pure rage. A shiver of fear poured over her.

She nodded her head ever so slightly and gave him a deliberately bland smile. She'd die before she let him see he still had the ability to unnerve her with that icy glare from his cold blue eyes. He gave her a caustic once-over. She held the smile with an effort.

While her host hung up his heavy coat, she gazed defi-
antly at her former nemesis.

Shane Macklin was a couple of inches over six feet, almost a foot taller than her five feet three inches. His hair
was a thick shock of tawny blond. It still tumbled over his
forehead in a manner that made women want to smooth it
into place.

His eyebrows and lashes were dark, an attractive contrast to his blue eyes. The hard angularity of his face
seemed even more formidable now than it had years ago
when she'd last seen him... when he'd accused her of being a fortune hunter and told her to stay away from his
brother. His brother, Ty, had been twenty-one at the time,
hardly a babe in swaddling clothes.

Shane, she remembered, had been twenty-four. The wise
older sibling, he'd been determined to protect his baby
brother from the clutches of an eighteen-year-old vamp.

She noticed he looked as lean as a timber wolf in his
lawman's uniform. And about as predictable.

A hand on her arm startled her.

"Our table is ready," Jack Norton said, giving her a
curious glance before guiding her across the room.

If she were going to live here, she would have to do better, she thought, chiding herself for her silly reaction. She
couldn't let a caustic stare upset her. The Mighty Macklin
would just have to get used to seeing her around. She lifted
her chin to a stubborn angle and took her place at the table with Jack.

"Adrianna will be late," he said with a husband's
knowledge of his mate. "Why don't we order a drink while
we wait?"

Tina murmured agreement. "I'll have a glass of white
wine and a cup of coffee, unleaded," she told the waitress.

After Jack gave his order and the woman left, Tina re-
alized she could see Shane every time she glanced at Jack.
She wished she'd chosen the chair taken by the attorney.
That way she'd have had her back to Shane.

"Something bothering you?" Jack asked.

"Not at all." She ignored the withering gaze across the
way and turned her head to stare out the window.

Jack twisted around, saw the two men at the other table
and waved. The four of them were practically the only ones
left in the posh restaurant, besides the waitress and bus-
boy. There were a lot of noisy skiers out on the slopes,
however, zipping through the fresh snow and enjoying
themselves. Tina tried to remember the last time she'd been
happy and carefree like that....

"That's the county sheriff," Jack told her when he
turned around. "Shane Macklin. The other one is Rafe
Barrett, the owner of the resort. He recently got married."

Her heart lurched, then steadied. "Shane?"

"No, Barrett." Jack perused her face curiously. "You
know Macklin?"

She nodded, feeling the heat seep into her face. She
hoped she hadn't made an utter fool of herself, jumping to
conclusions that way. Not that it mattered to her if he was
married.

"I had the impression you'd never lived in the area."

"I did when I was nine. My mother and I came here after my grandfather died in an accident. My grandmother
was ill and passed away a few months later. And then there
was the summer I stayed with Anne. I was eighteen. She
helped me get a scholarship to the state university."

Actually, Tina suspected Anne of providing the money,
but the woman had never admitted it. Until that summer,
Tina hadn't even realized she had a godmother. Her

mother had handed her a letter from a Miss Snyder one day and told her to do what she wanted.

The letter had been an invitation to spend the summer as a paid companion to an elderly lady. The lady had been Anne, her godmother, a woman of immense wisdom. They'd become friends.

A mist blurred the menu for a second before Tina blinked it away. Without Anne's encouraging presence, she didn't know whether she could stay in the town. While her godmother hadn't stipulated that she live there, she had asked Tina to keep the house for one year before deciding to sell it.

So here she was, committed to living in the community for a year, by her own decision, while she wrote her great exposé on the evils of war. And of men, she tacked on, giving Shane Macklin a look in kind when he continued to watch her as if she were a suspect at a crime scene. Maybe he thought she was planning a robbery.

A giggle behind her stopped the visual clash. A pretty, rather breathless woman stopped at the table.

"Hello, you must be Tina Henderson. I'm Adrianna. I suppose Jack told you I'd be late." She laughed again, a sound so jolly that Tina had to smile.

"He did mention it." Tina shook hands with the other woman. Adrianna was in her late twenties and had the rushed air of a busy mother who typically ran an hour behind schedule.

"The baby-sitter was late," Adrianna explained. She gave her husband a kiss, then plopped into the chair with a distracted air, removing her knit hat, shrugging her coat over the back of the chair, finding a place for her purse and generally creating an amusing chaos for several minutes.

Finally her order was given and she settled back with a sigh. "Ah, it feels good to slip those shoes off. I can't stand heels, can you?'' she asked Tina, as if they were already old friends.

"No. I rarely wear them."

"Wise thinking. I'm going to stick to flats for the rest of the winter. I nearly fell in the parking lot. There was only one spot left and it was icy. Tell me how you got to be a hardened TV reporter at your delicate age."

Tina instinctively liked the woman. Dashing from one subject to another without a pause, Adrianna was without subterfuge. A person didn't have to wonder what she thought or meant, she'd tell you flat out. Tina admired that quality.

"I went to work as a researcher for a wire service right after college. They sent me to Rome when they realized I was pretty good in Italian. Finally, I was allowed to write some stories—after I threatened the boss time and again with bodily harm."

The Nortons laughed appreciatively at her droll account of some of her escapades. Tina had once been captured by a jealous husband who wanted her to take messages to his estranged wife. Another time it had been more serious. A terrorist had refused to speak to anyone but her after reading her article on the making of a radical. That had catapulted her into television.

The fame had led to an international career. There had even been a TV miniseries about the event, with a famous actress playing her role. She wondered if the local people had seen it. Her glance strayed to the nearby table. She looked away when Shane's gaze shifted to her again.

"So it was easy," she said with a laugh and a shrug as her hostess exclaimed in horror.

By the time they finished the meal, Tina was relaxed. Two glasses of wine and some friendly companions had gone far in easing her nerves...added to the fact that Shane had moved his chair so that their eyes didn't meet every time they looked up. And the fact that he had deliberately avoided glancing her way after those first jolting moments of recognition.

Over coffee and dessert, she, Adrianna and Jack talked about her inheritance.

"Are you going to rent out the house?" Adrianna asked. "I know a couple who are looking for a place."

"No, I'm going to live there, at least for a while."

"How long?"

"Adrianna," Jack warned in a tone that said she was encroaching on other people's business.

"That's okay," Tina interjected. "For a year," she said. A tremor ran along her nerves. She felt committed, she realized.

"Oh, good. Do you play bridge? A group of us meet every two weeks, taking turns at each other's houses. We could use another warm body." Adrianna laughed merrily. "Don't worry about your mind. We're all atrocious players."

"That's because they gossip the whole time," Jack put in.

"Well ... maybe," Tina hedged, not sure about plunging into the social stream.

"Oh, do. We'd love to have you," Adrianna told her, ignoring her husband's teasing.

Tina felt herself warming to the woman's natural friendliness. It felt nice to be wanted. Her grandparents had resented her. Her mother had loved her, of course, but even as a child, she knew she'd been a "mistake."

Later, Anne Snyder had made her feel welcome, as if she'd come home...until Shane Macklin had let her know exactly where she stood in his estimation.

"When I get the house in order," she said.

"It's fine," Jack assured her. "The roof has been replaced, and everything has been checked and is in good shape."

Tina wanted very much to go to the house and explore it from top to bottom. Her personal things had arrived a month ago. She had given up the lease on her flat and shipped everything from Italy at that time, traveling with only one suitcase while she visited her parents and half sister in Portland.

Now it was on to her new career....

Shane pushed his chair away from the table. "Well, it's back into the cold, cruel world for me, although I'd like to sit here and watch the snow for the rest of the day."

"Don't work too hard," Rafe advised, not at all sympathetic. He stood when Shane did and glanced at his watch. "Speaking of work, I have an appointment in exactly one minute."

"I'll say hello to Jack on my way out," Shane said. He waved goodbye to his host, then ambled over to the threesome at the nearby table. It was mere curiosity, but he wanted to know what she was doing back in town, looking like a million dollars and more beautiful than she'd been ten . . . no, eleven years ago.

She wore blue slacks and a sweater of dark gold. Over the sweater she wore a vest of gold, black and deep blue, sort of an Indian design. Her eyes, when she glanced at him, looked more blue than gray, he noted. It was startling. As if she were someone he didn't know.

Except he did know her. Or her kind. After his mother died, his father had gotten caught by a fortune hunter. It had cost the family a lot of money to get rid of her. His father's health had deteriorated rapidly during the nasty divorce and he'd died of a heart attack shortly after that.

The following summer a sexy eighteen-year-old had come to town and nearly caught his brother in the same trap. Luckily, he'd put a stop to that little scheme. He looked over the expensive outfit, the trim black boots hugging her feet, the gold watch on her wrist, and wondered who'd paid for them.

"Hello, Jack, Adrianna," he said. No trace of the strange tumult he felt inside sounded in his voice. As sheriff, he couldn't allow personal feelings to interfere with his duty.

"Hi, Shane," Adrianna said, rushing into conversation in her usual friendly, energetic way. "Guess who this is?" She pointed at Tina as if she were a prize out of a Cracker Jack box.

"Tina Henderson," he said.

Adrianna made a moue of disappointment that lasted about a half a second, then she grinned. "Right. International reporter and celebrity," she added, to make sure he understood the importance of their luncheon guest.

He swung his gaze to the woman who'd haunted his dreams for months after she'd left town all those years ago. She was quietly composed, not even the flicker of an eyelash giving away her inner thoughts or feelings at seeing him again.

"Hardly that," she said, correcting Adrianna's ecstatic introduction.

"More," Shane contradicted. "The rising star of nighttime broadcasting, according to the latest edition of *People* magazine."

He suppressed the questions that rose to mind and forced himself to remain coolly cordial. She was probably passing through the area and hadn't been able to resist the temptation to drop in and show the locals how well she was doing.

Meeting her eyes, he realized she recognized the under-current of suspicion in him. For a taut second, they engaged in a visual duel, and he was reminded of the past, when she'd looked at him with the same insouciant defiance, a slight smile at the corners of her mouth as if daring him....

He had dared once. He'd kissed that mouth. He'd tasted the honey. And he'd never forgotten the feel of those soft, pouty lips under his. She'd resisted at first, then her mouth had trembled ... and parted ... and responded, just for an instant. Then she'd bitten the devil out of him!

A stirring in his body warned him of the dangers of the memories. One thing he didn't need at the present was another problem to contend with. His duties as sheriff, plus those to his family, gave him enough headaches. He didn't need more.

He'd find out what the hell she was doing here ... and how soon she planned to leave.

A slight frown appeared on Adrianna's face. The attorney's wife sensed the hostility between them, he realized. He forced the anger into abeyance.

"What brings you to these parts?" he asked. He glanced out the window as a group of skiers paused below, their laughter pealing out above the sound of the wind. "Are you on vacation or just passing through?"

"Neither," she answered calmly.

That didn't make any sense. The anger stirred again. She was being deliberately evasive. "So why are you in town?" He sounded sharper than he'd meant to, which earned him surprised glances from Jack and Adrianna. He sighed internally. This was going to be a hard day in more ways than a mere snowstorm could account for.

"Is this an official inquiry?" his antagonist countered.

He frowned in frustration. Antagonist? Hardly. When he'd been twenty-four, she'd driven him right over the edge with the cool challenge in those stormy eyes and the half smile that had lingered on her lips. At thirty-five, he had more control.

Against his will, his gaze flicked to her mouth.

Her lips, as delectable as cream puffs, were outlined in a darker shade of the lipstick she wore. With total recall, he remembered how incredibly soft those lips could be.

His sense of self-preservation had already burned to a crisp in the heat of that kiss when the first punishing touch abruptly changed to something else...something that had been beyond anything he'd ever felt before with a woman.

Remembering that day, he felt his anger flare anew. The spiteful little vixen had bitten him! Otherwise—he drew a deep breath and admitted what he'd known unconsciously for years—otherwise, they would have made love, there by the river....

He realized the Nortons were giving him odd looks. It wasn't fair to involve them in the ancient quarrel. She'd left town the day after that kiss and hadn't returned. Until now.

"No, not official," he finally answered. "Just neighborly interest. It isn't often someone famous drops in."

"I'll be living here for a while," she said softly.

He felt the jolt of disbelief clear down to his boots. "How long?" he demanded, a thousand complications coming to mind—Ty and his problems with his wife; Jonathan, their four-year-old son; and now...this.

"A year. Maybe more."

Shane smiled in relief. "You'll never last that long in a backwater like Riverton," he predicted.

Her smile faltered, then returned. "You're so sure," she murmured. Her lashes dropped lower over her eyes. "The Mighty Macklin has spoken. Who dares dispute him?"

He felt the heat creep into his ears. Damn, but she made him feel like a crass youth.

"Riverton was once my home," she reminded him. She spoke softly. "I was happy here as a child...."

She let the thought trail away, and for a second she looked wistful. He hardened himself to her allure.

"I loved roaming the woods or standing on a mountain with a wide-open vista, feeling that the world was mine to do with as I pleased," she continued.

He'd felt that way once. Long ago. Before a gold digger had snared his father and another one had tried to nab his brother. He wouldn't be fooled by her "poor, world-weary me" act.

"Well, then, welcome back," he said, resisting the urge to tell her to stay away from his family. He'd keep an eye on her personally and see that she didn't upset the status quo.

"Thanks."

"Tina," Adrianna put in, ending the unspoken battle between the other two, "you must come to the April Fool's Ball Friday night. Do you think we can get an extra ticket?" she asked her husband, clearly expecting him to accomplish this miracle.

He looked doubtful. "Well, I'll ask—"

"I have an extra ticket," Shane said. "If you want to go." It looked like his duties would start immediately.

"No, thanks, I'll be busy."

"Oh, you must," Adrianna insisted. "It will be the perfect time to meet everyone in the county. It's held here at the resort, and the proceeds go to the library fund. We'll pick you up."

"I can do that," he volunteered. "Where are you staying?"

She hesitated, as if she didn't want him to know.

Adrianna had no such qualms. "At the Snyder place. That would be perfect, since it's just across the river from your house."

He blinked in surprise, expecting she'd be staying at one of the motels along the interstate or perhaps at the resort. "The Snyder place," he repeated. "No one has lived there since Anne died last year."

"Tina inher—"

"We need to go, Adrianna," Jack interrupted firmly.

Shane put two and two together. "You inherited it? The Snyder place?"

"Yes." She was as cool as buttermilk.

"Isn't it super?" Adrianna enthused.

"Yeah," he agreed, all his suspicions confirmed. "Just dandy."

Chapter Two

Tina almost expected Shane to be waiting for her when she left the resort and pulled onto the county road. She kept looking in her rearview mirror for a flashing blue light.

She was being silly. No one had any reason to pull her over. No one could order her to leave the country—as one head of state had done when she'd looked too closely into his illegal activities, or as Shane had done when she'd gotten too close to his family.

When she came upon a speed limit sign, she quickly checked to make sure she was driving slowly enough, then laughed at herself. She'd probably imagined all the tension between her and the lawman back at the restaurant. There was no reason for it.

Putting it out of her mind, she drove through Riverton to the edge of town. At the end of a quiet street stood the neat brick house that had belonged to Anne Snyder and was now hers.

She stopped in the driveway. Again she felt a sense of homecoming, as if Anne's gentle spirit were there to welcome her. Anne, who had been wise and comforting, who had urged her to forgive weakness in others and who had made her see her own strengths.

"I'll miss you," she said aloud.

Her breath became frosted in the air, and she shivered in her new coat, a Christmas present from her family. Suitcase in hand, she walked up the snow-covered sidewalk to the front door. The lock opened smoothly. She stepped inside.

The house was warm. A lamp was on in the living room. Wood and kindling were laid in the grate, ready for a match to be put to them. The smell of cooking food filled the air.

Tina left her suitcase in the hall and went into the kitchen. A note from Anne's housekeeper, Mrs. Perkins, was stuck on the refrigerator with a souvenir map-of-Oregon magnet. The brief letter welcomed her, told her dinner was in the oven and said the housekeeper would be over the next morning.

Tina opened the oven door and sniffed the delectable aroma of a casserole. She found the refrigerator stocked with milk, orange juice and a large bowl of salad greens. Homemade rolls were there, too, ready to be popped into the oven when she wanted them.

A nostalgic yearning overcame her, as it had those first days in Rome when she'd felt so far from everything dear and familiar.

Homesickness was a strange malady for someone who'd never felt she truly belonged anywhere, she mused. She wondered why it seemed important that she find roots. No answer came to her.

Well, there were things to be done. She couldn't stand around all day thinking about it.

Grabbing her suitcase, she checked out the four rooms to the left of the wide entrance hall. One was a master suite, complete with private bath and a sitting room. Anne had used the sitting room as her office. Tina touched the desk and felt comforted.

You're strong, she could almost hear Anne say. *What you make of your life is up to you. Other people's weaknesses and mistakes don't have to be yours. Overcome them.*

But sometimes that's awfully hard, she wanted to tell her mentor. Sometimes strength felt like loneliness.

She found boxes of her personal belongings stored in the closet. Leaving her suitcase in the master bedroom, she hung her coat on the hall highboy, then peeked into the other two rooms.

One was a comfortable bedroom with its own sitting area complete with coffee table and wicker sofa. The bed was covered with a white chenille spread. The room had been her retreat on that summer visit so many years ago.

The other room was a *solarium,* as Anne had called it. A sun room. The Mexican tiles soaked up the sun's warmth—when the sun made an appearance—and stayed warm far into the winter night.

For several minutes, she watched the snowflakes fall at a slant, driven by the wind from the north. When the flurry let up somewhat, she could see the river, a steel gray ribbon running along the southern edge of the town and the property.

Across the river, she could barely make out the house that sat on a knoll amidst the pine trees, lording it over the extensive sorting and storage barns of the orchards.

The Macklin home . . . where she hadn't been welcome.

Restless, she returned to the bedroom and worked for a couple of hours arranging her clothing. When she found her ski parka and warm ski hat, she pulled them on and headed out for a walk.

In a few minutes she was at the town square. It didn't take long to get there. Riverton was tiny, not exactly a one-horse town, but there was one grocery store, one drug-store-gift shop, one hardware store, one farm-supply business and so forth.

Surprisingly, there were two cafés, a tea shop and a posh restaurant. The old yarn store had been enlarged and was a sort of general arts-and-crafts house now. A sign in the window indicated basket weaving classes were beginning next week.

She walked the three main blocks and turned into the park that lined the river all the way back to her new home.

The Macklins had owned the property on both sides of the river. Apparently the town had bought the land to preserve it in its natural state. On the other side of the river, pear orchards stood in dark rows against the snow.

There among the fruit-laden trees of summer was where Shane had confronted her, telling her to leave his brother alone. She'd told him he couldn't tell her what to do. Then she'd challenged him. "Make me," she'd said, a smile of defiance firmly in place.

He had. The kiss had caused her to leave town a week before she'd planned to return home to prepare for col-lege. It had melted her resolve to hate him.

Remembering, she felt anger flare anew at her wild, un-controllable response to him. In self-defense, she'd bitten him, or else they would have made love, there by the river....

The wind hit her all at once, and she realized she was cold. Turning back to town, she went into the tea shop. The mouth-watering scent of cinnamon tickled her taste-buds.

The woman behind the counter removed a tray of hot raisin buns from an oven. "You're just in time," she called out, smiling and indicating the tray.

"I'll take one," Tina decided, "and a cup of tea."

"What kind?"

There were many varieties to choose from, and gourmet coffee as well, which was ground only as it was needed. Tina made a selection from among the herb teas and sat at a table near the window so she could watch the snow, which was coming down much harder now.

She hung her hat and parka on a coatrack.

"Snow's getting worse," the woman said, bringing the snack.

"Yes. I may have made a mistake, setting out for a walk in this weather. I forgot to change to snow boots."

"Someone will give you a lift home. Where do you live?"

"At the other end of town. The Snyder place." She introduced herself and in turn found out the woman was the owner of the shop.

"I always wanted to try my hand at business," the woman said, "but my husband was against it. I sat around for a couple of years after he died, went to California for the winter and stayed with my daughter last year. I decided to open this place when I came back. Now I'm too busy to leave."

Tina smiled at the obvious pride the proprietress took in her shop. She stocked tea and coffee from all over the world, plus carried a selection of jams, jellies and candy made by local people.

"I encourage my friends to make things for me to sell," she confided. "It gives them extra money for Christmas and such."

A little women's lib taking place here, Tina thought in approval. Everyone needed a sense of personal worth.

Just as she was feeling comfortable, a large figure appeared at the door. Shane Macklin came in, bringing the cold with him.

Tina hugged herself as the chilled air swished past. The closing of the door stopped the draft.

"I knew you'd be in," the owner said with a satisfied smile.

"Smelled those buns all the way to the interstate." He slapped his black felt hat against his thigh, then hung it on a peg next to Tina's. He did the same with his coat. He'd taken two strides before he noticed who was at the lone occupied table. He stopped abruptly.

"Looks like I'm not the only one with a nose for your cooking, Bess," he drawled.

"This is a new neighbor—"

"I know her," he interrupted.

"Well, have a seat. I'll have your stuff in a minute." Bess bustled about behind the counter.

His eyes questioned Tina as he laid a hand on the chair opposite hers. She nodded, her heart pounding hard as it had earlier when she'd seen him. No need to get nervous, she reminded herself sharply. She was bound to run into him, since he lived in the same community. She just didn't like it.

He pulled out the chair and folded his tall, lean body into it, looking perfectly at home in a tea shop.

Perhaps it was his height that gave him that supreme air of confidence. The world looked up to tall people. Being rather short, she'd always felt at a disadvantage compared to her male colleagues. She'd learned to use her elbows to get to the front for an impromptu interview with some important person.

Now that wouldn't matter anymore, she realized. She had a contract to write a book and a house to do it in. She wouldn't have to compete for her own space ever again.

"Bad weather to be out," Shane commented.

Tina flicked him a glance, then observed Bess as she measured coffee beans and ground them, placing the fresh grounds in a filter atop a large mug. She poured in hot water and brought the mug to the table along with a plate of warm raisin buns. Two, Tina noted.

"Yes," Bess agreed. She turned to Tina. "Say, here's your ride home. The sheriff can drop you off. She walked down," she explained to Shane.

His eyes, as blue as a summer sky, as cold as an icicle, speared hers. When Bess bustled off, pleased with her Good Samaritan effort, he leaned back in the chair and studied Tina casually. "Didn't take you long to look over your inheritance, did it?"

"No. After all, I stayed with Anne when I was here that summer eleven years ago." Tina waited tensely to see what he would say about that past visit.

He watched her, examining each feature of her face until she felt as if he'd branded her. "Do you have to live here a year to keep the place?"

"No, of course not." She lifted her chin. "I chose to stay."

"Why?"

"Why not?"

"Touché," he said softly, surprising her. "No reason, I suppose, but I can't help wondering at your motives. Why would an important person like you stay in a hick town like this?"

Because everyone needs a home, a place to belong. She didn't say it. She'd never expose her heart that much. "The peace and quiet? The warm welcome?" she suggested, tongue in cheek.

He grinned ruefully. "Guess I asked for that one."

She noted the two lines across his forehead and the one between his eyes. He looked like a man with problems. Her natural instinct was to draw him out in sympathy. She suppressed it.

"What about your big television career?"

"I'm on leave for a year."

He mulled this over, but didn't remark on it. He pushed the hot water through the filter, set the device aside and took a sip of coffee. "Ah, that warms the heart," he murmured.

She doubted it could reach his, but she refrained from saying so. They ate in silence. She was aware of him, she realized. Of his lean, masculine power, of the grace in his movements as he lifted his fork, of the craggy planes of his face.

The admission alarmed her. She *had* moved here for peace and quiet after the hectic pace of the past few years, not to finish that... that strange episode of long ago.

After that kiss, he hadn't said a word. Neither had she. They'd stood there by the riverbank, their chests heaving in unison, their eyes shocked and angry at what had happened.

Then he'd turned and left.

She saw him pause now and look at her, a question in his eyes. She realized she'd been staring at his mouth, at two tiny, almost invisible white lines at the base of his lower lip.

He raised a hand and ran a finger over the scars where her teeth had sunk into the flesh. He was probably recalling that it had taken only one kiss to frighten her away before.

"You won't run me off this time," she said. She immediately wished she could recall the words. They sounded juvenile.

"Did I the other time?"

She took a calming breath. "Yes."

"I'm sorry."

Whatever she'd expected from him, it had never been an apology. "For what? You wanted me gone."

"Yes, but..." He thrust his hand through his hair. "I used my strength against you. I've wanted to apologize for that for a long time. Did Anne tell you I came by the next day?"

"Yes."

"You had already left."

"You'd made it plain I'd better get out of town."

"I know. I thought you wanted my brother for the Macklin name and fortune."

She smiled coolly. "I did."

Tina sat in front of the fire in her gown and robe. She held a note from her benefactress, Anne Snyder, in her hand. She'd found it in the middle drawer of the desk. She opened it with shaking hands.

My dear Tina,

By the time you find this, I will be gone. I can truly say I've had a good life—in fact, a joyous one since I

met you. You have no idea how your letters brightened my days. Mrs. Perkins can tell you how often I
sent her to check the mail these past months. Each
word was treasured.

Thank you for accepting the gift of this house. I'd
love to think your family will grow up safe and happy
beneath this roof, but that is an old woman's wish,
and you're to pay no attention to it. Live where your
happiness abides.

From time to time, I have written to you little tid-
bits of my life that may touch yours. You will find the
notes tucked here and there. When you've found them
all, I hope you'll be wise enough to understand and
strong enough to forgive.

It was signed with Anne's familiar signature.

Tina read it through once more. She didn't understand
the cryptic last paragraph, but the rest of the letter was like
Anne, making her feel special and welcome. There were no
ghosts in this house but gentle ones, Tina reflected.

She hoped she'd be as happy as Anne had been in the
sturdy brick house, but she wasn't sure if that was possible, considering her neighbor across the river.

With a sigh, she folded the note and laid it on the lamp
table. She was tired after several hours of unpacking boxes
and finding places for her books on the shelves in the sitting room. She'd also set up her computer and printer.

That done, she'd taken a shower, then eaten the casserole along with the homemade dinner rolls. As long as
she'd been busy, she hadn't had time to think. Idle now,
her mind returned to the tea shop where she and Shane had
talked.

The tension between them had condensed into an almost tangible substance, like a cloud forming on the peak

of a mountain, when she'd admitted she'd wanted Ty for his name and fortune. She'd faced the developing fury in Shane with a fatalistic calm.

"At least you're truthful about it," he'd muttered, his tone low, controlled, but surprised, too.

In long, thoughtful remembrances of that summer during her years abroad, she'd realized it wasn't Tyson Macklin she'd wanted, but the prestige and position that went with the name. She'd wanted to show the town that she could be somebody.

However, from the first time she'd met his older brother, Ty had been safe from any machinations on her part. From that moment all her dreams had been of one man, a man who, with his kiss, had destroyed those young, foolish dreams once and for all.

She'd never forgotten the moment he'd jerked back from her, startled by her defensive attack. The warmth of his blood had mixed with the heat of his kiss on her mouth, while the contempt in his eyes had told her how much he despised her.

How young she'd been, thinking he might love her....

A shaky sigh escaped her. It was annoying that he still had the power to get her emotions in a tangle. She was a mature woman now, not a girl with fantasies dancing in her head.

At the tea shop, she'd managed to laugh and make light of that confrontation so long ago. The mighty Shane Macklin would never know the effort it had taken to do that.

The flames in the grate before her blurred. She blinked rapidly and fought a longing that she couldn't name. She glanced at Anne's note, not sure whether she'd stay the year or not.

One day back, and her resolve was already shaken.

Shane had made sure she knew his younger brother was now a married man and a father. His tone had been fiercely protective when he'd mentioned his nephew. Passing on that news had been his primary reason for joining her, she decided. He'd wanted to make certain she knew his family was still off-limits to her.

For the briefest second, she felt a return of the anguish from that first encounter, when he'd made her feel an outcast, unworthy and unwanted. She pushed the emotion aside impatiently.

When she'd prepared to leave the tea shop, he'd insisted on paying both their tabs, then escorting her to his truck, driving her home through the storm and seeing her safely in the front door.

How gallant, she thought mockingly. He was ever the gentleman…except when he was riled. She wondered how it would be to have someone like him on her side, to be friends rather than enemies.

She didn't need anyone to take up her cause, she reminded herself sharply. While she wasn't an outgoing person who collected people like a dog picked up fleas, she'd always had friends to play with and confide in while growing up.

Of course, there had been the usual mean kid in school who'd taunted her about her lack of a father, but she'd learned to live with that. She no longer cared about the identity of the man who'd abandoned her and her mother so long ago.

When the fire sank into ashes, she went to bed, relatively content. Her first meeting with Shane hadn't been as nerve-racking as she'd thought it might be. On the other hand, it hadn't been as easy as she'd hoped, either.

* * *

The sun on the snow was absolutely breathtaking. Tina sat at the table, sipping a fresh cup of coffee, and admired the scene. The backyard swept down to the river in an unbroken fantasy of pure white. Every shrub and tree wore a fluffy shawl of snow.

She watched a blue jay alight on a twig. Its weight dislodged a chunk of snow. A startled rabbit took off in a mad stampede, probably thinking an owl was about to nab it. She laughed.

The ringing of the doorbell caused her heart to speed up, but the caller was Mrs. Perkins, the housekeeper who had been with Anne for almost twenty years.

"Hello. Come in. Would you like some coffee? I just made a pot," Tina bubbled, glad to see a welcoming face.

"Good morning. I wondered if you'd be up and decided you would. You were an early riser when you visited before," Mrs. Perkins recalled, following her into the kitchen. The woman put her coat and scarf over the back of a chair and sat down.

"I'm so glad to see you." Tina poured coffee into a clean cup, refilled her own and resumed her seat at the table in the breakfast nook of the large, old-fashioned kitchen. "I wanted to thank you for the food you left. Everything was delicious."

"Good." Mrs. Perkins added sugar and milk to her cup. "I wanted to be here in person, but I have a new position now."

"Oh, of course." Tina was relieved. She'd wondered how to tell the housekeeper she couldn't afford to have her every day. She'd been careful with her money and had saved enough to live on for the foreseeable future if she was frugal. Her budget didn't include daily cleaning service.

"The Macklin housekeeper retired last year, and Shane told me to come on over when I needed a new place." Her smile became sad for an instant. "Everyone knew Anne wouldn't last out the year. After I wasn't needed here, I moved over there. That house needed putting in order," she declared on a brighter note.

Tina smiled at the woman's self-satisfied tone. She could imagine that Mrs. Perkins would have things running smoothly in no time.

"A young person like you doesn't need an old biddy like me around, anyway. You probably don't stir up more than a smidgen of dust, little thing like you." The housekeeper gave her a critical once-over, as if she thought Tina's size indicated a lack of proper eating habits.

"I can be pretty messy when I'm working," Tina confessed. "I tend to let the dishes pile up in the sink."

"Hmm, well, I could come over once a week or so."

"That's okay. I'll manage."

"So tell me what you've been doing these past few months. Anne kept me up to date from your letters. She was right proud of you, she was. Said she'd always wanted to go off and see the world herself."

Tina told the friendly housekeeper about the book she was going to work on. They talked for over an hour.

"Lands sakes, I've got to get back," Mrs. Perkins commented, checking the time. "Shane will be home, wanting his lunch before long. Why don't you come join us?"

"Uh, I can't. I still have so much to do."

"You sound like Shane." Mrs. Perkins shook her head, as if despairing over young people and their strange ways. "He works all the time, too."

"Fighting off all the women who throw themselves at him, I'll bet," Tina said dryly.

Mrs. Perkins nodded primly. "There was one woman visiting over at the ski resort who near drove him mad. She called a dozen times a day. He finally had to tell her he wasn't interested, in very plain terms."

A chill crept along Tina's spine. She knew very well just how plainspoken he could be.

"That man never has a minute to himself," the housekeeper lamented. "He's always taking care of some problem in the county or for that brother of his."

"Maybe Shane should let Ty learn to handle his own problems," Tina suggested.

"My feelings exactly. With Ty and his wife separated, it's even worse now than before."

"Ty and his wife are having problems?"

"Yes. Nearly from the moment they married. It's no secret," Mrs. Perkins hastened to add.

The impact of Shane's talk in the restaurant hit Tina. If Ty wasn't happy with his wife, he'd be vulnerable. Shane had been warning her not to interfere between the two. She did a slow burn.

What had she ever done to earn his unjustified mistrust? She'd left when he told her to, hadn't she? She hadn't tried to lure Ty into marriage. In fact, she'd refused the offer when he'd pleaded with her to elope with him. Big Brother didn't know about that, she was willing to bet.

"Shane has all the responsibility of a family with none of the joy," Mrs. Perkins added darkly. She picked up her coffee cup with an indignant gesture. It wasn't hard to discern where her loyalty and sympathy was directed.

"I'm sure if Shane had wanted a family, he could have had one without undue difficulty."

Although, with his overbearing disposition, a woman might think twice about embroiling herself in his life. He'd probably tell her how many times a minute she should breathe.

The older woman sighed worriedly. "After what he went through with his stepmother, I don't think he'll ever marry."

"I didn't know he had a stepmother." Tina pictured his being sent to bed with nothing but bread and water for some minor offense such as laughing in the house.

"He doesn't now, but he used to. She married his poor father less than a year after the first wife died." Mrs. Perkins leaned forward and spoke in a near whisper. "Caught the poor man when he was out of his mind with grief, don't you know?"

"How terrible," Tina commiserated. "How old was Shane?"

"Twenty-three."

"Oh, after he was grown." Her sympathy evaporated.

Mrs. Perkins bobbed her head up and down. "The marriage lasted less than a year, then the new wife took off for New York. Sued for divorce, she did, and tried to get half of everything poor Mr. Macklin owned. It's said she tried to get the son, too, but I don't know about that."

"Shane?" Tina stared at the housekeeper.

"She was a shameless hussy. But even her fancy lawyer knew they couldn't get all she wanted. Shane worked out a settlement, but his father didn't get to enjoy it for long. He dropped dead of a heart attack a month after the divorce. That woman had been a pure torment for him from the day he brought her home."

Mrs. Perkins sat back with a heavy sigh, as if human nature were too much for her. Tina was quiet, absorbing this information and putting it with the rest of what she knew about Shane.

"Ty was at school during all this ruckus," Mrs. Perkins continued, "and Shane had had to fly up there and get him out of some scrape or other a couple of times. Now Ty and his wife are fighting like two cats. I think they both need a good smack, acting like spoiled kids when they have that little boy to raise."

After Mrs. Perkins left, Tina washed her cereal bowl and spoon and started on her tasks once more. The housekeeper had given her several facts to mull over. It sounded as if Shane had gotten the proverbial stepmother from hell.

With his usual skill, he had vanquished the woman just as he had the eighteen-year-old who'd dared invade his turf.

For a moment, Tina regretted that they hadn't met first, before she and Ty had, before a horrible woman had trampled on his grief for his mother, before all the bad things had happened to make him a hard, distrusting man.

Then she mentally gave herself a shake. Whatever Shane Macklin was, he was no concern of hers.

Besides, she had Friday night to worry about. If she didn't hear from him, she'd call and say she couldn't go to the ball. She'd tell him she was coming down with a cold. Yes, that sounded like a wise decision.

With that off her mind, she got on with settling in. The house made her feel welcome in ways she couldn't express. For the first time, she felt she truly belonged.

Chapter Three

Tina picked up the phone. Tomorrow was Friday, the day of the ball, and she had to reach Shane Macklin. She called the number she found in Anne's desktop directory.

"Hello," a woman's voice answered on the first ring.

Expecting Mrs. Perkins to answer at the Macklin residence, Tina hesitated before greeting the unknown female. The telephone banged down in her ear. Startled, Tina hung up.

She checked the number in the phone book. It was correct. Exasperated with her own timidity, she dialed again. This time she was prepared for the impatient voice on the other end of the line.

"May I speak to Shane, please?" she requested. She felt odd, calling to break an engagement when he had another woman in the house. Well, whoever his guest was, Tina had to speak to him.

There was a long pause. Then the woman demanded, "Who's calling?"

Definitely hostile. Tina gave her name.

"Shane's not here."

Tina wondered what he'd done to anger his paramour so early in the day. She thought about leaving a message, but decided the woman probably wouldn't deliver it. She had another idea. "May I speak to Mrs. Perkins?"

"I'll get her."

This was so grudgingly said and the interval before the housekeeper answered was so long that Tina almost decided to hang up and try later.

"Hello, Tina," Mrs. Perkins finally answered in her cheerful tone. "I've made apple turnovers. Would you like to come over?"

"Uh, no, thank you, Mrs. Perkins. I, uh, called to...that is, could you take a message for Shane from me?"

"Of course. That poor boy was called out at four this morning. Bad wreck on the interstate. He hasn't got back yet."

That explained the girlfriend's ire, Tina decided. She didn't like being left alone, nor being disturbed so early. "He was going to stop by for me tomorrow night for the ball—"

"Why, that's wonderful," Mrs. Perkins broke in. "It's about time he started getting out with a pretty girl."

Tina wondered what his houseguest looked like. Probably ravishing. Her voice had been sultry in spite of the acrimonious tone. Some men liked fiery women.

"Actually, I think I'm coming down with a cold and won't be able to go," she said to the housekeeper. "If you'd tell him for me, I'd really appreciate it."

"I'll do that."

Mrs. Perkins sounded so disappointed that Tina felt the heat rise up her neck at the fib. "Thank you."

Before she could say goodbye, Mrs. Perkins inquired about how she was taking care of herself. "Drink plenty of fluids," she cautioned.

"I will," Tina promised. When she finally hung up, she felt limp with relief. That was one thing off her mind ... although she would be sorry not to see Adrianna and Jack.

She made a pot of tea with lots of lemon—following Mrs. Perkins's advice—and turned on the computer. After running some checks to make sure the equipment hadn't been damaged in transit, she started to work.

First she wanted to finish typing in all her notes. By marking key words, she'd be able to get a cross-reference file set up in the computer. That would make the actual writing easier.

At five o'clock, she turned the computer off, stood and stretched wearily. She'd forgotten to go for a walk and get some exercise. It wasn't wise to let herself get lazy.

She looked out the window at the snow-covered landscape and gave a soft exclamation of pleasure. Dusk had painted the shadows on the lawn in shades of lavender. Purple-gray clouds on the horizon were tinged with gold around the edges, while the patches of clear sky were deep indigo.

Between snowy banks, the river flowed like liquid pewter. Glints of gold and lavender danced over its restless surface. She thought of all the land it touched on its way to the ocean and felt somehow linked to the others who lived along its borders.

She drifted out of the sitting room, which was now her office, and into the sun room. From there she could see across to the Macklin house, its brick chimneys jutting from among the pine trees. She noticed smoke coming from one chimney.

A picture came to mind—Shane and his guest curled on a comfortable sofa in front of the fire, enjoying a hot toddy while he told her of his day.

She gripped the windowsill as something hard and achy coursed through her. An unbearable loneliness slowly overtook her normally bright spirit.

The inexorable need of one human for another, she decided, rationalizing her mood. It caused women to accept lovers, to marry under the most appalling conditions of war and danger, to take the risk of having children when the world was falling apart....

She heaved a deep sigh. Enough of that. She'd take a shower, put on warm pajamas and rustle up something for supper.

Going into the master bedroom, she quickly shed her wool slacks and sweater and headed for the bathroom. Fifteen minutes later, she emerged.

She shivered in the chill of the bedroom. Her hair, which she'd blown dry, curled around her bare shoulders. Quickly she pulled on warm lounging pajamas made of cranberry-colored velour. Thick, fuzzy scuffs kept her feet toasty.

Before going into the kitchen, she laid a fire in the living-room grate and turned on the gas jet to get it started. She flicked on the floor lamp by the easy chair, adding a soft glow to the shadowy room. Just as she started out, the doorbell rang.

The two-toned chime pealed through the silent house and died away without an echo. Tina paused, the hair on her neck prickling. The moment seemed portentous.

The chime sounded again.

She chided herself for being silly. Glancing at her casual attire, she decided she was properly covered for answering the door. Probably the paperboy wanting to know if she'd subscribe to the *Daily News*. She'd forgotten to call—

The bell dinged three times in rapid succession. She hurried down the hall. Before opening the door, she peered through the peephole installed in the solid oak.

"Oh," she said. She opened the door.

Shane looked her over, leaving no part unnoticed. She felt heat build inside and sweep outward to every extremity.

"Mrs. Perkins said you were coming down with a cold," he said. "She sent you some onion soup."

Tina saw that he held a large glass jar filled with homemade soup in one hand, a plastic bag was in the other. Before she could say a word, he somehow maneuvered past her and stood in the hall. She closed the door.

He headed for the kitchen as if he lived there, too.

"She needn't have done that," Tina protested, trotting at his heels like a well-trained cocker spaniel.

He opened the plastic bag and removed a loaf of homemade bread and a small plastic jar. "According to Mrs. Perkins, this will knock a cold right out," he told her. "I can vouch for that. It's worked several times for me."

"Really—"

"Go sit in front of the fire. I'll fix a tray."

"Oh, but really—"

"I know where everything is. Unless you've changed things around from where Anne had them."

"Well, no, but—"

"Fine. It'll be ready in ten minutes." He opened a cupboard and removed tea bags from the box.

She stood there, uncertain about allowing this invasion, then left the room in a huff. This was her space. He had no right to barge in and take over. She'd explain that very carefully when he finished his good-neighbor act.

Settled in a large easy chair in front of the fire, she prepared several speeches to tell him exactly what she didn't like about him being in her home.

"Here we go," he said. When he came in, she noted that he'd removed his heavy jacket and hat. He carried a large brass tray that had been hanging on the wall in an attractive grouping. Two quilted place mats were draped over his arm.

He placed the tray on the coffee table, then raised the arm of her chair. Hidden inside was a wooden leaf that came up and over her lap like an airline tray. He spread one of the place mats over it, then put a bowl and a small plate on it.

The vapor of hot onion soup tickled her nose. A stack of toasted bread, golden with melted cheese, tempted her palate.

He took a seat on the sofa. "Ah," he said, like a weary traveler at last arriving home.

She watched in disbelief as he put a place mat on the coffee table and set out another bowl and plate.

"I didn't know you had an invitation to dinner." She cast him a caustic glance to let him know his company wasn't wanted.

"Mrs. Perkins had a meeting tonight. She told me to see that you ate your soup. It seemed easier to eat with you." He bit into a piece of toast.

"What about your guest?"

His eyebrows rose in question.

"When I called earlier, a woman answered the phone."

He frowned, looking definitely irritated. "My sister-in-law, I suppose. She's staying at the house for a while."

Tina took a mouthful of soup and found it delicious. She realized it had been six hours since she'd had a sandwich for lunch. Mulling over his statement, she finished every drop of the soup.

"Don't Ty and his wife live with you?" she asked, picking up a toast wedge and munching on it.

"No." He polished off the last of his supper and stood. "They have their own place." He stacked the dishes on the tray and left the room.

She replaced the chair tray and turned off the gas jet. The logs had caught and now burned cheerily. She returned to the chair and sat with one foot curled under her while she watched the flames.

It seemed strange to eat a meal with the enemy, she mused. Although he was much more domesticated than she'd ever dreamed the Mighty Macklin would be. His presence made her nervous.

When he returned, he again carried the tray. This time there was a ceramic teapot and two cups and saucers on it. He poured the tea and handed her a cup, then took one for himself.

She stared at the pale liquid in the cup. "What is this?" she asked. She detected cinnamon, cloves and lemon. Some kind of liquor, too, she thought.

"Mrs. Perkins's version of a hot toddy. Drink it. It's part of the cold remedy." He gave her a lazy perusal. "You sound better already," he remarked.

She went on the defensive. "I'm not going to the dance," she stated, needing to get her decision out in the open at once.

"Adrianna will be disappointed." His gaze was assessing, as if he evaluated every word she spoke for hidden motives. "She apparently thinks of you as a friend."

He made her feel guilty that she'd even tried to get out of going. "Well, I like her, too, but..."

"But?" he encouraged.

She gave him a level stare. "You hardly had a choice about stopping for me."

"You think Adrianna stampeded me into it?"

Tina nodded.

"I volunteered, remember?" He watched her over the edge of the cup, the rising steam a barrier to his thoughts.

She sipped the aromatic brew. It had a hefty addition of brandy in it, she realized. She drank it more slowly. Her head already felt light.

"Yes, but why?"

He poured another cup of tea for himself and topped her cup. "So I can keep an eye on you."

Anger rampaged through her. Her hand trembled as she brought the cup to her lips, holding it like a shield in front of her face. "Just what do you think I'm going to do?"

He yawned, then rubbed his eyes. She realized he looked tired. "I don't know," he admitted. "I just don't think a sexy woman who happens to be beautiful, rather famous and living alone is a good thing in these parts right now."

"I assure you, I have no designs on the community's virtue," she said hotly. She clinked the cup onto the saucer and plunked both down on the coffee table. Rising, she paced the room in quick, angry strides.

Her nemesis spread his arms over the sofa back and leaned his head into the corner, his narrowed gaze following her every move. "Maybe not, but some of the community might have designs on yours."

If you have any. He didn't say it, but she was sure he was thinking it.

She turned to the fireplace and laid her palms against the mantel. She hated violence, but at that moment she experienced an urge to hit him again and again until he took back his doubts and suspicions about her. Whatever her motives for dating his brother years ago, they certainly didn't apply at the present.

"Thanks for your concern, but I can take care of myself. I've done so for a number of years," she informed him.

"And in places much more dangerous than Riverton, I'm sure," he added. "Don't underestimate a small town. Its residents have all the emotions of the world at large."

She tried to decide if this was a warning for her not to get involved with the townsfolk. It didn't take a genius to see he didn't want her within a hundred miles of *his* territory. Taking the poker, she broke open a log so it would burn evenly and added another to the grate.

Finished, she sat on the raised brick hearth and looked at Shane. He was asleep!

She stared at him, unable to believe he'd go to sleep in her presence. After all, he seemed to consider her one of the more dangerous members of the human species.

He moved, slumping further into the sofa. She checked the teapot and found it still half-full. Leaving the pot and her cup, she took the tray to the kitchen, then returned to the living room.

Shane had shifted again. His feet hung off the end of the sofa. His boots were real working boots, not city-slicker ones with high heels and pointed toes. His uniform fit his tall frame perfectly. She wondered if the cellular phone clipped to his belt bothered him, but decided he wasn't feeling a thing.

She remembered that Mrs. Perkins had said he'd had a call early that morning. He obviously hadn't rested since then.

A town like Riverton surely didn't have much crime....

However, it was next to the interstate highway. Lots of strangers passing through these days. And the area was growing. It had doubled in size since she'd lived here.

Her gaze was drawn to his belt. She wondered if he ever wore a gun and if he'd ever been shot at. A lawman's job was dangerous. A strange feeling, something like fear, went through her.

She poured another cup of the spicy tea and sipped it, feeling its warmth spreading through her on the inside while the fire warmed her back when she sat on the hearth again.

Shane slept serenely, his head on the sofa arm.

A plink against the window drew her attention. Snow was falling again. She placed the empty cup on the table and sat in the easy chair. The house was quiet. She felt at peace with the world for the first time in years.

Odd. She hadn't even known she'd been in contention with it. She yawned and closed her eyes.

Shane woke slowly, painfully. He was cold. His body ached. Hell, no wonder. He'd fallen asleep on the sofa again.

He rubbed his eyes, which felt as if someone had thrown sand into them, and pushed himself upright. It took a supreme effort. His head felt weighted with lead. Looking around, he realized he wasn't in the den at his place. He was at Anne Snyder's house.

And Tina Henderson was asleep in the easy chair.

He mentally groaned. Just what he needed—a rumor about the sheriff and the famous war correspondent making the rounds. He focused on the clock on the mantel. Damn, almost two o'clock in the morning. He couldn't believe he'd fallen asleep like that.

If anyone had noticed his truck parked in her driveway until all hours there would be hell to pay. That would really set the gossip mill to grinding. He could imagine the smirking grins of the men at the barber shop, a favorite hangout of the town's geezers, who yakked as much as a bunch of women.

Why the hell had she let him sleep?

Every muscle in his body made itself known as he surged to his feet. He pinched the bridge of his nose in an attempt to hold back the headache that was starting to pound behind his eyes.

Tina shifted in the chair, her head sliding down until it rested on the padded arm, her arms crossed over her chest as she tried to stay warm. The fire had smoldered into ashes long ago.

He cursed again. Edging around the coffee table, he stopped near the big easy chair, intending to shake her awake. He had a thing or two to say to her....

She looked small and defenseless, curled into a ball in the chair. For some reason she reminded him of his nephew, her face young and trusting in sleep. Not at all the way she looked when she was awake, he realized.

When she gazed at a man with those stormy eyes, she was wary, guarded...a woman who gave nothing of her inner self away. Only once had he seen emotion reflected in those translucent gray depths. Even now he wasn't sure what it had been.

Anguish? Had she really been hurt when he'd told her to leave his brother alone, or worse yet, to get out of town?

He doubted it. The heart of a gold digger had no soft spots. He'd learned that lesson well with his stepmother. He'd better remember it.

Yet watching her sleep gave him strange feelings inside, as if he wanted to hold her...protect her...make her trust him until those inner barriers dropped and he saw the real person.

He cursed again, not silently, but low, under his breath. She heard him.

"What is it?" she asked, startled. She sat up and looked around, as confused as he'd been upon finding himself awakening in a strange place.

When she raised her face to stare at him in bewilderment, a surge of hunger, so strong it caused an ache to settle someplace deep inside, ripped through him.

"Shh," he soothed, bending forward, drawn to the rosy hue of her lips, which looked incredibly soft in the light of the lamp she'd left on.

She pushed the dark swath of hair away from her face. "What time is it?"

"Almost two o'clock in the morning," he told her, controlling the hunger with anger. He stepped back. "Why did you let me fall asleep? Do you have any inkling of the gossip this will stir up in town...hell, in the whole county?"

Her eyes opened in an incredulous expression, then she smiled coolly at him. "What's the matter, Sheriff? Afraid your sterling reputation will be tarnished?"

He suppressed the desire to shake her. If he touched her once, he might not quit until it was too late to stop. "Not mine, honey, yours. The small-town double standard is still alive and kicking in these parts."

"I'm sure it is." Her tone was frankly mocking. "Thanks for your concern."

She uncurled herself from the chair and stretched with the sensuous grace of a cat. Her breasts were momentarily outlined against the soft material of her outfit. He realized she wore no bra. The blood pounded with a dull roar through his ears—whether in anger or passion, he couldn't tell.

Having a man sleep over didn't seem to bother her, so why the hell was he getting all steamed up about it?

He remembered who her neighbors were and gave a low groan of frustration. "Emma Tall lives next door. She and her husband own the local hardware store. She's the biggest gossip around."

The wind blew with an eerie sound around the house. A flurry of snow hit the window. He watched the sway of very feminine hips while his nemesis, as he was beginning to think of her, walked to the window.

"It's snowing again," she said. "It might be dangerous out on the road. I haven't heard any snowplows come through."

"They'll be over on the interstate, keeping it open." He thrust a hand through his hair and worried about getting stuck in her drive. That would be all he needed—a tow truck coming to pull the sheriff out at—he glanced at the clock—two-fifteen in the morning.

"Umm." She leaned forward, putting her forehead to the window like a kid gazing outside, longing to be in the snow. She yawned, then turned around. "I'm going to bed. Do you want the guest room or a blanket for the sofa?"

He stared at her, feeling more than surprised, almost shocked—the way he had earlier when she'd admitted, as cool as a frosted shake, that she'd been after Ty for his name and fortune.

This woman threw him off balance. He didn't like it.

"It would be warmer to share," he drawled, watching her closely for a reaction. Hell, maybe she did want him. Maybe she was one of those cosmopolitan women who took their pleasures where they found them.

She moved her shoulders in an impatient gesture. "That wasn't an invitation," she informed him crisply. "But even I'm not heartless enough to throw somebody out in the cold at this hour. The damage has already been done to my reputation, if what you say is true, so you may as well stay until morning. I'll even cook you breakfast." She tossed him a sardonic grin.

Heat burned its way right down his backbone. He tried to think, but it was no use; he didn't see any graceful way out of the situation. And she was right. A few hours more or less wouldn't make a damned bit of difference to the local gossips. Besides, if he stayed until morning, maybe the neighbors would think he'd just arrived, rather than spent the night.

"Bring me a blanket. I'll take the sofa."

When she left the room, he built up the fire until it burned brightly, warming the cold room. He heard the furnace click on. She must have turned up the thermostat.

She returned in a few minutes, carrying a pillow, two flannel sheets and a wool blanket. "Do you think this will be enough?"

"Yeah."

"What time do you need to get up?"

"At six. I'll be awake." He always woke without an alarm.

She nodded, glanced around and walked out. "Good night," she called back softly from the hall.

"'Night," he automatically responded.

He shucked his boots and pants, laying them neatly over the arm of the chair. He glanced at the cellular phone and thought of calling the office, then decided against it. Everything seemed quiet. If he was needed, the dispatcher would call.

After preparing his bed, he put his shirt on the chair and crawled between the covers. His thermals would serve well enough for pajamas. Of course, at home he didn't sleep in anything.

His last thought was of his hostess, a surprising, puzzling woman. He wondered if she slept in the seductive outfit she'd had on....

Tina made breakfast as quietly as she could. She stirred the eggs with a plastic spatula, which made no sound against the skillet. Shane was still asleep.

She grinned. It was almost seven. Apparently, his internal alarm clock had switched off.

The microwave dinged, startling her. She removed the rasher of bacon and placed the strips on a platter. Peeking into the oven, she saw that the biscuits were done to a golden brown. She took them out and dumped them into a cloth-lined basket.

Leaving the kitchen, she crept down the hall and into the living room. Shane was snoozing like a baby. Quietly. He didn't snore. A sense of tenderness came over her as she watched him.

The lines had been smoothed from his forehead. He looked peaceful in the gray light of morning. She hated to wake him.

Glancing out the window at the sky, she sighed. It was still cloudy. The snow had stopped, but the wind blew over the house with a relentless sound. She shivered, thinking of the chill factor for the people who had to be outside in the unfriendly elements.

Screwing up her courage, she looked at her guest, wondering if he woke like a bear or a kitten in the mornings. Well, only one way to find out. "Shane," she said.

He opened his eyes at once. She saw instant awareness in him. He knew where he was, where he'd spent the night. It had bothered her at first, knowing he was merely steps away. It had taken her awhile to fall asleep. She'd woken a few minutes after six, had washed and dressed, then gone to the kitchen.

"Breakfast," she told him and hurried out. Her hand tingled. She'd wanted to sit beside him and brush the tumbling curls off his forehead.

Putting plates on the table, she wondered what it would feel like to wake with him. She sucked in a shaky breath. What was the Linda Ronstadt song? "I Know a Heartache When I See One." Yeah, that was it.

Shane came into the kitchen. He was dressed. She'd noticed his clothing lying on the chair when she'd wakened him. He'd been wearing blue thermal knits. A thermal top, she corrected. She was making assumptions about the bottoms.

He must have washed his face in cold water, for it had a healthy pink glow—along with an enticing stubble. She wondered how rough his beard would feel against her skin early in the morning.

Heat slithered through her. She hastily put the thought aside. "Good morning."

He gave her a sour glance. "It's seven o'clock," he announced, as if this were somehow her fault.

"Yes," she said equably.

"I usually wake up...." He let the thought trail away. "How much snow did we get last night?"

She looked out the window. "Two or three inches."

"Damn."

Well, now she knew—he woke up growling like a bear. She placed the meal on the table, ignoring the slight tremor she seemed to have developed during the night.

"There won't be any tire tracks. I forgot about that."

She tried to figure that one out, but gave up. She poured two mugs of coffee and put them on the table. "Do you want some orange juice or milk or both?"

His laser glance swept over her, then the table. He sighed and took a seat. "Juice, please."

She prepared it and joined him. "Why are we worried about tire tracks?"

"I thought the neighbors might think I'd dropped by this morning on...um, official business. I could tell the geezers I'd had to warn you about snow tires. By the way, you'll need them if you try to get over the pass on the interstate."

"I have aggressive treads with four-wheel drive," she informed him, proud of her foresight.

"Umm." He frowned heavily and bit into a biscuit. "Well, maybe no one will notice the tracks."

"What tracks?" She gave him an exasperated glance.

"That's the trouble. There *aren't* any." He took another bite of biscuit. "Did Mrs. Perkins send these over?" he asked.

"Of course not. I made them. If there aren't any tracks, how could they be a problem?"

He sighed heavily. "My truck. I can hardly say I came over this morning when there aren't any fresh tracks in the snow behind the blasted truck. That's the first thing Emma Tall will notice."

"Perhaps everyone doesn't have as suspicious a mind as yours," Tina suggested. Heaven forbid that anyone should link the pristine Macklin name with hers, she thought waspishly.

"She does," he assured her. "You won't be able to make a move without her reporting it to the whole town."

"I really don't see what difference it makes. I learned long ago that people will think what they want to, no matter what." She gave him an insouciant smile. "So I vowed never to let other people's opinions bother me."

He ate in silence for a few minutes. She noted that he'd eaten two biscuits and was starting on a third. At least her cooking met with his approval.

"You seemed to take mine to heart," he said thoughtfully after a while. "When I told you to leave, you looked...hurt."

He had no idea how she'd felt, she reflected. She'd wanted something from him...approval, kindness, acknowledgment of her as a person...she wasn't sure what. She certainly hadn't gotten it.

She stared at her plate, filled with a strange yearning and a restlessness that bedeviled her soul. When she looked up, he was watching her, waiting for an answer.

"I was angry," she informed him, "not hurt."

He ignored her statement. "Did I get too close to the truth that day? I was right. By your own admission, you were after the Macklin name. If I hadn't sent you packing, you'd have lured Ty into marriage before he knew what hit him."

She could almost hate him for thinking that of her. He thought he was right, but he didn't know the workings of her heart. Only Anne had seemed to detect the inner feelings she kept so carefully concealed. She suddenly missed the older, wiser woman's counsel.

He looked around the kitchen, then back at her. "Yet Anne must have thought you were pretty special to have left her home to you rather than her niece."

"Her niece?" Tina had known there had been a nephew, deceased, whom Anne hadn't been close to. She hadn't realized Anne had also had a niece.

"You must know," he said, studying her with a narrowed gaze. "Anne's niece—great-niece, actually—is my sister-in-law, Ty's wife." He paused as if to let this sink in, then continued, "This time you got the money without having the bother of a husband along with it."

Chapter Four

Tina considered hitting Shane on the head with a heavy object. Except the object would probably break, and she'd have to clean up the mess.

"I didn't know about your sister-in-law," she said with great calm, given how she felt. "Jack Norton handled everything. He said Anne had few relatives and none she was close to."

Tina couldn't imagine having a relative in the same town and not being close to her, especially someone as wonderful as Anne.

"Hmm," Shane said.

Which could have meant he did or did not believe her, not that it mattered to her.

He buttered a fourth biscuit and reached for the jar of homemade jam. "Did you make this, too?"

"Hardly. I found the jam in the pantry."

He added a generous dollop of jam to the biscuit and polished off the meal. "That was good," he said when he'd finished.

"Thanks."

"What's wrong?"

"Not a thing," she said with a mendacious smile. "You just barge in, make yourself at home, spend the night, eat my food and accuse me of being an opportunist who robbed your sister-in-law of her inheritance from her only living relative. Nothing to be upset about in that scenario."

He shrugged, picked up his cup and tried the coffee. "Perfect," he murmured. To her surprise, a smile crinkled the hard, attractive planes of his face.

A slight indentation—she wouldn't dare call it a dimple—etched a line at the corner of his mouth. Wary and alert, she watched him, expecting him to say something harsh.

He drained his cup, eyed the pot regretfully and stood. "I've got to go," he told her.

She trailed at his heels down the hall, almost jogging to keep up with his long stride. *"Arf, arf,"* she muttered, irritated by the way he made her feel. He was just so damned confident, doing as he pleased in *her* house.

"What?" He stopped for his jacket and hat, which were hanging next to her coat on the highboy, and gave her a quizzical glance.

"Oh, nothing."

"Are you always a grouch in the mornings?" he inquired.

"Moi, a grouch?" She feigned amazement. "Look who's talking—Mr. Sunshine himself."

He watched her with a thoughtful expression. "Sorry. Things have been . . . difficult this week."

Things like his sister-in-law? she wondered. How often did the woman stay at his house? Maybe that was the reason he let himself fall asleep here. Maybe he hadn't wanted to go home and listen to a litany of complaints.

And maybe she was getting soft in the head, feeling sorry for Shane Macklin. From her own experience, she knew he had no problem speaking his mind. If he wanted his sister-in-law gone, he'd tell her to leave.

After putting his jacket and hat on, he paused again and studied her. She was aware that she wore no makeup, that her jeans were old and her blue flannel shirt had faded to silvery shades.

The silence built. She noticed the loud ticking of the clock in the kitchen echoing through the hall. Her heart thudded at the same rate, heavy and slow and, for some reason, afraid.

He stared at her lips. She knew he was remembering that other parting years ago. For a moment, she wished...she wished...

The unbearable longing for things she couldn't name rose in her. She pressed a hand to her throat, terrified of feelings she didn't want to acknowledge. A tremor ran through her.

"I've got to go," he muttered. He opened the door and stepped outside into the frigid air. "I'll see you at six-thirty," he said. He bounded off the porch, through the fresh snow and into his utility vehicle. He waved, not at her, but next door.

She looked in time to see the curtain drop on her neighbor's window. She closed the door and watched Shane back out and drive off. His tire tracks were the first ones in the snow that morning.

* * *

Tina hung the sophisticated black-sequined pants outfit back in the closet. What the heck did a person wear to an April Fool's Ball, anyway?

She remembered she had a blue-and-white domino cape. Court jesters—the king's fools—had once worn similar garb. That should be appropriate. She was a fool for going with Shane.

She decided on a blue lace dress lined with beige silk— her one French-designer outfit. It was demure, yet rather provocative at the same time. Her hands shook as she finished dressing.

Really, there was no need to be nervous. A country ball was nothing. She raised her chin and gave herself a stern examination in the mirror. She could handle it.

Six-thirty seemed early for a ball. She paced the living room, wishing she'd told Shane she was *not* going. She'd call—

Too late. He was turning in the drive.

She stared at the expensive sports car, not sure he was inside. A tall, masculine figure climbed out and crunched through the snow on the sidewalk. She'd made a brave-hearted attempt to clear it away that morning, but mostly she'd worked off a lot of tension before giving up partway to the drive.

Her heart gave a gigantic leap as he came up the porch steps into the light. He wore a dinner suit, which looked elegant on his lithe frame. He was handsome and distinguished and mysterious.

She'd never seen him in formal attire. The summer they'd met, he'd worn jeans, and shirts opened halfway— sometimes all the way—down his chest while he worked in the orchards. When she'd put her palms against him to push him away, she'd touched bare flesh, lightly furred with tawny hair across his chest.

Forcing the disturbing image from her mind, she opened the door. He stepped inside, crowding into the hall, invading her space.

"Well, the little beggar girl gets to meet Prince Charming," she said, her voice husky rather than cynical as she'd meant it to be. She dropped into a sweeping curtsy to hide the sudden case of nerves that overtook her.

A hand on her arm pulled her upright, not exactly roughly, but not in a friendly way, either.

"Come on, Cinderella," he said, his tone dry as straw. "Midnight will be here before you know it."

"Oh, I'll know." Then the magic would disappear and she would go back to being the despised intruder in their midst. "But until then..."

She gave him a saucy glance. No matter how many qualms she felt about being with him, she was determined not to let him know. She'd be so cool he'd think he was with an icicle.

He frowned thoughtfully at her from his superior height. "You're in a strange mood tonight."

"Be careful," she warned in a playful whisper. "It's April Fool's Day. All may not be as it seems."

"With women, it rarely is."

"Ah, thus speaks the cynic." She tilted her head to study him. His gaze wasn't cold tonight. It roamed over her with restless energy, then returned to her face. She felt warm and feverish, not like an icicle at all.

"For instance," he went on, ignoring her quip, "you look like an angel—small, adorable...untouched."

His voice cascaded over her like the liquid notes of a gypsy violin. Her heart quivered with each vibrant inflection.

His voice dropped to an intimate level. "But I know there's fire inside, and more of the temptress than the angel," he added, giving her a cool assessment as if he'd noted all her charms and found them amusing.

"Gee, thanks." She managed to inject just the right note of sardonic humor in her voice. "Shall I take my warm coat? I have a short cape." She held up the domino.

He reached for her heavy coat. "Wear this in the car. You can wear the cape when we go to the ball. It has a nice dramatic flair. The artsy crowd will love it."

She let him help her into her coat. When she had her purse and the cape in hand, they went out. The air was so cold it made her teeth chatter. In fact, she felt cold clear through.

Clinging to the banister, she walked carefully down the steps. High heels were precarious at the best of times. On an ice-slick surface, they were plain stupid. When her foot skidded, a strong hand caught her elbow.

"You're going to break your neck," Shane said impatiently.

She was swung up into strong arms. She clasped her own arms around his neck instinctively. "Don't," she protested. "I can make it on my own."

"Be still," he ordered. "If I fall, we both might bust our bottoms." He grinned at her, and she recognized a taunting spirit of recklessness in him.

She was enchanted. This close, she was aware of his shaving lotion, of the clean scent of his shampoo, of the fresh-shaved smoothness of his cheeks. She wanted very much to kiss him.

It would be easy. Their mouths were so close. An abrupt stirring inside her had her gritting her teeth and trying to remain as still as possible. It was hard not to melt against him.

The crusted snow broke under their combined weight, and Shane wavered for a second before regaining his balance. She held on for dear life, her face pressed into his neck.

"Open the door," he murmured near her ear.

She did as he said. He placed her inside the car. Across the yard, she saw the curtain fall into place. On a defiant impulse, she waved to Mrs. Tall. So did Shane.

He was still grinning when he got in his side of the car and started the engine. He'd enjoyed the slight taunt to her nosy neighbor.

It was a delightful side of him, she realized. Playful, but not mean spirited. Endearing. She drew her coat tightly around her, troubled by the feelings that threatened to block her common sense.

"You don't weigh as much as a sack of cotton," he commented. He looked her over before putting the car in gear. "I forget how tiny you are when we're in the midst of a battle."

"I'm not tiny. Short, maybe, but not tiny."

He chuckled at her retort. "And with the heart of a tigress," he tossed at her. "And the teeth."

"The better to bite you with, my dear," she said in a deeper voice, a warning that he'd better not tangle with her.

"Ah, yes." He touched his lower lip.

She was silent, thinking of the past. He'd apologized to her for the punishing kiss. She would have to be as magnanimous about the bite. "I'm sorry for that."

He flicked her a glance as they pulled onto the pavement. "I deserved it."

Her heart went into high speed at the sudden intensity in his gaze. When he looked back at the road, she clasped her hands together. Desire, hot and pungent, poured through her like liquid heat.

It was dangerous to feel like this. She was in over her head and not sure which way was up. She tried to think of some wise words her mentor might have used to guide her, but none came.

Oh, Anne, what am I doing here, riding through the night with my nemesis? This can't be wise, can it?

"We're going to have dinner with friends of mine before we go to the ball," Shane informed her.

"I wondered why we were going so early."

She dreaded meeting his friends. She could imagine the speculation in their eyes. If they knew about him being at her house last night...

"Rafe Barrett's wife was in Europe with the foreign service. You might know her—Genny...um, I forget her maiden name."

"I didn't know many people. I moved around a lot the past five years. I was rarely in one place for very long."

"I see. Pretty exciting life," he commented. "You'll be bored with us local yokels."

"A wise person once told me only boring people are bored, that life is what a person makes of it," she said softly.

"Anne."

"Yes." She watched him in the dim light from the dash and broached a point she'd wondered about. "You knew where things were in her house."

He slowed on a narrow bridge. The road was shiny with ice. "I stopped by to see her occasionally after you left. We got to be friends." He seemed to think about this last statement. "She wouldn't give me your address at college."

"You asked for it?"

He nodded. "I was going to apologize, remember?"

"I wonder why Anne didn't give it to you. I never told her about us, about what happened." Tina stared into the darkness, perplexed at the news.

His laugh held a cynical edge. "She said I was to leave you alone, that you didn't need me in your life right then."

"Really?" Tina was surprised by Anne's attitude.

"She also said you would come back someday. I wonder... Did she tell you she was going to leave you the house? Or did you suggest it?"

"Of course not!" She curled her hands into fists. "I would never have accepted the house if I'd known there was a living relative. She wrote that her nephew had died years ago."

"Yeah. He was a banker in Medford. He had a heart attack on his way to work one morning. Anne said it was a blessing he went quickly, saved his family a lot of trouble." Shane smiled. "She was something, wasn't she? Acerbic and witty, yet she could be kind. She knew how to listen."

"Sometimes she heard more than a person wanted to tell," Tina murmured, remembering how often Anne had seemed to gaze right into her soul. But no one, not even Anne, had known of her feelings after that episode down by the river... nor of the tears she'd shed.

He pulled to a stop at the ski resort. Instead of getting out, he hooked a wrist over the steering wheel and watched her for a long minute. "She said you hadn't received the richness of life that you deserved."

Heat flamed in Tina's face. Sometimes she'd suspected Anne had felt sorry for her. She raised her chin. "That was a long time ago—"

"She said it last September, shortly before she died. I've often wondered what she meant."

"I'm sure I don't know."

"Maybe someday we'll find out." He swung out of the car and helped her out. She removed her coat and put the cape around her shoulders. All the way to the door of the lodge, she was aware of his warm clasp on her arm.

Inside, they went to a private dining room down the hall from the restaurant where she'd first seen him.

"Hello. Come in," Rafe Barrett called, crossing the room to meet them at the open door. "Tina Henderson," he said, giving her a warm handshake. "You're as pretty in person as on the tube. I've enjoyed your broadcasts."

She thanked him, then followed as he led her and Shane into the smaller, more intimate room.

Votive candles burned on a table set for six, she noted. A sinking sensation grabbed her middle. While she'd never minded going to the various embassies as a reporter, she stayed away from parties as a rule. She'd seen too many love affairs induced by a common nationality and loneliness to trust the social setting.

The women standing across the room smiled at them as they approached. "My wife," Rafe said. "Genny used to live in Paris."

Genny Barrett welcomed Tina cordially. She was a lovely woman, a bit older than Tina, with dark hair and green eyes. She had a scattering of freckles over her nose and cheeks. Her dress was emerald velvet.

"I saw you once," Tina said, her reporter's instincts aroused. "You were visiting…um, in Egypt, I think. There was an embassy party. You were there with your uncle, an ambassador." She looked at Rafe. "Your father—is he by any chance Ambassador Barrett?"

"Yes," her host replied.

"It's a small world," a masculine voice commented at the door in an amused voice.

Tina whirled. "What are you doing here?" she demanded, her surprise giving way to delight.

Gabe Deveraux came forward, his arm around the waist of a tall redhead in a long black skirt and a white blouse. Her old friend gave her a quick hug.

"Looks like Old Home Week," Shane commented dryly, giving her a sharp glance. He shook hands with Deveraux and said to Tina, "This is Gabe's wife, Whitney. Whitney, Tina Henderson."

"I'm glad to meet you," Tina told the other woman.

The redhead returned the greeting. Her smile was warm and genuine. "We saw you on television. Gabe said he knew you."

While their host was mixing drinks, Tina found a moment to speak to Gabe. "Your wife is lovely. You look happy."

He nodded and let her see the contentment in his eyes. "Marriage," he said. "You should try it."

When she'd known him, there'd been an anger in him that he'd kept carefully under control. She sensed it was gone. A lump came to her throat. She and Gabe had dated some, then remained good friends when things didn't work out, seeing each other occasionally when they were in the same part of the world.

"Gabe and I worked on a couple of cases together," their host commented when they were seated. His gaze flicked to Tina. "How did you two meet?"

When she hesitated, Gabe answered, "Tina and I both happened to be in the wrong place at the wrong time. We were caught in the crossfire between two warring factions."

"He saved my life," Tina put in after his brief explanation.

"He just has to play the hero," Whitney said when he protested. Her manner was droll, but her eyes were filled with loving pride. Husband and wife exchanged smiling glances.

Tina looked away from the happy couple, trying not to be envious. Maybe someday she'd find bliss, too.

"Ah," Rafe said, "here's our meal."

There was speculation in Shane's steady gaze while the first course was being served. The meal was French cuisine and very good. Tina was aware of Shane's warmth beside her while she chatted with her host and he talked to their hostess and Whitney. She glanced at Gabe, her old friend, and smiled.

"What are you planning on doing now that you're one of our famous residents?" Genny Barrett inquired at one point.

Everyone looked at Tina.

She felt herself blush. "I'm going to write a book on war from the perspective of the women and children caught in it."

"That could be pretty grim," Deveraux said.

"War is grim," Rafe Barrett put in before she could answer.

Tina saw his wife give him a comforting smile. "Be sure and notice the decorations tonight," the woman said, tactfully changing the subject. "They were made by local elementary-school students."

When the meal was over, they went to the ballroom, where the dance was already in progress. A table had been reserved for them.

A troop of actors dressed as jesters pranced among the crowd, juggling various items and playing jokes on the guests. Clown cutouts decorated the walls all around the room. Tina's short cape, which she wore around her shoulders in the cool room, was noticed at once by the troop.

"One of our own," a jester in yellow-and-purple satin cried.

She was whisked off. They added her to the act by having her toss rings, balls and teacups into the air for them to juggle. When two of them made a saddle by crossing their arms, she was lifted onto it and carried about the room in a great rush while they shouted, "Make way for the queen, the Queen of Fools! Make way!"

Just when she was beginning to wonder if she'd ever get away, Shane appeared. He plucked her from the two jesters and looped an arm around her shoulders. "The queen wishes to dance," he said.

The men staged a mock joust, as if fighting him off. One of them shouted an alarm, "He has stolen the queen! Where are the guards? The mortal has taken the queen!"

His partner laughed. "The more fool he. The queen will turn him into a dancing pig."

Waving their arms like windmills, the jesters ran off into the crowd. Shane lifted Tina's hands to his shoulders. He linked his together behind her back.

The top of her head barely came to his shoulder. He glanced at a couple dancing past, their cheeks pressed together in romantic bliss. "You're too little," he said. His eyes roamed her face, their summery blue shimmering with thoughts that seemed suddenly dark and deep and unreadable.

"I know." Her heart was tripping all over itself. For a moment, she forgot that they were enemies. "It's hard to dance with someone short."

"There are other ways. You're so light, I could lift you right off your feet."

She felt as if she'd float away at the slightest breeze. "To dance?"

He smiled slightly. "Yes."

A wave of giddiness washed over her. She recalled that she'd had two glasses of wine with dinner. Or had it been three?

Shane took a deep breath. She felt a shudder go through him. She leaned her head back and gazed at him, aware of the heat that spread slowly between them. For the space of a heartbeat, she saw the bright flare of hunger in his eyes, then it was gone.

"The jesters were right. You have turned me into a dancing pig...or a fool...." His voice was a deep, soft rumble that mixed pleasantly with the music. "Only a fool would play with fire."

"Yes."

He gazed at her through narrowed eyes. "You feel it, too."

There seemed no point in denying what they both knew. She said nothing. Dreams that had once seemed far-fetched suddenly took on new possibilities. She gazed at him, lost in the wonder of the moment, in the music that strummed in her blood.

"You sometimes have such an innocent look," he murmured. "I can't decide if you're a beguiling enchantress who will fill my life with magic or a devil-woman sent to torment me."

She smiled at his plaint and the frustration he experienced trying to figure her out. This was more of himself than he'd ever revealed to her before. "How much wine did you consume?"

"Not enough to make me numb," he muttered.

He pulled her closer, until she had no choice but to rest her head on his chest, her body tucked intimately against his. He moved them in a slow shuffle, dancing in a circle in the same spot.

It was the second time she'd been in his arms. The first time superimposed itself on this one like a double-exposed snapshot. There'd been anger in him then, but not now.

"Relax," he growled into her hair. He rubbed his nose back and forth in the tresses, taking a deep breath as he did. "You smell so damned good. What kind of perfume are you wearing?"

"None. I mean, it's soap and shampoo, not perfume."

"Hmm," he murmured.

Enchantress, he'd called her. She felt they were both caught in a spell. If she didn't watch herself, she'd end up melting at his feet like a candle set too close to a fire.

The next hour passed in a blur of enchantment. Shane introduced her to the mayor, who had a booming voice and a happy manner, and the mayor's wife, who was a calm, smiling woman.

They danced several times and chatted with the resort owner and other couples they met. Everyone made her feel welcome; everyone wanted to hear about her life.

"It isn't as exciting or dangerous as it sounds," she explained modestly. She didn't want to mislead people, but they seemed intent on treating her like a heroine. She met the owners of the local newspaper, the *Riverton Daily News*.

"I write the living, food and social columns," the wife, Dolly Adams, explained the operation of the paper. "Clint does the front page, letters to the editor and the typesetting on the computer."

"We could use some help," Clint told her. "If you want a job, just show up any day at seven a.m."

"He isn't joking," Dolly informed them with an impish grin. "The mayor dropped in one day to talk about an item for the paper. The collator had quit, so Clint, who knew he was a retired airplane mechanic, put him to work fixing it. The poor man didn't get out of the office until seven that night."

"Remind me not to go down there," Shane muttered in an audible aside. The group around them laughed.

Tina drank two glasses of champagne punch, then refused any more. She was already floating on a cloud.

Shane was attentive, but rather quiet. His gaze was warm when he looked at her. After dancing once more, she sighed deeply as they started back to the table. "Tired?" he asked.

"Yes, I think I am."

"We'll say good-night to the others and leave."

They returned to the table and thanked the Barretts. The newspaper owners were there, too.

"Isn't it interesting," Dolly mused, pointing out the Deverauxes on the dance floor, "that Whitney and Gabe both returned to this area because of an inheritance? Rafe recently bought back the ranch his uncle left him, and now here's Tina, who also came back because of an inheritance. I think there's a feature article here—a sort of returning to one's roots."

"Or stealing someone else's," a feminine voice remarked in an acidic purr.

Tina looked around. Behind them stood a couple. She easily recognized Tyson Macklin. His hair was the same tawny shade as his brother's, although his eyes were a lighter blue. He wasn't as large as Shane, nor as broad, but the physical likeness was there.

The woman with him was a lovely blonde of average height whose generous bustline filled a low-cut sequined bodice. Her eyes were blue with gold flecks. Right now, they were shooting venomous looks at Tina. Anne's niece, she deduced. Ty's wife.

"Pull in your claws," Shane advised his sister-in-law in the uncomfortable silence that followed her accusation. "Tina, you remember Ty. This is his wife, Ronda."

"You're lovelier now than eleven years ago," Ty said, taking her hand in his. He looked tired. His smile was tinged with a bitterness that hadn't been present all those years ago.

Tina eased her hand free. She felt sorry for him, she realized. He'd always been at a disadvantage compared to his older brother; now he was apparently trapped in a marriage that wasn't working out. She wondered if he loved his wife.

Watching the blonde speak to the others in the group, Tina saw that Ronda had adopted a brave, silently suffering front. It was an obvious bid for sympathy from her audience and about as real as a three-dollar bill.

She also noticed the lines of discontent around the woman's mouth. A person used to getting her own way, she concluded; one who didn't take kindly to being thwarted. One who flirted her way through life, but kept her nails sharpened for use against anyone who didn't fall for her charm.

A chill crept up Tina's neck and along her scalp.

Glancing at Shane, she found he was also watching his sister-in-law. His gaze had softened, and he looked completely taken in by that poor-brave-me act. Tina was amazed.

Was he in love with Ty's wife?

"Who's with Jonathan?" Shane asked during a pause.

"Mrs. Perkins," Ronda answered.

Shane frowned. "She had a movie planned for tonight."

Ty's wife dropped her gaze flirtatiously and looked petulant. "I was bored. When I mentioned the dance, she kindly volunteered to watch Jonathan so I could come."

Shane looked at his brother.

Ty shrugged. "She called me. I'm always handy as an escort . . . when she can't get you."

The sardonic statement revealed a lot of animosity, Tina thought. Her heart went out to Ty. His life couldn't have been easy these past few years. Yet he and Shane had been close when she'd first met him. He'd looked up to his older brother then.

Shane let out a deep breath, as if forcing himself to relax. "I'm taking Tina home now. I'll talk to you tomorrow," he said to Ty.

"Sure, Big Brother." Ty strode off toward the bar.

"I think I'd like to leave now, too. May I catch a ride?" Ronda asked. "Ty was so difficult on the way over."

To Tina's shock, there were tears in the woman's eyes. Maybe she'd misjudged Shane's sister-in-law. Maybe she was sincere. But if Anne hadn't cared for her . . .

"I'll come back for you," Shane offered.

Ronda nodded, managing to look disappointed and eager at the same time. It gave Tina an uneasy feeling. Glancing toward the bar, she saw Ty drink half a glass of liquor in one swallow.

"Don't get mixed up with Ty," Shane advised cooly on the way to his car. "He has enough troubles without the Lolita of his youth returning to tempt him."

Tina stiffened. "I agree. It must be hard to watch your brother cut in on your wife."

Chapter Five

Anger surrounded Shane like a dark aura. Tina waited for the fury to break around her. He didn't speak until they were in the car on the road.

"Just what the hell did you mean by that nasty remark?" he demanded, his hands clenched around the steering wheel in a manner that suggested what he'd do to her neck if he had a chance.

"It's obvious. You take the wife's side against her husband. That's interference, in my book."

"I'm not on anybody's side," he growled, casting her a feral glance before looking back at the ribbon of light cutting through the darkness.

Peering out the window, she saw only patches of stars. Clouds dotted the sky, bringing the threat of more snow. Spring had never felt so far away, and she had never felt so alone.

She decided not to add any more fuel to Shane's flaming temper. She'd keep her mouth shut. After all, what did she know about anyone's life here? She was an outsider.

"I believe in the sanctity of marriage," he informed her after a silent five minutes went by. "I've tried to talk sense into both of them. Neither Ty nor Ronda will listen. Jonathan is caught in the middle of the mess."

"Jonathan is your nephew?"

"Yes." A worried line appeared between his eyes at mention of the child.

"How old is he?"

"Four. The kid needs both his parents, especially now. He hasn't been well lately."

"What's wrong with him?"

"The doctors don't know or won't say. They're running tests." This last was said with an exasperated twist of his lips.

"I see."

She couldn't help the softer note that invaded her tone. It was the one thing she couldn't bear—for children to hurt. In a world at war, whether between parents or countries, children were the losers.

Shane heaved a deep sigh. "That's what I'm telling you—stay away from Ty. He needs to solve the problems he has, not compound them with . . . complications."

"What about you?" she inquired coolly.

"What about me?"

"You're going back to pick up his wife at the ball. Why not let her husband take her home? Maybe part of the problem is you."

Shane cursed under his breath. "Ty knows I'd never do anything underhanded. I'm trying to help them patch things up."

She knew she should let it drop—after all, she hadn't come back here to get tangled up in other people's disputes. "It seems to me the best way to do that is to stay out of it."

He pulled into her drive and turned off the engine. In the sudden silence, they could hear the wind moaning through the fir trees. Her neighbor had left an outside light on. It cast long, eerie shadows through the trees. The shadows pitched to and fro in a frantic dance on the snow, driven by the commands of the wind.

"Since when did you become an expert on marriage?" he asked with more than a trace of sarcasm.

"Sometimes an outsider sees things others miss. As long as your sister-in-law can go running to you for sympathy when things go wrong with her husband, she will."

"Thanks for the advice. Now I won't have to write Dear Abby."

Tina had to smile, thinking of Shane sending his problems to an advice columnist. "With your ego, I'm sure you think you should be writing the column for her."

He leaned toward her. In the dim light reflecting off the snow, she could barely make out his features. She didn't have to see him clearly to know how penetrating his direct blue gaze was, nor how it could cut right into a person's heart.

"You said that before...eleven years ago," he said quietly, an odd note in his voice.

"What?" Whatever she'd expected, it hadn't been that he'd recall the past.

"About my ego. You told me that the best thing I could do for Ty was to stay out of his life. You said my ego was so colossal that I thought I could play God...."

His voice trailed off. For a moment, she was thrown back to that day he'd come to her at the river instead of Ty.

She'd maintained an outward calm, smiling all the time he told her off. Her insouciance had made him furious.

The touch of a warm, rough finger on her mouth caused her to jump.

"You're remembering," he said.

She pulled away, but he caught her chin and brought her around to face him.

"I've never forgotten your eyes...cloudy eyes that never reveal your thoughts. What are you thinking now?"

"That it's darned cold out here and, as much as I'd like to debate the philosophy of life with you, I really should go in."

She saw the flash of his smile, then it was gone. He leaned closer. She tensed. Her eyelashes felt incredibly heavy. She wanted to close her eyes, but knew she mustn't. That could be taken as an invitation for him to kiss her.

"I remember your fire," he murmured, his gaze dark and searching. "You were soft in my arms...hot... responsive—"

"No, I wasn't. I didn't."

He traced the line of her lips, making them tingle unbearably. She licked the sensation away. Her tongue touched his finger. She heard him draw in a sharp breath while a tremor of undefined longing went through her.

She shouldn't have gone to the dance. She'd known, deep inside, how it would be...dancing with him, being in his arms...feeling his warmth, the strength in his body, the gentleness of his touch. She shouldn't have gone.

"You trembled in my arms that day," he said. His breath fanned over her mouth. "I was shaking, too."

"I was angry," she said, "just as you were."

"That's something I've been wondering about ever since." His lips were closer. His breath deepened, became heavy.

"What?" she whispered, barely able to speak.

"Was it all in anger?"

"Yes." She closed her eyes. "Yes."

"Was it?" His lips touched hers.

It was the softest grazing of flesh on flesh, but it was like a lightning bolt striking. Her breath hung suspended between one eternity and another.

His mouth brushed softly over hers, again and again, then pressed ever so gently, parting her lips. His tongue dipped briefly inside.

"You taste so damned good," he said.

"The champagne..."

"No," he whispered. "You."

He covered her lips possessively, hungrily, and probed slowly, sensuously beyond them, following the line of her teeth, the curve of her mouth, then delving deeply into her while stars swirled madly behind her closed eyelids.

All power of reasoning left her. She knew she shouldn't allow this, but it was too hard to think why. His wonderful stroking of her mouth started an upheaval inside her that spread into faint nervous tremors throughout her entire body.

His arms slipped around her, drawing her as close as possible. It wasn't enough. She clung to his broad shoulders as if he were her only anchor in a world gone berserk.

He shifted, cracking his knee on the gear shift as he did so. When he cursed softly, she drew back from his arms with an effort.

"That's what I get for trying to make out in a parked car," he said ruefully, then added in an almost irritated tone, "but that's what you do to me—make me forget things I should remember."

Reason returned. Tina released her grasp on his suit lapels. She hadn't been aware that she'd been holding on. Realizing how foolishly she'd behaved, she pushed against him, wanting to be free from his embrace, but he didn't let her go.

Permitting that kiss to happen had been the height of folly on her part. Her lips still tingled from the effects. She licked them and tasted the faint flavor of the brandy he'd consumed before they left the ball.

"Such as?" She was proud of her cool control.

"Such as—why did you return to this two-bit town when you had the world in your hand?"

His suspicions hurt in ways she couldn't begin to explain. She hated it that he saw her as a fortune hunter out for the main chance, yet her pride wouldn't let her argue with him. What would be the point? He wouldn't believe anything she said.

"I—I need to go in," she said, disturbed at the slight break in her voice that betrayed emotion.

"Yes, else the neighbors will have something new to talk about." A slight smile flicked at the corners of his mouth, then disappeared. He looked harsh and firmly in control of his emotions once more, his breathing calm and easy.

She suppressed the insane desire to see him trembling in her arms from the passion they shared. She wanted him to feel unsure and vulnerable and filled with the same unbearable longing as she, for things she couldn't begin to explain.

That would be the day. Tell this man, with his confidence, his control, his cynical view of life, how she felt so he could laugh at her? Never.

But his heart had pounded hard beneath her palms when they'd kissed. It wouldn't have taken much to propel both of them over the edge . . . to disaster.

Hastily, she reached for the door. One finger hit the edge of the handle and she felt a nail break in the brittle cold.

"Wait," he ordered, stopping her frantic haste to get away. "I'll help you. The sidewalk is slippery."

She sat still while he got out and came around to her side of the luxury car. She was composed when he opened the door. Then he scooped her into his arms.

"The neighbors will think I've forgotten how to walk," she remarked dryly, resigning herself to the inevitable. She didn't know why he thought he had to carry her. "A helping hand would probably be sufficient."

"You're such a midget, it's easier to carry you."

"I may be a fraction short, but I'm hardly a midget."

"Right. If you weigh a hundred pounds, I'll eat my hat."

"With ketchup or without?" she inquired sweetly. "I weighed a hundred and ten the last time I checked."

He let her slide down his hard length to the porch, which was a step above where he stood. She had to look up only a couple of inches to meet his eyes, had to lean forward and stretch up ever so slightly to meet his lips.

The frown line appeared between his eyes. He caught her to him. "When you look at me like that..."

She turned her face away and stepped back.

His hand tightened on her back, then he slowly released her. That he didn't want to let go was obvious. A thrill ran along her nerves at his reluctance. He followed her to the door, waited while she fumbled with the key and finally opened the door.

The wind rushed through the house. From the back they heard a sound like glass shattering. Shane moved her aside and stepped into the hall ahead of her. "Wait here," he ordered in a terse whisper before moving soundlessly to the car.

She started when she saw him return with a pistol in his hand. He moved silently down the hall.

With an effort, Tina closed the front door against the wind, which had gotten steadily stronger during the evening. She tiptoed along the hall, aware of the beat of her heart and the fear she felt for Shane. If a burglar was in the house, he might shoot before Shane had a chance.

"It's okay," he called out just as she reached the kitchen.

When she entered, she saw him studying the window above the sink. Then she saw the glass . . . and the rock.

"Someone threw a rock through the window?" She stared at the evidence. It seemed a personal affront, as if someone didn't want her there. Which was silly. She'd been in town less than a week.

"Yeah. The wind caused another sliver of glass to fall out when you opened the front door. The back door is still bolted, and I don't see signs of anyone entering."

Tina stopped beside him and stared at the rock and shards of glass lying in the stainless-steel sink. "Why would someone do that?" she wondered aloud, perplexed by the apparently random act of violence.

"Made any enemies since you arrived in town?" he asked.

Only your sister-in-law. "Not that I know of," she said.

He shook his head. "Kids, probably. This place is a good target. It's the last house on the street. With woods on one side and the river behind you, there's a great deal of privacy."

He frowned thoughtfully, his gaze flicking from the window to her. A cold blast came through the broken pane and she shivered, feeling invaded by the vandalism, made vulnerable by it.

"I'll see if I can find something to cover this until you can get it fixed tomorrow." He headed for the door leading down to the old root cellar. "Don't touch anything."

He returned with a piece of heavy cardboard, then sorted through a drawer until he found the masking tape. He cut the cardboard to fit and taped it over the hole.

"Don't go outside," he advised. "In the morning, I'll check for footprints in the yard. It was most likely some kids goofing off. I don't think you'll have any more trouble."

She thought of gangs of wild youths in black leather, sinister and tough, running around looking for trouble. She thought of guns and knives and things that hurt.

"Are you afraid to stay here alone?" Shane asked, a curious note in his voice.

"I . . . no, of course not." She shook off the images.

He reached out and took her hand. It was icy cold. "You're trembling," he said, his voice deep and quiet, making her shake even more.

She ordered the shaking to stop. "I've never been vandalized before." She glanced at him, then away, afraid of the emotions he stirred to life. It wasn't some unknown prankster she feared, but him and the way he made her feel, she realized.

"Something like this can make a person seem vulnerable."

"Yes." She removed her hand from his warm clasp. "I'm all right. It's late. You'd better go."

"How about a cup of cocoa?" He spoke casually, but she detected a hint of something more—sympathy?—in him. He went to the stove, found a pan and poured in milk to heat.

Tina sat at the table, only then realizing she still had her coat on, her purse and cape clutched in one hand. She took the heavy coat off and laid her stuff on a chair.

"Why don't you change into something comfortable?" he suggested. "The cocoa should be ready when you get back."

"I . . . all right." It seemed a sensible idea. She went to her bedroom. After a moment's indecision, she put on her thick lounging pajamas and fuzzy house shoes. She clipped the broken nail and washed her face before returning to the kitchen.

"Just in time." Shane put water in the pan and set it back on the stove, then brought two mugs to the table. "You're still trembling," he said when she lifted it to her mouth.

"I always do. It's reaction." She avoided his eyes, embarrassed that he should notice her one weakness.

As a war correspondent, whenever she returned to Rome after witnessing the aftermath of violence, she'd tremble for days.

"You've got to harden yourself," her editor had told her once after a particularly harrowing assignment. "You're an excellent reporter, but you've got to be tough to last in this business."

"People died," she'd said, haunted by visions she couldn't erase. "How do you ever get used to that?"

The nightmares would sometimes stay with her for months. That was the reason she'd returned to Riverton. She hadn't been able to distance herself from other people's suffering. It was a weakness she couldn't seem to overcome.

Shane studied her, a perplexed expression in his eyes. He listened when the clock began to strike the hour. "Midnight," he said softly when the last *bong* died away. "The ball is officially over, Cinder-girl."

"Totally," she said and sighed. She managed a wan smile. "I guess I'd better clean up the glass before someone gets cut."

"Leave it," he told her. "I'll take care of it. You'd better go on to bed. You look beat."

"Thanks. That's just what every woman loves to hear."

His gaze skimmed along her loose pajama top, which was high necked and long sleeved, then settled on her face. She'd washed the makeup off when she'd changed clothes. She knew her face was pale, her hair disheveled.

Slowly, his perusal changed. His face took on a forbidding moodiness. He looked angry, but she instinctively knew it was more than that. He wanted her, and it bothered him.

Tension hummed between them like electricity on a high-voltage wire. Her breath became tumultuous, difficult. She held herself rigid, unwilling to let this strange, hurting need overtake her common sense.

"I wonder what you're thinking," he mused aloud. "Your eyes don't reveal your thoughts. You're the only person I've never been able to read."

She shrugged and kept her eyes on the steam rising from the chocolate. If he knew what she was thinking now—how she'd like to touch him . . . how she'd like to snuggle against him . . . how she'd like to make love with him until time dissolved—he'd probably be shocked.

"I'm a simple soul," she insisted. "You're the one who keeps his cards close to the chest."

His smile was harsh. "I learned to do that a long time ago."

"Because of your stepmother?" she ventured, then wished she hadn't. It was none of her business.

A grimace of distaste appeared and was gone in the blink of an eye. "She was one of the lessons in life I learned well."

"And I'm another," she concluded.

"You I haven't figured out yet. But I will." There was a wealth of meaning in that declaration…and a warning that she didn't miss. He wanted her, but he didn't trust her. He thought she was up to no good, as her grandmother would have said.

He finished the cocoa and took the mug to the sink. "I'll clean up this mess."

"I can do it—"

"There might be a clue," he cut in. He found a plastic bag and secured the stone inside, careful not to touch the smooth granite with his bare hand. Next he cleared the glass away, then washed the pan and the mug he'd used.

"Stone is too porous to hold fingerprints," she pointed out.

"How do you know that?"

"I once dated a man who was an expert," she replied coolly.

"Deveraux," he said, watching her closely. "I thought there was more to you two than a professional relationship."

"He was my friend."

"And lover?"

"My friend," she repeated.

He didn't pursue the matter. Instead, he peered out the window. "Perhaps I should stay over," he muttered, glancing at the clock. "With a reporter's curiosity, you might go out searching for clues and mess up any prints before I see them."

"I won't. You have my word. There's no need for you to stay. I'm fine now." She stood and held out a hand. "See? I'm hardly shaking at all."

He glanced at her hand. "Stay in the house," he ordered. "Keep your doors locked at all times, even during the day. Someone could walk in on you when you're working." He frowned. "I don't like you being here alone. In a small town, word gets around."

"I'll sleep with a brick doorstop under my pillow," she promised in a mock-serious tone, in control once more.

He nodded, making her feel guilty for her flippant reply. People who threw stones could be dangerous. She followed him to the front door. "I'll see you in the morning," he promised.

After he left, she bolted the door, turned on the porch light, which she'd forgotten earlier, and went to bed. It was a long time before she slept.

All her misgivings about living there returned. Shane Macklin stirred up too many controversies inside for her peace of mind. Plus she had a feeling someone didn't want her in town.

Dingdong.

Tina sat straight up in bed, startled out of a sound sleep. She glanced at the clock. Barely six. What had awakened her?

Dingdong. Dingdong.

The impatient two-tone chime of the doorbell answered that question. A neighbor must have an emergency. She leapt from the warm covers and rushed to the front door.

Peering through the tiny spy hole, she saw Shane on the other side. "Hurry up and open the door," he called. "It's cold out here."

She spared one thought for her appearance, then, with a frown, unlocked and opened the door. She unlatched the storm door and pushed it open with her foot. He hurried inside.

"Breakfast," he announced.

"At six o'clock on a Saturday morning?"

"I came to fix the window."

He headed down the hall. She rolled her eyes to heaven, ran her fingers through her hair to smooth it somewhat and followed at his heels.

He held up the bag he'd brought in. "Cinnamon buns, still warm from the oven, compliments of Mrs. Perkins."

"I didn't think you'd stayed up all night, or what was left of it, baking rolls for breakfast," she told him, not disguising her waspish tone.

"Hmm, you are a grouch in the morning."

She gave him a sour glance and headed for her quarters. There, she washed her face, brushed her teeth and combed her hair before hurrying back to the kitchen. Shane was at the table. The coffee maker gurgled merrily on the counter. She took her seat.

"But you're also beautiful," he remarked. He took a bite of cinnamon roll while he looked her over.

All at once, his teasing good humor disappeared, replaced by something she couldn't name. Then it, too, went away. He looked at her with frank desire. She took a big drink of milk while her insides burned to cinders. They ate in silence.

He looked extraordinarily handsome that morning. He wore a deep blue V-neck sweater over a white shirt, which was opened at the collar. Tawny curling hair was visible at the throat.

"I'd better get to work," he said. His voice was husky.

She looked into his eyes, then away. For a second she felt impossibly young and foolish, like a girl in the throes of her first love . . . as if she were eighteen again. . . .

"You really don't have to bother," she said coolly. "I can get someone to do it."

"It's no bother. I measured the glass last night and brought a matching pane from an old window in one of the sheds."

There didn't seem to be anything to say to that. When he went out, she tossed the napkins and paper plates in the trash and went to her room.

After a quick shower, she put on soft suede-cloth pants in a rich brown. Over a deep russet sweater, she added a vest that matched the pants. Heavy socks and brown suede oxfords completed the outfit. A russet scarf held her hair away from her face. She added lipstick and a dash of blush before returning to the kitchen.

The cardboard was gone, she saw, and the windowpane replaced. An empty cup was on the counter. The coffee was ready. She poured a cup, sipped it, grimaced, added some tap water and sipped again. Better.

Leaning against the counter, she peered out the window. Shane was studying the ground, walking from the old stable, which held a lawn mower and outdoor furniture, to the side of the house. He bent and held his hand against a track in the snow to measure its length.

Her heart seemed to tighten as she watched him work. Last night she would have made love with him if he'd pressed only the slightest bit. She wanted him with a compelling need that had never changed, not from the first moment she'd met him.

Was there only one person who would make her feel this way? Why did it have to be Shane Macklin? She clenched her hands as confusion washed over her in crashing waves of irony and despair.

She remembered those first years in Rome. In loneliness and desperation, she'd turned to someone—a wonderful man who had accepted it gracefully when she'd told him she'd rather be friends, not lovers. Gabe Deveraux was a rare man and a true friend. She was glad he'd found happiness.

With a sigh that spoke of the loneliness she now felt, she prepared a fresh pot of coffee, then knocked on the window to attract Shane's attention.

When he entered the back door, the cold air swirled in with him, making her shiver all the way down to her comfortable shoes. She hugged the vest around her as his gaze ran over her slacks and the russet sweater. He pulled off his heavy winter jacket and hung it on a peg.

"Find anything?" she asked huskily.

He looked rested, in spite of not getting much sleep. "Some prints, but they're not very clear. He must have dragged his feet. There was only one person."

She was relieved. "A random act of vandalism. It happens everywhere these days."

"Yeah." He poured a cup of coffee into the mug on the counter and took a hearty swallow. "Umm, either my coffee improved a lot upon standing, or you made a fresh pot. What's your secret?"

"Well, I start with cold water and half as many coffee grounds," she suggested.

He grinned and her heart turned over. She quickly looked away. In snug jeans and black boots, he looked solid and powerful.

"You aren't in uniform, so I assume you're not working today. Why didn't you sleep late?"

"My mom used to ask me the same thing. I wake about the same time each day. It seems to me that when the sun comes up, it's time to rise and shine. Mrs. Perkins said you were the same. I thought you would be up." He looked her over, the way the housekeeper might have, and seemed to approve of her appearance.

"I see."

A loud *chirr* broke into the conversation. It sounded like a large cricket. She glanced around for the cause, and saw Shane pull the portable phone out of his pocket.

He answered, then listened. His brows drew deeper into a frown. She could detect a feminine voice at the other end of the line across the kitchen. It sounded angry and accusing.

"Something came up," he said. "I forgot."

Tina realized he'd forgotten all about returning to the ball for his sister-in-law last night. So had she.

"There was a, um . . . an emergency." He glanced over at Tina, and his eyes seemed to darken with mysterious thoughts.

Her ears suddenly felt hot as she listened to his end of the conversation. She was glad the scarf covered them so he couldn't see her embarrassment.

"I'll be busy all day. Perhaps you should talk to Ty yourself," he suggested. "Maybe you can work it out between the two of you."

Tina stared at him in surprise.

He listened for another minute, then said goodbye. After taking his place opposite her at the table, he inquired with a grave demeanor, "Was that the politically correct thing to do?"

"Yes." She picked up her cup and took a drink to hide the shock of his deferral to her suggestion.

"Maybe I'm not as egotistical as you thought," he suggested.

She wondered if she'd hurt his feelings with her accusation. "Maybe. Thanks for fixing the window. What do I owe you?"

"Nothing."

It felt strange to have him doing things for her. Of course, part of it was in his official capacity, but still . . .

Stop it, she ordered her too-active imagination. He was doing his job and being a good neighbor. And keeping an eye on her, she added, so she didn't tempt his baby brother into mischief.

For a moment, she thought of trying to see how far she could tempt the tough, hard-edged sheriff himself.

A frisson swept over her like a cold north wind.

"Someone walk over your grave?" he asked.

She looked at him in confusion.

"You shivered."

"Oh. No, I . . ." She lapsed into silence.

He took a deep breath, then stood. "I've got to go to the office." He grabbed his coat off the peg and let her precede him down the hall.

She stopped at the door and looked up at him. A mistake, she realized at once. His gaze fastened on her mouth.

They watched each other warily, their chests moving as their breathing deepened.

Time wavered and dissolved. She licked her lips and thought she could detect the taste of him, as if he'd just kissed her.

He made a sound deep in his throat and reached for her, pulling her up on her toes. She spread her hands over the warmth of his sweater just as his mouth covered hers. This was no grazing of the lips, but a full-scale, mouth-to-mouth kiss.

His tongue swept inside and demanded a response. She gave it to him without reserve. The yearning broke free inside her.

She strained upward. His jacket slipped to the floor, and his hands cupped her hips, bringing her completely into the embrace of his thighs. She felt his muscles flex against her as pure, rampant need took control of her senses.

Melting . . . she was melting.

When she looped her arms around him, he released his grip and let his hands slide up her ribs. His thumbs touched the sides of her breasts. He caressed her there while his tongue played havoc in her mouth.

It was only a few steps from the hallway to her bedroom. She felt him take those steps without breaking the kiss.

The backs of her legs touched the mattress, then she was lowered gently and his lean, hard body came to rest beside her, his thigh capturing both her legs.

"You should have come to *me* all those years ago," he murmured, kissing along her neck. "You should have been mine, not Ty's."

She stiffened as the words penetrated her haze of passion. Shock swept over her at her wanton response. And what he obviously thought of her—that she was available to any Macklin male for the taking.

"Don't," she said when he cupped her breast. Spirals of electricity shot off into her nether regions. "Let me go."

When she struggled, he lifted his head, his eyes narrowed in disbelief. "You don't mean that."

Desperation seized her as he moved slightly away from her. She wanted to snuggle against him, to experience his warmth forever. No, no, no . . . "Yes, I do. Let me go, Shane."

He pushed up, then stood. He drew a deep breath and closed his eyes briefly. When he opened them, he was in control once more, and his gaze was filled with loathing. "You're right. This would be a mistake of the first magnitude."

Before she could think of a reply, he'd turned and gone. She heard the door close after him. It was like a slap in the face, a reminder of the cold reality of life. She'd not forget again.

Chapter Six

Tina stared at the rain through the swishing windshield wipers. The weather had changed abruptly over the weekend. The cold wind that had been blowing fiercely from the north shifted to the south. The snow turned to a gray, misty rain.

Heading into her drive, she pushed the button on the remote control. The garage door had slid smoothly open by the time she reached it and pulled inside.

The pickup truck that had followed her from the exit to the interstate stopped on the blacktop a few feet behind her.

Through the rain-beaded back window, she identified the face of Ty Macklin at the wheel. She popped the trunk lid and climbed out of the station wagon. Ty also got out and came toward her.

"Hi. Need a hand?" he asked.

Her first inclination was to tell him no, she didn't want him in the house. Then she realized how ridiculous that was. Whatever he might have become during the years since she'd last seen him, he wasn't an ogre she had to avoid—which would be impossible in a small town, anyway.

"Sure," she said casually.

He hefted two plastic bags of groceries while she carried the third and the gallon of nonfat milk. He swung the lid closed and entered the kitchen after her.

"Shall I make coffee?" she offered. "Or is this an official call?"

"Official?" He gave her a puzzled glance and placed the bags on the counter next to hers.

After putting the milk away, she started a pot of coffee. "I thought you might be the deputy sheriff or something."

"Not me." His snort of laughter was laced with bitterness. "Only Big Brother gets to wear the white hat."

"It was black, last time I saw him in it."

"Black, then," Ty acknowledged. He sat on the stool at the breakfast bar and watched while she put her groceries away. "How have you been?"

"Fine," she said. "Is this a social call?"

"Yeah." He paused, then smiled. A dimple very like his brother's appeared in his cheek. "You weren't quite so suspicious when I came around before."

"You weren't married then," she crisply reminded him.

"Marriage," he said. "Life's a bitch and then you die."

There was just enough caustic humor in the statement to pull at her heartstrings. She saw the disillusionment in his eyes for a second before he laughed again. "Feeling sorry for yourself?" she inquired, but in gentle tones.

A hint of color swept into his ears, a trait he shared with her, she realized. She felt sorry for the young man who'd found out that his older brother couldn't always come to the rescue and make everything right.

"Maybe," he admitted. He blew across the surface of the coffee when she plunked a mug in front of him. He sighed, then smiled, a genuine smile this time. "I just came by to say hello and see how you were doing. Are you glad to be back?"

She thought it over. "Yes, I think so."

"Everyone in town is trying to figure out why you'd come to a dirt-water place like this to live. They think you should have settled in Washington—the capital, not the state."

"I'd been wanting to write this book for about three years. Anne knew about my ambitions to make it as a political writer. I think this house was a way of giving me my chance."

"She told me when you left that you wouldn't return until you were a success. I guess she was right."

Tina absorbed this insight regarding herself and realized it was true. She'd had to feel she could hold her own against Shane Macklin in order to live here.

"Anne knew more than I realized," she murmured.

"You never told me you were leaving," Ty tossed out suddenly, a frown furrowing his forehead. For a moment, he looked tired . . . and older than his brother, she realized.

"It was best that way. I can't stand drawn-out goodbyes," she said, making light of their youthful fling. She wondered how much of Ty's feelings had been defiance of his family.

A lot, she decided.

She'd continued seeing Ty due to pure anger when she'd overheard Shane telling him that she was a fortune hunter, out for what she could get. Shane had made it clear the day Ty had brought her home for a garden party that she was persona non grata at their elegant mansion.

She and her unexpected guest were silent for a moment. She wondered if Ty's memories about that summer were as troubled as hers.

"You make good coffee," he said at last.

"Mrs. Perkins taught me."

"She's with Shane now. Ronda despises the woman. I think that's because Mrs. Perkins wouldn't take over our house."

Tina said nothing. She moved from one foot to the other, ill-at-ease with the conversation.

Ty glanced around the kitchen. "Ronda resents you. She claims you got her inheritance. But she got plenty from her father, and Anne left a healthy trust fund for Jonathan."

"I'm glad," Tina said sincerely.

He studied her for a moment. "I believe you are."

Another doubting Macklin. "I am," she said firmly. "I have work to do." She gestured vaguely to indicate she had scads of chores.

"Here's your hat and what's your hurry?" He set the mug on the counter. "I wonder if our marriage would have been as miserable as the one I have if you'd accepted my offer years ago."

She sucked in a sharp breath at the question. "Don't ever start thinking that," she warned tersely. "I turned you down then. I'd do it again."

"Oh, I know. Once you saw Shane there was no one else in your sights. He might have considered having an affair if you'd offered, but he'd never have married you."

"I don't think this topic is of interest to me." She didn't need anyone explaining Shane's opinion of her. He did it quite well himself.

Ty sighed. "I'm sorry, Tina. I'm not being a very good neighbor. I really came over to bid you welcome and to say I'm glad to see you again." He walked toward the door, then stopped. His eyes, blue like Shane's, were bleak. "You went off and made something of your life. Don't throw it away here in Riverton." He opened the door, went out through the garage and ran to his truck through the pouring rain.

She'd never felt so sorry for anyone in her life.

Shane lifted his nephew down from the truck. Jonathan loved to ride with him, especially when he turned on the lights and siren. He hadn't needed them on the trip to the barber shop.

It was Wednesday, and as usual, all the old geezers were hanging around, drinking coffee from the tea shop across the street and talking. Doug, the barber, was busy working on the thin fringe of hair that circled over the ears and behind the head of Mr. Tall, who ran the local hardware store.

"Hey, there, young fella," the barber called out to Jonathan. "How about pumping this chair up a notch or two for me?"

Shane watched the boy rush over to push on the pedal that lifted the barber chair a bit higher. His thin leg pumped industriously, and Mr. Tall rose in the air another inch.

"That's fine," the barber said.

Jonathan watched as Mr. Tall got his biweekly trim. He clambered up in the seat when Doug was ready for him.

"Uncle Shane said I could get it short on the sides and long in the back," he said proudly.

"He wants a queue," Shane explained with an indulgent smile.

"We're going out for lunch when we finish," Jonathan told the barber, holding still as the drape was tied around his neck.

"I saw that reporter woman go into the tea shop awhile ago," Mr. Tall informed them. "Maybe Ty will be with her."

Shane felt a hot ball of anger collect in his gut. "Why would you think that?" he asked, with just the right amount of interest in his tone.

"He's been over a couple of times . . . yesterday and the day before, Emma said. Understand they used to see each other right steady back some years ago when the girl was staying with Anne."

"Yes, they were friends," Shane confirmed.

"Too bad about Ty and his wife," one of the other men piped up. "Young people just fly off and get a divorce nowadays and the devil take the hindmost." He gave Jonathan a sympathetic glance.

The gossip had started, Shane realized. He'd learned that Ronda had seen a lawyer over in Medford on Monday. Great. Just what they needed, with the latest test results on Jonathan due by the end of the week.

He sighed. He'd talk to Tina, make her understand that Ty couldn't afford a scandal just now, not when there might be a custody battle looming on the horizon. Next, he'd talk to his brother and Ronda about what they were doing to their son.

Marriage wasn't just for the good times. It was for all time, as far as he was concerned. A couple who had kids had an obligation to raise those kids in a stable environment.

"Next."

He was roused from his introspection and took his seat in the chair. Using the handle, Jonathan let it down so the barber could reach his uncle's hair, which had gotten way too long and unruly.

It had been a hell of a month, Shane reflected, then realized it was only the sixth day of April. The month had barely started.

Tina wished the talkative Bess would hurry her order. Since seeing Shane and a towheaded little boy go into the barber shop across the street, she'd been in a tizzy to rush home.

Running?

Yes. There, she'd admitted it. The way Shane made her feel frightened her. She'd thought, after all this time, that she'd be immune to him. She wasn't.

And there was the complication of Ty. He'd stopped by the house yesterday for a brief chat. She felt a softening within. Ty needed a friend.

She glared at the utility vehicle with the sheriff's decal on the side. Shane should have been the friend Ty went to.

Well, their problems weren't hers. She was *not* going to get mixed up in the affairs of the Macklins.

"Here we are," Bess announced, startling Tina out of her introspection. The tea-shop owner placed the order on the table.

"Thank you. It looks delicious."

"I'll bring you another pot of tea." Bess hurried off.

Tina lifted the sandwich, then paused before she took a bite. Shane and the boy—his nephew, she presumed—were leaving the barber shop. Instead of climbing into the truck, they crossed the street.

She realized they were heading for the tea shop. Just her luck. Her tummy did a nosedive to her toes as she watched them splash through potholes filled with the rain that had been falling off and on for four days.

The child was thin and winter pale, but she could tell he was going to be tall like the Macklin men. At present, his hair was the cotton blond often found on children, but he would most likely inherit the thick, tawny locks of his father and uncle. He held his uncle's hand and skipped along beside him, chatting all the while and gazing up with adoring eyes the same shade of blue as his father and uncle had.

Shane should have a son of his own.

She laid her sandwich down without tasting it. Wild, hurting sensations ripped through her. Images of Shane walking with a child on his shoulders, holding another by the hand, came to her. She saw them in the meadow by the river, laughing and skipping stones while a woman laid out a picnic lunch, smiling and watching them with all the love she felt reflected in her eyes. . . .

No! Dear God, what was she thinking?

When the door swung open and the little bell jangled merrily to announce their arrival, she kept her eyes on her food, unable to meet the cynical gaze of the man who had shattered her youthful fantasies with his punishing kiss.

"Come in, you two," Bess called out. "I thought you might be by today. I put the stew on early."

"Jonathan and I couldn't come this close, then pass up a chance at your stew, Bess. It's the best." Shane hung his hat and coat on the rack. He helped his nephew with his wrap, then he and the boy walked over to Tina's table.

She was forced to look up and acknowledge them. "Hello."

"May we join you?" he asked.

She nodded warily, forcing all emotion from her mind. After they were seated, Shane introduced her to Jonathan.

"Hi," the boy said in friendly tones. "What kind of sandwich is that?"

It obviously never occurred to him that his questions might be intrusive or that he might be rebuffed. He was as confident as his uncle in his expectations of life.

"Vegetarian," she said. "It has sprouts and shredded carrots and cranberry sauce. Would you like a taste?"

He glanced at his uncle, who nodded assent. "Please," the child requested politely.

She cut a corner off, laid it on a napkin and placed it in front of him. He ate it with relish.

"Would you like some more?" she asked.

"Um, no," he decided. "I'll wait for the beef stew. Uncle Shane and I always have that. It sticks to a man's ribs."

"That sounds like something your uncle might say." She gave Shane a glance, then picked up her sandwich and tried again. This time she managed to chew and swallow, although her throat was dry.

Bess brought a huge bowl and a cup of stew and set them before the two males. A basket of crackers and homemade bread accompanied the meal, along with two glasses of milk. She brought Tina a new pot of tea.

"How's the work going?" Shane asked her.

"Fine. I'm still putting my notes in order."

"I suppose it's a nuisance when people drop by without an invitation. They tend to do that in a small town. Sometimes you have to tell them not to."

She wondered if he knew of Ty's visits and recalled that Shane had been to the barber shop, where Mr. Tall had gone earlier. She'd been thinking of telling Ty she was too busy to visit, but the subtle warning in Shane's message angered her. Big brother didn't trust her or Ty, it seemed.

Shane ate all of his meal, but Jonathan didn't have much appetite. He ate barely half. She remembered that Shane had said his nephew wasn't well. The child did look pale, and there were lavender shadows under his eyes, as if he didn't sleep well.

Again she felt her heartstrings tugged by a member of the Macklin family. There was a quietness about the child that didn't ring true. His eyes held a bright intelligence. His expression was alert, but he seemed tired.

"Finished?" Shane asked.

She detected the worry in his eyes as he visually measured the amount of food left on his nephew's plate.

"Yes, sir," Jonathan said. "Thank you. It was very good." He wiped his mouth and laid his napkin on the table, neatly tucked under the edge of his plate in a grown-up manner.

"You haven't finished your sandwich," Shane remarked to her.

"I'm like Jonathan. My eyes were bigger than my tummy."

Jonathan laughed at that and asked her what she meant.

"It means I thought I could eat more than I really could." She poured a fresh cup of the aromatic tea, added a small amount of brown sugar and took a sip. She gazed out the window at the mist, which had started falling again.

The buzz of the portable phone interrupted the silence. While Shane answered, two groups arrived for lunch, laughing and talking so that the peaceful shop took on a lively air.

Tina listened while Shane reported in to the dispatcher. She learned there'd been a seven-car pileup on the highway. Shane stood and spoke to Jonathan.

"Come on, sport. I'll take you home. I have an emergency."

"Can't I come, too, Uncle Shane?"

"Not to this one. People are hurt and need help."

Tina could easily imagine the scene. "I'll take him home," she volunteered. "If you don't mind him walking."

Shane flicked his gaze to her, then out the window, then back. "Are you expecting Ty later?"

"No. I meant I'd take him to your house. It isn't that far to the bridge and across the river."

He shook his head before she finished speaking. "Mrs. Perkins isn't in this afternoon. If you can keep him at your place, I'll send a deputy over to pick him up as soon as I can. Would that be too much trouble?"

"Not at all."

He tossed money onto the table to take care of the meal. "I'll get your lunch."

"That's okay. I can—"

"You're doing me a favor," he told her sharply. "It's the least I can do."

She didn't argue.

"Will I see you again?" Jonathan asked his uncle.

"Probably not today. Later this week we'll go for a ride."

The boy brightened up. "Great!"

"Do what Miss Henderson tells you."

"I will."

When Shane had gone, Tina and Jonathan sat there in silence. More people came in. "Shall we go?" she finally asked. "Bess might need our table."

They put on their coats and hats and started down the street in the light mist. When they came to an intersection, she wondered if she should take his hand. The problem was solved when he slipped his hand into hers. Once across, they continued to hold hands the rest of the way to her house.

"What do you like to do, Jonathan?" she asked.

"I don't know."

She tried to think what might entertain a four-year-old. She had no books for his age group. Recalling that he wasn't feeling well, she tried to think of quiet things they could do. Perhaps make something....

"I was going to bake some cookies this afternoon," she said, going up the sidewalk to the front door. "Would you mind helping?"

"No, I'd like that." He gave a happy smile.

So grown-up, she thought. And trusting. He followed her into the house without hesitation. After they'd hung up their outer wear, they headed for the kitchen.

"I saw a cookbook on the shelf here just the other day," Tina mused aloud. She rummaged through the pantry until she found it.

The book flopped open when she laid it on the counter. She saw a note and picked it up. It was in Anne's familiar writing.

My dear Tina,
The recipes in this book have been used by my family for three generations. I'm delighted that you're thinking of trying some. The old-fashioned brownies on this page were favorites of mine when I was a child.

I hope you'll like them, too.

Tina gazed at the graceful signature and put the note aside to add to the other letter she'd found. She glanced at Jonathan. "Did you ever visit your Aunt Anne, who lived in this house?"

He nodded. "Uncle Shane used to bring me here. And once I came with my mom, but she and Aunt Anne didn't like each other," he explained with a child's candor.

"Uh, well, I thought we'd try some recipes from this book. It has belonged to your family for...let's see...you'd be the fifth, no, sixth generation. That means your great-great-great-grandmother was the first to use it. I think."

"Wow."

"Yeah, pretty impressive. I have things that belonged to my grandparents, but your folks go back to the first settlers who came over with the wagon trains. Did you know that?"

He shook his head. "With horses and all?"

"Right."

"Were they soldiers?"

"No, they were farmers. They brought fruit-tree seedlings with them all the way from back east." When he looked disappointed, she added, "It was a very hard journey and very important to keep the roots of the tiny trees damp so they wouldn't die. I once read a story about it, about how the son of the first Macklin family worried about the trees when they came over the mountains because it was so cold. He put the seedlings inside his shirt and kept them warm until they reached the valley. He was only a little older than you when he did that."

"Really?" Jonathan's eyes gleamed with pride.

"Really. He was very smart. He helped his father plant the very first orchard in the valley."

"Did he ride a horse?"

"Umm, yes, I'm pretty sure he did. Everyone did in those days, you know." She smiled. Horses were big with him, it seemed.

"My dad's going to get me a horse just as soon as I'm old enough to take care of it myself," he told her proudly. "When I'm six, I think."

"How nice." She'd been assembling the ingredients for the brownies while they chatted. She turned the oven on. "Okay, shall we start on these? You stir and I'll drop the stuff in. Can you do that?"

"Sure."

She positioned a stool so he could reach the bowl and spoon. Soon they had the brownies mixed and poured into a baking pan. She put the pan in the oven.

"There," she said, closing the oven door and setting the timer for thirty minutes. "Now we just have to let them bake."

Jonathan climbed down from the stool and went to the window. "I can see Uncle Shane's house," he said in surprise.

"Yes, it's close to mine, but you have to walk down the main street to the bridge to cross the river."

"I live down the road—down another road—from his house."

"I see." She resisted the urge to question him, although she wondered how often he stayed with his uncle or Mrs. Perkins. Why hadn't Shane taken the child to his mother or father?

"My mom has gone to Medford," Jonathan volunteered. "She and my dad had a fight last night. Dad went out."

"Shall we build a fire in the living room while our brownies are baking? Then we can make hot chocolate to have with them."

She distracted him from further confidences with a number of chores until they were at last seated in front of the fire with brownies and cocoa. After eating, she noticed his eyes drooping.

She pulled off his shoes and laid him on the sofa where his uncle had slept. After placing an afghan over him, she washed their cups and resumed her place in the easy chair. She opened a magazine and read until she heard the sound of a vehicle outside the house.

Shane turned off the engine and sat in the truck until Ty's pickup pulled in behind them. Then he got out and waited for his brother. Together they walked toward the house without speaking.

Shane sighed. "Ty," he said, making an attempt at civility. He and his brother had said some harsh things to each other that afternoon. He bit back the frustration he felt. The family was going to hell in a hand basket, one might say.

"Yeah?" Ty asked dully. His face was pasty, the blue of his eyes brilliant against his red-rimmed eyelids.

"About Tina—"

Ty stopped and turned on Shane. "What is it, Big Brother?" he snarled. "More advice?"

"Yes," Shane snapped, his own temper exploding. "Stay away from her. You have enough problems."

"You're damned right about that," his brother agreed on a cynical note. "But she isn't one of them. She's a friend. She listens without judging. You know, sometimes it's nice to have a friend like that." He leapt up the three steps and reached for the door chime. Before he could ring it, the door opened.

Shane, standing on the steps, controlled his anger with an effort. He saw Tina glance from Ty to him.

"What is it?" she said.

"Is Jonathan here?" Ty asked.

"Yes, he's asleep." She pointed toward the living room.

Ty swept past her. She waited with the door open until Shane came up the steps and into the house. In the living room, he heard Jonathan awaken and exclaim, "Daddy!" with a happy squeal.

Shane motioned for Tina to go ahead of them. They went down the hall and into the warm, cheery room. He saw she'd built a fire.

Ty held his son in his arms, his face pressed into the boy's neck. Shane felt his heart constrict in love and pity for the man and the boy. The Macklin men had bad luck in their women, it seemed. Ronda was making threats about keeping the boy away from his father, and Ty's drinking wasn't helping things.

Neither was having Tina acting the sympathetic friend. He'd have to put a stop to that. Since his brother wouldn't listen, he'd have to make her see reason....

"Ready to go home?" Ty asked his son.

"Sure. Dad, guess what? We made brownies that were real old. Tina said my great-grandmothers made 'em too."

"From Anne's grandmother's cookbook," Tina explained. Her smile was spontaneous and sweet. Shane wondered what it would be like to have her look at him in the unguarded, friendly way she did his brother and nephew. Well, she'd dislike him even more when he reminded her again to stay away from his family. This time he'd see that she knew he meant business.

"Yeah, and one of our grandfathers brought the pear trees in his shirt. Did you know that?" Jonathan squirmed out of Ty's embrace and grinned at them. "Did you, Uncle Shane?"

"Yeah," he said. "Remind me to show you some pictures of the first orchard."

"Super."

Ty collected Jonathan's coat and hat. When he'd dressed the boy, he turned to Tina. "Thanks," he said gruffly, "for your help today. Sorry you had to be bothered with a . . . family problem." He lifted his son in his arms and headed out, nodding to his brother as he passed him.

"It was no trouble. Jonathan was a big help."

"Right. We did lots of things, Dad."

Shane reluctantly smiled as his nephew recounted all the helpful things he'd done for Tina. It seemed she was good with children. That was a surprise.

He sighed and removed his hat. A fine mist clung to the waterproofed felt. He hung it and his coat on the highboy in the hall while she saw the others out. When he glanced up, she was watching him with her opaque gray eyes, not giving any thoughts away. It wasn't the way she'd looked at Jonathan. He'd seen kindness in her gaze.

Hell, she'd *liked* his nephew. She didn't like him.

"Got any coffee?" he asked. He would try to tactfully ease into a conversation about his brother. After all, she had helped him out in a pinch.

"Yes. I made a pot earlier." She went into the kitchen.

He followed and sat at the table. Through the windows he could see the roof of his house over the pine trees. Below the knoll the house sat on, the fruit trees ran in orderly rows right down to the riverbank. On this side of the river, the lawn, still dormant from winter, rolled in gentle swales to the boulders that lined the Rogue River.

Inside, the scent of brownies lingered in the air, mingling with the spicy aroma of cedar boughs lying in a basket and of wood burning in the fireplace.

He'd always liked this house, he reflected. He had come to Anne whenever life got too hectic and he needed a breather, a place of quiet to rethink his direction. She'd been a good listener.

So was the present occupant, according to Ty.

Tina brought the coffee. He noted the pleasant perfume that surrounded her, a sort of clean smell, like soap and talcum powder. Her hair brushed her shoulders, a rich dark brown, very shiny, but without red highlights. He reached out and touched it.

She froze in place.

He looked into her eyes and saw emotion there, but he couldn't read what it was. If there weren't so many other things on his mind, he thought he'd like to know what made her tick, this small woman who didn't betray her inner being to anyone.

Except maybe Anne.

Leave her alone, Shane. She'll come back when she's ready to face you again.

And here she was.

"Have you eaten dinner?" he asked, letting his finger slide down the lock of hair.

"No."

"I'll take you out."

"I made chili earlier. If you'd like some..." She pulled away from him and hooked her hair out of the way behind her ear.

"That would be nice."

"You—you look tired," she ventured, going back to the stove. "So did Ty."

Shane grimaced at the mention of his brother. Things were tough there. "He and Ronda had a fight last night. He went out and tied one on. One of the deputies brought him home at three this morning. I kept Jonathan while he slept it off."

"Where was... Never mind, it's none of my business."

He watched her efficient movements while she heated a pot of chili and set out crackers in a blue bowl. He drank the coffee she'd given him. "Ronda came over to the house this morning and left Jonathan. She had an appointment with her lawyer in Medford."

"For a divorce?"

"Yeah, but there isn't going to be one."

Calm gray eyes studied him for a minute. "Thus speaks the Mighty Macklin," she mocked softly.

He shrugged. "I had a talk with Ty. I think he'll try to patch things up with Ronda. They need to stay together because of Jonathan."

She ladled the chili into bowls and brought them to the table. "That could be worse for him. I mean, if they argue all the time."

"They won't. They're going to try counseling."

The heaviness in his spirit was like a weight pulling him downward into hell. He looked at Tina as she sat opposite him at the table. Why had he stayed after Ty left?

Answer—he hadn't wanted to go home to an empty house. Mrs. Perkins was down in Ashland helping her daughter, who was pregnant and had two other children. She'd be gone all week and probably the next as well, she'd called to say. He hadn't felt like rattling around in the gloom by himself.

Certainly he didn't expect sympathy from his hostess for his worries. Why should she care?

"Shane, what's wrong?" she suddenly asked, looking directly into his eyes.

He wanted to talk to her, he found. He wanted to tell her of his frustration with his family, of his worries about his nephew, who had been ill with colds and flu all winter and had lost weight.

He shook his head slightly, amazed at the idea. When had he ever needed the comfort of a gold digger? he asked cynically. When had he ever needed anyone? He was the family problem solver. He had been for years.

"Nothing," he said.

"Shall we have brownies and coffee in the living room?" she suggested when they finished.

He nodded and helped her clear the table. "I wanted to tell you we caught the vandals. Some kids formed a secret club. The window breaking was part of the initiation. After a lecture and a tour of the jail, they decided to go straight."

She laughed and picked up the plate of brownies and the pot of coffee. He carried the cups. They went into the living room.

While he added fresh logs to the fire, she refilled their mugs. Then, going to a wall unit of shelves and cabinets, she opened a pull-down door and poured brandy into two snifters. She carried these to the coffee table and set them by the mugs.

She chose her favorite chair. "What happened with the accident at lunch? Was anyone hurt?"

He settled on the sofa. "Yes."

"Not . . . killed?"

"No, but two people were hurt pretty bad. A young girl, no more than sixteen, will be lucky to walk again."

She wrapped her arms across her chest, remembering the shattered bodies she'd seen, the lives wrecked by injuries that couldn't be described. Shane, in his job, saw them, too.

"I used to shake for days after seeing the aftermath of violence," she murmured. "I wondered how people could do that to each other. No cause was that noble...."

"Car wrecks are worse," he said, continuing her thought. "They're not even for a cause. A careless moment, and lives are ruined for no reason, no reason at all."

"Yes." She gave him a sympathetic glance.

He speared her with a hard, determined stare. "That can happen in people's lives, too. Sometimes, in moments of despair or weakness, we do foolish things."

Cold air settled around her like a shroud. "Why don't you just say whatever it is you want to say?" she invited, letting no emotion show on her face.

"I think it would be better if you didn't get involved in the Macklin family problems. It...could be awkward, especially if things end in a divorce and a custody battle." He paused, then finished in a harder tone, "If you don't discourage Ty from dropping by, I'll have to think of a way to do it for you."

Chapter Seven

Tina watched a drop of moisture collect and run down the windowpane. She sighed and turned off the computer. She hadn't gotten any work done that morning. Nor the day before.

Restlessness pervaded her spirit until she couldn't stand to sit still. She'd walked for miles, but that didn't help much, either. Anger churned in her.

Shane had practically accused her of being a home wrecker. As if she had anything to do with Ty's marital problems. According to Mrs. Perkins, the couple had been quarreling since Day One.

If anyone had a problem, it was Shane. She grinned wryly. True to her nature, she'd reminded him of her view of the situation. They'd ended up having a flaming row.

"Why don't you try being a friend to your brother?" she'd demanded. "You might try asking him what he wants from you, rather than telling him what you think he should do."

She shook her head in exasperation. She was absolutely, positively *not* getting involved—

The ringing of the telephone halted her advice to herself. She answered with a defensive note in her voice, but it wasn't her nemesis.

"Tina? This is Dolly Adams. From the newspaper."

"Oh, yes. How are you?"

"Not so good. That's what I'm calling about. The dumbest thing happened. I fell and broke my ankle."

"I'm terribly sorry," Tina at once sympathized.

"Well, the problem is—I know this is an imposition— but do you think…would it be possible for you to…Clint is just going to lose his mind…."

"Dolly, do you need help at the paper?" Tina asked, smiling.

"Yes," the other woman said with a great deal of relief in her voice. "Do you think you could do the feature articles for a few weeks, just until I get the cast off? I can handle the rest."

"I'd be glad to do whatever you need."

"Bless you. I'll tell Clint, so he can stop tearing his hair out. He doesn't have all that much left."

Tina laughed with Dolly when she heard the man protesting in the background. "When shall I come in?" she asked.

"Today wouldn't be too soon, if that's possible. The paper is supposed to go out this afternoon, but we aren't finished."

"I'll be there in five minutes," she promised.

After hanging up, she went to her bedroom and donned a pair of ankle boots. She put on lipstick, then checked her outfit in the mirror. The black wool slacks, black sweater and black, gold and blue vest would do.

With a quickening feeling of excitement, she slipped into a raincoat and, pulling the hood over her hair, hurried out into the mist. She'd covered half of the three blocks to the newspaper office when a horn honked and a truck pulled to the curb beside her.

"Need a lift?" Ty called out.

She hesitated, then climbed in.

"Where to?" he asked.

"The *Riverton Daily News*. I'm their newest reporter." She told him of the accident.

"Tough luck," he said. "I guess that means you can't have lunch with me?"

She shook her head. "Ty, you need a friend, but that person isn't me. Why don't you talk to Shane?"

"Why? So he can lecture me on family duties and all that?"

"So you can stop feeling sorry for yourself. Maybe it's time you started taking charge of your life. You have a wife and a darling little boy. How is he, by the way?"

Ty shrugged, his jaw set in the stubborn mode of the Macklin males. "The doctors have decided he's just run down. They've put him on iron and vitamins."

"Oh, good. Well, here we are." She was relieved that they'd arrived at the newspaper building. She opened the door and climbed out. "You have a family," she said softly, "something I've always wanted. Your son adores you. Your brother loves you. Make peace with your wife. Be happy." She smiled. "End of lecture."

He smiled, too. There was a sardonic twist to his lips, but it was still a smile. "I take it this is the goodbye you forgot to say all those years ago?"

She nodded. The Macklins didn't need her. They had each other. She hoped Shane would be happy when he learned she'd decided to do as he'd requested. Ha, he'd probably wonder what she was up to now.

"Goodbye," she said softly and closed the door.

Ty waved and drove off.

She watched the pickup disappear into the parking lot next to the ranch-supply store. She felt a nostalgic fondness for Ty. It had been like a dream come true when he'd asked her for a date that first time. Funny, she couldn't remember if he'd ever kissed her.

Surely he had, she mused, heading toward the door. But after meeting Shane, all she could recall was the older brother's suspicious attitude toward her, his frosty greeting when Ty had taken her to the garden party and introduced her…and finally, that kiss under the pear trees that had melted her defiance and sent her scurrying for safety.

Why wasn't she running now? After that episode in her bedroom last Saturday, she should take off and not look back. Until she'd protested, he'd seemed to think she was his for the taking.

She lifted her chin. She belonged to nobody but herself. She wouldn't run from anyone, ever again. She had a right to live where she pleased.

Anyway, all that was behind her. She would put the Macklin family out of her life. In the future, she'd avoid the whole bunch of them like poison bananas. Satisfied with this decision, she went inside to start her new job.

"Well, that's it," Clint Adams said in satisfaction. The paper had been run through the presses, collated, folded, labeled and tied into bundles. The driver and his helper were at the loading dock, tossing the bundles into the truck for transportation to the post office or the delivery people.

Tina, smiling, placed her hands in the small of her back and stretched. "I'm going home."

It was Friday, a week since she'd come on board. She was so tired she could hardly stand. She'd never realized what a labor of love it was to put out a small-town paper with a staff of six, one of whom was the secretary-receptionist-typist and another of whom was the maintenance man, who kept the computer-controlled printing presses running as smooth as a greased track.

Besides herself and the Adamses, there was one other reporter, a recent college graduate who covered the local sports news, accidents and police reports. Together they'd put out sixteen pages of articles, feature stories, advertisements and lots of pictures of local doings. The comics page came from a national service, thank goodness.

"Wait," Dolly requested. She sat at her desk with her injured foot propped on a cushioned stool. She'd missed only half a day of work with her injury.

Tina hooked her hair behind her ear and sat on the corner of the desk. "Don't tell me we have a weekend story to cover?"

"Well..." Dolly clapped her hands together, something she did when she was particularly excited about an idea. "I've had this brilliant idea to do a series. Clint likes it, too."

"A series?" That sounded interesting. "On what?"

"A day in the life of the mayor, the local pediatrician, the police chief." Dolly smiled excitedly as her idea took hold. "We could do the sheriff, too—sort of contrast his day to that of the local police."

Tina felt her interest dim, then brighten. She could start with the mayor. By the time they were ready for the sheriff, Dolly would be well, and she could gracefully retire.

She glanced around the cramped, noisy office. She'd missed working. She liked being with people more than she'd realized. She liked interviewing the local politicians and sniffing out stories, from accusation of graft in the school system to photographing the beauty queen in the spring pageant.

Dolly and Clint had made her welcome as a valued member of their team. They'd praised her stories and her style until she'd laughingly threatened to quit if they didn't stop. They made her feel wanted and worthy of their trust.

"I'll start Monday," she promised.

The paper came out weekly, on Friday. Other than special events, they had the weekends off. She used that time for her own project and for housekeeping. Not that she did a lot of that.

Dolly nodded. "Go home and nurse that cold. We can't have you coming down sick."

"I will." Her nose was stuffy, her voice croaky.

She left the office and walked down the street in the rosy twilight. On an impulse, she headed for the river. She'd stroll through the park to her house.

There was a haze of green on the ground, she noted, and on the pear trees across the river. The buds were swelling, ready to pop into bloom after the late winter.

The air was chilly with the departing of the sun. She zipped her jacket up to her throat when she felt the wind pick up. Earlier she'd been outside without even a jacket on, the day had been so warm.

Spring at last.

It brought a strange, painful joy to her heart. Hope reborn, she thought, after the starkness of winter.

She hadn't seen any of the Macklin family that week, thank heavens. That was probably why she felt so chipper. She'd had time to get her equilibrium back. With Dolly and Clint, she had all the friendship she needed, plus work she loved.

The shadows were deeper along the tree-shaded path. Usually she met a jogger or two, but there were none today. It was as if she were the only person in the world.

Nearing her house, the park narrowed until it came to an end at her property line. Here the path ran along the fence that divided the yards of the other houses on her street from the park.

At the end of the path, she easily climbed the wooden rails and jumped lightly down on her own land.

Instead of going inside, she lingered on the banks of the Rogue and watched the sunset darken the water to pewter. The rain last week, as well as the melting snow on the mountains, had turned the river to a torrent that cascaded over the boulders, throwing up white plumes.

"Hi, Tina," a young voice called.

She glanced across the river. Jonathan stood on the opposite side, upstream from her. She noticed that the bank had been eaten away by the rushing water. The child stood on a thin ledge. He waved and jumped up and down to get her attention.

"Jonathan, get back," she called.

Too late. The water-soaked earth began to crumble. Jonathan scrambled backwards, but the landslide moved faster, as if determined to trap the human who had dared venture too close.

He fell into the water with a cry.

Tina looked around wildly. There was no help anywhere. The boy's head bobbed to the surface, disappeared, then came up again. He thrashed against the churning water.

"Look out!" she screamed as he was hurled toward a boulder. "Grab hold. The rock. Hold on!"

He managed to turn toward the huge block of granite. With arms outspread, he was swept up onto it, the force of the water holding him against the stone. He pulled himself up higher and clung with all his strength. Even from there, she could see the terror on his young face.

"I'm coming," she called. "Hold on. I'll be there."

She dropped her purse and kicked off her shoes. In a second, she was out of her coat. Judging the force of the water, she leapt over the fence and ran upstream so she would be carried down to Jonathan. She dived in and came up fighting for breath.

The water was shockingly cold. She sucked in air, got her bearings and struck out in a strong crawl as the current bore her irresistibly down river.

Her knee hit a submerged rock. The pain raced along her leg. She ignored it and forced herself to kick harder. She was coming up on the boulder where Jonathan lay, his strength spent.

Unable to stop, she slapped into him, clutched for the boulder and was torn away like a leaf by the current. She got hold of the child's shoulder and brought him with her.

He roused himself and wrapped his arms around her, locking them behind her neck. She turned on her back so his face was above water. "Hold on. I'm going to swim for shore. Warn me if I'm about to hit anything."

He nodded. His face was chalk white.

A short way downstream, the river curved. She didn't fight the flow, but let it carry her. By kicking and using her arms, she angled them so that they would wash up on the sandbar in the bend.

When she felt the rough edge of a hidden ledge with her hand, she gave a cry of thanksgiving. Turning, she pushed them upright out of the water and stood. The water tugged at her waist, but she kept her balance. Carefully feeling her way, she managed to reach the bank and pull them to safety.

For a while she lay there, breathing hard, clutching Jonathan to her fiercely as if the river might snatch him away again.

She became aware of the cold again when she heard his teeth chattering and felt his thin body shaking. She got them both upright and looked him over.

He'd lost his shoes in the torrent. His pants, shirt and windbreaker were soaked. His lips were blue.

"Come on. We have to get inside." She lifted him into her arms. He dropped his head against her shoulder as if exhausted. She started walking, aware of the chills coursing through her own body.

It seemed forever before she saw the elegant veranda of the Macklin mansion facing the river. Like Jonathan, she couldn't stop shivering now. Fortunately, her feet were numb. She no longer felt the sharp imprint of rocks on her soles.

The house was dark. She crossed the smooth paving stones of the veranda and tried the door. Locked. She knocked on the glass panels, but there was no answer.

"Jonathan, where do you live? Look up! Where do you live?"

He raised his head and peered into the growing dark. The trees were silhouettes against the sky, the shadows beneath their branches deep. He pointed toward the east.

The wind hit her like a solid wall when she stepped off the veranda. Her legs were made of lead, so heavy she could hardly lift one, then the other. She pushed on. Finally, she saw lights ahead of them.

"Jonathan, is that your house?"

He didn't answer. She peered down at him, but could only detect the pale oval of his face nestled against her throat. He'd stopped shaking. She knew that was a bad sign.

His legs no longer gripped her waist, but hung limply, hitting against her thighs with each step.

Don't let him die. Please, don't let him die.

She leaned into the wind and concentrated on putting one foot in front of the other. Hypothermia. It could kill....

At last they reached the lawn, crossed it.... At the front door, she tried the handle and found it locked. She put her finger on the bell and kept it there. Inside, she could hear the musical tones chiming over and over.

Finally, the door opened.

"What's going on?" Ty's wife demanded. She stared as if she didn't recognize either of them.

"J-Jonathan f-fell in the r-river." Tina couldn't keep her teeth from chattering. "He n-needs h-help."

The irritated scowl changed to shock, then worry. Ronda snatched the boy from Tina's arms and rushed toward the stairs, leaving Tina standing in the open door.

She stepped inside and closed the door. Her legs buckled. She caught at a table, steadied herself and went up the steps. The floor heaved up and down under her feet.

In the upper hallway, she heard Ronda's voice, talking in strident tones to someone...paramedics, Tina thought.

"Hurry. He's unconscious. What should I do?" Ronda demanded. "Yes, I will. Yes. Yes. Hurry."

Tina heard the bang of a telephone being hung up. Help was coming. They'd save Jonathan....

She leaned against the banister, then slipped downward. Her head ached terribly. Annoying black spots danced in front of her eyes, then clumped together, becoming thicker and thicker. Finally, they obscured her vision entirely. Fortunately, she could still hear.

"Wake up, Jonathan. Mommy wants you to wake up. Jonathan, wake up!"

A sound like a slap reached Tina. *Don't hit him. It was an accident.* Tina's tongue wouldn't form the words. She needed to get home. A warm shower. Yes.

Holding on to the railing, she scooted down the steps on her rear. Her legs wouldn't cooperate. At the bottom, she managed to stand up. She realized she'd stopped shivering.

She wished someone would turn the lights on. It was so dark, she couldn't see a thing.

The wail of a siren became louder. An accident. She needed to get there... to cover it. Her job... to see... oh, God, she didn't want to see... blood... blood everywhere when people got hurt.

"What the hell is going on?" someone asked.

She couldn't see the man, but she thought she knew the voice. It was coming from a great distance, though.

"Need help," she said. Was that her? That hoarse croak? Her lips wouldn't work right. So stiff... but not cold... not anymore.

"God, you're wet and chilled through. I thought it was Jonathan. Ronda said he was unconscious."

She opened her eyes. Shane's face wavered into view, then disappeared. The world tipped. Hands touched her. She was lifted into strong arms.

"You're a block of ice," he said.

"Jonathan," she tried to explain. "River."

"Shane! Thank God! Jonathan needs help. Come here. Put her down and come here."

The sharp commands roused Tina again. She tried to straighten up, but she no longer felt her body at all. She realized she was free of it . . . free and floating. It was marvelous. . . .

"Be still," a masculine voice growled near her ear.

She felt movement, then heard the man and the angry woman talking, but their words kept fading out, even though she tried to pay attention. More voices joined them.

"Let's take their temperatures," someone suggested.

She felt herself lowered onto something soft. She whimpered and clung to the warm arms that held her.

"It's okay," the man soothed. "I'll be right here."

"Don't leave."

"I won't."

The darkness came over her completely.

Shane stood aside while the medic checked Tina over. The man had already seen to Jonathan, who was on his way to the hospital, his body in shock from the drop in temperature.

Shane unclenched his hands and took a calming breath. He had a lot of questions, but no one to answer them. He deduced that both Tina and Jonathan had somehow fallen in the river. Why and how remained to be determined.

Ronda had been hysterical and unable to explain why her son was outside at twilight, playing near the river. She'd said she thought he was resting. She'd been on the phone and hadn't heard him go out. Then "that woman" had shown up with him. Ronda had accused Tina of trying to drown her son.

Shane shook his head. If she'd been trying to drown him, she wouldn't have walked a half mile in the near-freezing wind to bring him home. He stared at her lips, which were blue like his nephew's. She, too, was in shock.

He'd stripped her wet clothes from her and had put her under the covers until the medics could look her over. She was a small woman, but perfectly formed. He grimaced ruefully. He'd often thought of having her in bed, but not like this.

"She'll be okay," the medic announced. "Her temperature hasn't dropped into the danger zone. She needs to be kept warm, though. We'd better take her to the hospital for observation."

"No." The dark fan of lashes on her pale cheeks lifted. She looked at the medic, then at Shane. "No hospital."

The appeal in her eyes was something he couldn't deny. He forced a smile to assure her he'd take care of her. "I'll keep an eye on her, if that's what she needs."

The medic shrugged. "Give her lots of hot drinks until her temperature is normal." He packed up his bag.

"Jonathan?" she whispered.

"He's going to be fine," the medic answered. "So are you. Better rest for a couple of days before you decide to take a dip in the river again, though," he advised half-facetiously.

She smiled.

Shane's heart contracted. "What happened? Do you remember?"

She frowned as she obviously tried to recall. "The bank gave way. Jonathan fell. So frightened. I thought he was going to die. So awful...when children die...."

He took her hand. "Shh, it's okay. You saved him."

She glanced at him. "Did I? He stopped shivering. I thought—I thought..."

She closed her eyes and started to cry, silent sobs shaking her body as tears seeped into her hair at her temples. He stood there for ten seconds, then, when the medic moved aside, he sat on the bed and slipped his arms under her shoulders, holding her while she wept.

It gave him a strange feeling, to know she could cry.

Chapter Eight

Tina felt Shane's fingers smoothing away the tears from her temples. She stiffened as she realized what was happening. She was in the arms of her enemy, crying like one of those wimpy females she detested. Moreover, he hadn't said a word when his sister-in-law had accused Tina of trying to drown her son.

She pulled away, holding the sheet self-consciously over her breasts when she realized she was naked. She refused to think about how she'd gotten out of her clothing.

"I want to go home." She sounded pathetic rather than strong, as she'd intended. "Where are my clothes?"

Shane frowned, then nodded. "You're right. You can't stay here. I'll take you home."

She sniffed. He handed her a tissue. She wiped her eyes and blew her nose. "My clothes—"

"They're wet. I'll find you something." He left her. In less than a minute, he was back. He held a thick, fleecy robe for her to put on.

The color was champagne pink. She shied away from using anything of Ronda's, but didn't have a choice. Stretching one arm out from under the covers, she touched the soft material.

Shane had no thought for her modesty. He slipped the robe over her arm, pulled it behind her, pushed her other arm into the sleeve and swept the sheet aside in one easy motion.

Paying no attention to her glare, he lifted her as if she were no bigger than his nephew, set her on her feet and fastened the buttons down the front. He dropped to one knee and tugged on her foot.

"Lift," he ordered.

He slipped fleece-lined moccasins on one foot, then the other. She hugged her arms across her chest and started shivering again. He frowned at her before sweeping her into his arms. Instinctively, she flung an arm around his neck.

He grabbed a blanket from the bed and tossed it over her before hurrying down the stairs. Outside, he put her in the patrol truck, jumped in and took off. He turned in at the blacktop drive to his house. There he killed the engine, leapt out and came around for her.

"W-wait," she said, confused. Her teeth were chattering again. "I want to go h-home."

He paid no attention to her protests, but carried her inside and upstairs to a suite of rooms facing the river. He efficiently pulled back the covers on the bed, took the blanket away from her, then, as if he had every right, started unfastening the robe.

"D-don't," she ordered. She couldn't seem to stop his hands. They were everywhere—on the buttons...at her shoulders...down her arms as the robe slipped free...lifting her to the bed...yanking the moccasins off...pushing her under the sheet.

"Lie still," he said, forcefully holding the cover over her. "You're going to stay here where I can watch you. I'll be right back." He walked out.

She tried to sit upright, intending to grab the robe and get out of there before her captor returned. Her head spun dizzily, and she moaned as a wave of weakness ran through her. She lay down again abruptly.

The shivering grew worse. She huddled under the sheet and a thermal blanket and tried to will herself to stop shaking. She couldn't.

When Shane returned, she closed her eyes and pretended she wasn't there.

"Here," he said.

He slipped the covers down and urged her to sit up. Then he put a pajama top—his, she realized—on her. It was incredibly warm. He put thick socks on her feet.

"I warmed them in the clothes dryer," he told her, evidently proud of this idea. He covered her again and added the blanket he'd wrapped around her earlier. "You're still shivering."

"Reaction," she managed to say without stuttering. She forced her eyes open.

Shane stood by the bed, watching her with a worried frown between his eyes. "Was it like this when you were covering a story for CNN?"

"Afterward. When I returned to Rome. It's just reaction—"

"It's more than that. Your body temperature was way down. It still isn't up to normal. I have tea brewing." He left the room once more.

She hugged the warm cotton of the pajama top to her. It reached almost to her knees when she smoothed it into place. The shivers came in waves now, but she could at least control the chattering of her teeth.

When Shane returned, he carried a large thermal mug of the type made for commuters to use on their way to work. He sat on the side of the bed, his hip against the curve of her waist.

"Sit up," he coaxed. He stuffed two pillows behind her back so she could rest against them and brought the mug to her mouth.

She was forced to swallow. A drop ran down her chin, but he caught it on a finger and sucked it off.

"Too hot?" he asked.

"No." She removed one arm from the blankets and took the mug, determined not to let him see her totally helpless. She hated being vulnerable in front of anyone, but especially him.

He linked his hands together over one knee and leaned back to watch while she drank the sweet, hot tea. She felt the warmth flow all the way down her throat and into her stomach. As soon as she finished, he brought her another mug, just as hot, just as sweet. The cloying taste began to get to her, and she protested.

"You need it," he said, pushing the mug toward her mouth with one hand under the bottom of it.

Giving him an irritated glance, she drank the contents down, then set the mug on the table. She sank into the pillows with a sigh. The shivers had lessened to an occasional series of tremors.

"I'm all right now," she muttered sleepily. "You can leave. I don't need anybody."

Shane called the night dispatcher to check on things, then phoned the hospital. He talked to his brother, who had joined Ronda at the hospital from the Friday-night poker game at the feed store, which he, as sheriff, wasn't supposed to know about. He'd sent a deputy to the store for Ty after he'd gotten the hysterical call from Ronda and had called for an ambulance. Then he'd headed out himself.

It had been a shock to find Tina at his brother's house, wet clear through and semiconscious. He still hadn't found out how the accident had happened. Or why Ronda thought Tina would have a reason to drown her son.

His lips tightened. It was one thing for him to protect his family from a possible fortune hunter. It was another for Ronda to make wild accusations against her.

He returned to his room and sat by the sleeping woman in his bed. She had a surprising fierceness where children were concerned that reminded him of a lioness protecting her cubs.

Against his hip, he felt the shivers that still ran through her periodically. He realized he, too, was cold. His clothing was damp from where he'd carried her to the bed at Ty's house.

He went to a bureau and got out the bottoms of his pajamas and a long-sleeved sweatshirt. Glancing at his bed, he saw that Tina was resting still, her eyes closed. It stirred some emotion inside him to see her so pale. Even her lips—usually pink and plump as rosebuds—were colorless.

He changed clothes and put on a pair of sports socks to pad around in, then went down to heat some soup for supper. He'd fix some for her, too.

When he returned, he found her asleep, but restless. "Jonathan, don't!" she said. Her voice was hoarse. "Get back," she ordered. Her words became a mumble that he couldn't understand.

"Tina?" He called her name twice before she responded.

She opened her eyes and stared at him in fright. He knew the moment she recognized him and felt a flare of triumph. The fear left her, and she sighed in relief. Whatever else she might feel about him, she knew he wouldn't hurt her. She trusted him.

"Soup," he said. "Not as good as yours. It's out of a can."

"That's okay." She pushed upright and fixed the pillows.

He worried about her. She was definitely coming down with a cold or laryngitis. She must have been sick before she leapt into the river. He placed a tray across her knees.

With one hand, he pulled a chair close and sat down with his tray on his lap. "Can you tell me what happened tonight?"

"I walked along the river on my way home." She cleared her throat and gave a painful grimace. "Jonathan saw me and yelled hello. He was on the other side."

She paused, then continued the tale. Shane experienced a painful clenching inside as he envisioned the danger to both of them. The river was flowing at better than twenty knots with the recent rain and the spring snowmelt. A half mile farther, it dropped into a steep canyon, from which rescue would have been impossible. They could have died.

He tried to analyze the deep wrench that caused him, but couldn't sort it out. He had a sense of his life becoming more and more entangled with the woman who lay in his bed.

Maybe with her in his house—at his mercy, so to speak—he'd find out why she'd returned to the area.

He didn't really believe she'd heard of Ty's problems and decided to try to win him again. After all, she was a celebrity. If she were after money, she'd surely met wealthier people abroad than any she'd find in Riverton. The pear orchards made money, but not enough to put the Macklins among the country's richest families.

He watched his mysterious guest while she ate the hot soup. He wondered if she'd heard Ronda's wild demand that he arrest her for attempted murder.

Sighing, he shook his head. Things were not becoming clearer where Tina was concerned. They were getting more and more muddled.

Passion was part of the problem, he thought. He couldn't see her without becoming restless with needs he'd ignored for a long time. It had been two years, almost three, since he'd been intimately involved with anyone.

When the woman had demanded a commitment, he'd been unable to make it. His past experiences had crept between them. Hell, he knew better than to trust women, and that was a fact.

Against his will, his gaze was drawn to the delicate-looking female wearing his pajama top and sitting in his bed. She'd risked her life for a boy she barely knew. She trembled in reaction to emotional trauma when others got hurt. That didn't jibe with his view of her as a female predator after the main chance.

He could no longer put her in the same category with his stepmother—an out-and-out fortune hunter. Tina didn't fit neatly into any niche that he could find. So where exactly did she fit?

At last he gave up trying to figure her out and watched while she delicately sipped a spoonful of soup. Her lips, which had always fascinated him, pursed in a way that made him think of other things besides food. His body stirred in lustful need.

It would be a joy to make love to her, he thought, and was amazed at the idea. He'd never connected sex and happiness before.

"Through?" he asked when she laid the spoon down.

She nodded and glanced around. "I, um, need—"

"In there." He pointed toward the bathroom. Gathering the dishes, he started to carry them down to the kitchen. He noticed she didn't leave the bed until he was out of the room.

He smiled, his mood becoming cynical as he headed down the stairs.

She needn't be modest with him. He knew exactly what she looked like with nothing on. He knew how her breasts came to a rounded point, pert as a puppy's nose; how they stood out against the slenderness of her rib cage. He knew how she responded to his touch, thrusting upward to meet his hand. He knew every nuance of lovemaking he wanted to experience . . . with her.

Only with her.

Damn.

Tina was woken by her own cry, lashing out in her nightmare against fears she couldn't control or explain. She sat up abruptly and stared around the strange bedroom.

The walls were painted a soft shade of creamy white. One wall was decorated with several landscape paintings. Baskets, a copper pot holding a fern, plus ceramic pots with exotic palms lined the floor beneath the pictures. A reading table with a forest green cloth and two padded chairs formed a grouping at one end of the room. Built-in shelves and drawers occupied the other end. In the center of the room the huge bed backed against a side wall.

Shane was asleep in one of the chairs, his neck crooked at an awkward angle that Tina knew would make it sore when he awoke.

She realized where she was: in Shane's house...in his bed.... She couldn't remember how she'd gotten there...with nothing on but his pajama top and a pair of socks.

Oh...the river. Yes. She remembered the fright. Shane's nephew. She'd had to save him.

Shane's eyes flicked open. He sat up, grimaced, then rubbed his neck. He gave a low groan.

"Why are you sleeping in a chair?" she asked.

"Damned if I know."

He rose, stretched, then rolled his head in a slow circle to work the kinks out. Covering a yawn, he came to the bed and sat beside her. He took her hand in his and studied it thoughtfully. "Bad dreams?" he asked.

She realized she was trembling. She nodded.

"What about?"

Pulling her hand from his, she combed her fingers through her hair, then clasped her hands together to control the tremors. "I don't know. It's all mixed up. I always think someone is dying and needs me, but I can't get to them...."

"You saved Jonathan."

She looked away from his probing gaze. "It was... I just happened to be there. If he hadn't been trying to attract my attention, he might not have fallen in."

Shane enfolded both her hands in his and chaffed them, restoring the warmth. "Or he might have, and no one would have seen him until it was too late."

Again Tina tried to pull her hands from his, but he wouldn't let her go. She glanced up into his eyes, then down again. There were things in her she didn't want him to see. His touch was affecting her. It stirred feelings she didn't want to admit.

"Why did you do it? Why didn't you just scream for help?" His eyes, so darkly suspicious of her every motive, roamed over her face. "Did you think you could insinuate yourself into the Macklin family by acting the heroine?"

The haunting loneliness she'd experienced for the last eleven years came over her. She fought it, but like the trembling, she couldn't make it go away.

"Did it work?" she inquired with a mocking smile. The smile wouldn't stay on her mouth.

"Not with Ronda." His eyes crinkled pleasantly at the corners when he smiled, but the smile was without mirth. "Maybe it did with me...."

His hands moved up her arms, stroking slowly and gently. A violent shiver raced through her. He rubbed her shoulders, leaning forward until their faces were no more than a few inches apart.

She closed her eyes and tried the relaxing techniques taught to her by a doctor who'd treated patients with post-traumatic-stress syndrome. Nothing seemed to work.

The problem was, she wasn't sure if the shaking was caused by her dreams or by Shane's shattering presence.

"Feeling better?" he asked in a husky tone.

Slowly she opened her eyes, knowing she shouldn't, knowing she'd be lost to all reason if she gave in to desire.

"I should go," she said, her voice a thread of sound in the quiet room. She wanted to stay.

"You need someone to watch you."

She pulled her resolve together. "I can watch after myself."

He frowned slightly, studying her with a puzzled light in his eyes. "So stubbornly independent," he murmured. "Not a normal trait for a gold digger."

"Right. It's a ploy to confuse you." Her mocking laugh came out as a croak. Her throat ached.

His smile, genuine this time, was accompanied by a sigh of resignation. "You do that just by being here, just by *being.*" He smoothed her hair back from her temple.

She felt his breath blow lightly across her ear while he continued to lean over her. Gradually, in spite of his distrust, his presence became comforting to her, then arousing.

Her heart speeded up. She glanced at his lips, a hand span from hers, then away. She swallowed, fighting the desire to throw her arms around his neck and cling to his powerful frame.

He seemed so big, so strong, able to crush her with his hands, yet he stroked her temple as gently as a father would his child. It was unnerving.

She trembled again.

"Are you cold?" he questioned. Without waiting for an answer, he slipped down on the bed, the covers between them, and partially covered her with his body.

Heat rushed from him to her, warming all the cold, secret places of her heart, places she'd never known existed until now. Her bodily rhythms were troubled by his closeness.

First she breathed too fast, taking in great gulps of air that made her dizzy. When she tried to breathe slowly and evenly, she felt light-headed, as if she weren't getting enough oxygen.

She realized his lips were no longer a hand's width from her lips, but had somehow moved closer while she was trying to breathe. She lay very still, but she was aware . . . oh, yes, she was aware of him in every cell.

His fingers tunneled into her hair. Very slowly, he turned her to face him. Holding her head like a chalice, he moved ever so slightly closer, then sipped from her lips as if tasting a rare wine.

He drew back and paused. She tried to speak, but her throat would emit no sound beyond a raspy breath. He kissed her again, the merest touch of his lips.

"Kiss me back," he ordered in a low rumble, the need evident in the thickening of his voice.

"I . . . we shouldn't . . ."

Stay alert, she ordered, but a rosy haze seemed to shroud her thoughts. A loud hum invaded in her ears, but she couldn't tell if it was from within or without.

"I've wanted you here, like this, for years." He pressed his face against her neck and delicately stroked the flesh there with his tongue, leaving a moist, burning trail. "I wondered, after you left, what would have happened if you'd stayed . . . if you hadn't run from me. . . ."

"I didn't run." She couldn't let him think he'd scared her away—even though he had. Years ago, she'd learned it was better to face your enemies than to run, to smile rather than to fight. It drove them crazy. "I'm not afraid of anyone."

She smiled at him with an effort, to confuse him further. He chuckled, the sound a caress against her breasts as his chest moved. How had she become locked in his arms?

He laid two fingers on a pulse point in her neck. "Why is your heart beating so hard?"

"Why is yours?" she challenged.

"Because I want you like hell...and you're in my bed...and I can't think of one good reason to stop." He dipped his head and kissed along her collarbone, the heat of his mouth penetrating the cotton of the pajama top.

She caught her breath. Her heart felt jumpy, like a newly broken filly on her first ride outside the paddock.

"It might be a trap," she warned hoarsely.

That brought his head up. His eyes went as hard as Oregon granite. "Not for me," he informed her. "I don't play those games. Any woman who gets mixed up with me knows the rules."

"Do you make her sign a contract?" She turned her head and sneezed twice before she could stop. "Oh," she groaned, the spasm causing her throat to hurt unbearably.

Shane sat up and handed her a tissue from the night table by the bed. She used it and looked around helplessly. He tossed it into a nearby wastebasket, which he moved within reach.

To her surprise, he laid a hand on her forehead. "No fever that I can detect. But you'd better get some rest."

She was wary of this considerate Shane. It would be so easy to think he cared....

He pulled the comfortable chair to the bed and sank into it. He propped one foot on the quilt and crossed the other over it at the ankle. "Go to sleep," he advised with a sardonic twinkle in his eyes. "If you dare...."

There was some message in that statement, but she couldn't figure out what it was. Just before she drifted back to sleep, she remembered something she'd read once.

Be careful when a rogue is being charming. That's when he's the most dangerous.

She opened her eyes a crack. Shane had his eyes closed. She let her lashes drift down again. If she stayed in Riverton, they would make love. It was as inevitable as the sunrise.

Tina couldn't remember feeling worse. Her head ached. Her lungs burned. Her throat felt like raw meat. She had a cold.

It was Saturday morning. She'd awakened at six, when Shane had unfolded his long, powerful body from the chair and gone into the bathroom. Then she'd heard the shower come on.

He'd come out wearing a towel around his waist, and she'd quickly closed her eyes and pretended to be asleep when he'd glanced her way. She'd heard him moving around as he dressed.

Once, she'd opened her eyes and gotten a glimpse of him as he pulled on white cotton briefs. She'd clamped her eyelids shut tightly, but she knew she would forever remember the purity of his masculine form in the early morning light...the long, lean lines of his hips and thighs, the strong curve of his back as he'd bent down, the flex of muscles like smooth steel cables under his skin.

As soon as he'd left the room, she'd gone to the bathroom. It had been shockingly erotic to step into the shower, which was still damp and steamy from his use, and know he'd been there only minutes before. She'd never taken a shower with a man.

She'd washed quickly. The steam had helped open her sinuses. After drying, she'd put the blue-striped pajama top back on and the sports socks that came to her knees. She'd dried her hair, using his brush to turn the ends under, and brushed her teeth with toothpaste on a washcloth. Then she'd hurried back to bed, her heart pounding when she'd heard whistling from below.

She fluffed up the two fat pillows behind her and stared out the window as the sun peeked over the hill, changing the world from shades of gray to shades of gold. The earth reborn, she thought.

The clank of crockery drew her eyes to the door. Shane entered the bedroom. "Breakfast," he announced.

He was incredibly handsome in gray cords with a white T-shirt tucked into them. Over the T-shirt he wore a deep blue corduroy shirt, open down the front, the sleeves rolled back on his forearms. The color matched the blue of his eyes.

"Keep looking at me that way and I'll think you'd rather have me than breakfast," he murmured, giving her a deliciously wicked sideways glance as he bent over the bed.

"You'd be too tough," she said in a hoarse whisper. "I'd probably ruin my teeth trying to get through your hide."

Laughing, he released one tray—she saw he had two—on the bed, placed the other over her knees, removed his own plate and cup to the spare tray and took a seat in the chair.

"You could soften me up with a few nibbles," he suggested. He picked up his fork and began eating his overeasy eggs and sausage. He'd made himself four slices of toast to her two.

She noted he'd prepared her a poached egg, toast, oatmeal and juice. For some strange reason, his thoughtfulness touched her. Her eyes smarted, and she had to blink several times until she was in control once more.

It wouldn't do to let his care get to her, she reminded herself sternly. The situation between them was precarious at best. He made no secret of his hunger for her. And he knew she wanted him, too.

Could she risk her heart in an affair?

After it was over, then what? Like her mother, would she feel compelled to leave town in disgrace, knowing that everyone would be aware he'd tossed her aside when the newness wore off?

"Eat," he said, his tone lower and huskier than before.

She met his gaze. There was blatant desire in the fathomless blue depths. His eyes invited her to share it with him.

A storm of need broke over her. She quickly picked up her spoon and began on the oatmeal. Its heat soothed her throat and helped belay the nervous excitement that coursed through her.

When she finished eating, he took the dishes downstairs and returned with an insulated container of coffee. They drank in companionable silence. "It looks warm out today," she ventured.

He flicked a glance out the window, then returned to a steady contemplation of her. Strange little thrills ran along her skin.

"It's supposed to get up into the high fifties. But there might be a freeze later in the week."

"Would that hurt the fruit trees?"

"Yes." He seemed surprised at her question. "They're budding out now. A freeze could kill this year's crop."

"What do you do to prevent it?"

"We have heaters that we put around the perimeter of the orchards, plus wind jets to keep the air moving. Cold air settles into the low places."

"The whole valley is a low place," she murmured, watching the fruit trees sway in the morning breeze. She could feel the fitful longing deep inside her, growing and swelling like a bud on a tree. She knew the danger in that.

Holding her cup close to her mouth, she inhaled the rich aroma of the coffee and felt the steam soothe her throat as she tried to think of what she should do.

Go home.

She ignored the advice. She wanted to stay....

When Shane stood and prowled the room, she recognized the restlessness in him as well. He drank deeply from his cup and set it on the table.

"Either your coffee is better than the last time, or my tastebuds are completely useless," she said, forcing a light note.

"I followed your instructions," he told her. He stopped by the bed. After watching her for a minute, he sat on the side, his hip against hers before she scooted over.

"Then it's the coffee," she croaked, trying not to notice the way his gaze—dark and moody, almost resentful—ran over her.

"Why?" he asked in a low growl. "Why do I look at you and think of a thousand delights?"

"I—I don't know," she answered helplessly.

"You look so soft and innocent, and I want you so much, more than I've ever wanted anything... *anything.*" He repeated the word with a perplexed frown.

His breath became deeper, ragged with need he didn't bother to hide. He lowered his lips to hers. She turned her head at the last minute.

"I have a cold," she reminded him. "You'll catch it."

"I already have a fever," he murmured, his breath warm, coffee-scented, fanning over her temple and stirring the tendrils there.

His finger under her chin turned her face to his. All her muscles clenched in tormented longing and anticipation as his mouth hovered above hers. She licked her lips.

"The hunger grows." His breath touched her mouth. "I wonder if a kiss will be enough to satisfy it."

He paused and looked at her, waiting for her response....

Chapter Nine

Tina trembled when he moved his hand. His fingers brushed the tips of her breasts, which became taut and heavy at the same time. He watched her, his eyes delving into hers as if trying to probe into her soul. She stayed very still.

"I want to arouse you," he said, his eyes going dark with hunger. "I want to see you helpless in my arms, your body flushed with the passion I know I've kindled in you. I want your eyes—such stormy eyes, capable of hiding every thought—to gleam with desire... for me... only for me."

"Shane..." She couldn't say more. Currents like stray bolts of lightning ran randomly through her. She pressed her hands against the white T-shirt, intending to push him away. She *had* to push him away or else...

She didn't.

Of their own volition, her hands spread over his broad chest. She stared at their pale flesh color splayed against the white cotton. She pressed and felt the muscles contract, then relax under her palms.

"Yes, touch me like that," he encouraged. He lifted his hands to the headboard and leaned toward her.

Was that a plea in his voice? She looked at him. His eyes were closed, as if he were enraptured with her caress. The need was stark on his face. It enthralled her—captured her as nothing else would have—to have him need her.

She stroked him for a minute, then that wasn't enough. She wanted the feel of his flesh. Tugging at the material, she freed his T-shirt from his cords and ran her hands up under it.

He gave a throaty groan that echoed through her, stirring the hunger she tried to suppress. She knew she should stop before this madness carried them both too far....

Slowly, his eyes opened. He gazed deeply into hers. The moment became an eternity.

He lowered his head, his mouth opening as he touched her lips. He caressed her with his tongue, sipping and licking as if he couldn't get enough of her taste, going so slowly and carefully she never thought of holding back after that moment.

He touched her breasts again, the backs of his fingers brushing back and forth across the sensitive tips, first one, then the other until all her being seemed concentrated there.

She caught his hands and pressed them to her.

Shane felt her nipples beaded hard and tight against his palms and felt he was coming apart at the seams. She was so responsive, so *hot* when he got past that cool facade she showed the world. He shifted, raising his head to look at her.

Her eyes opened, and his breath stuck in his throat. They were gray and shining...molten silver...helpless and shocked and filled with desire so strong it drove him wild.

"It's all right," he assured her.

He didn't want to hurt her, only to love her until they both melted in the cataclysmic explosion their lovemaking would produce. He didn't even know how he knew that was the way it would be for them, he just did.

With strong, massaging motions, he caressed her breasts. She closed her eyes and arched upward to meet him. Her arms came around his neck, pulling him closer.

"Want you," she whispered. "So long...so terribly."

"Yes. A lifetime. I've waited for you. Anne said you would come back. I've waited...."

He heard the words, but they made no sense. The blood roared through his body, drowning out all thoughts that weren't of this moment, part of this magic.

Standing, ignoring her throaty cry of disappointment, he flung the covers aside. With hands that shook, he threw off his shirt and drew the T-shirt over his head. He kicked off the loafers. His hands went to his belt. He paused and observed her, waiting for her refusal.

None came.

Relief washed over him when she smiled at him. Her gaze was restless. Her eyes seemed dark now, the charcoal gray of storm clouds when the storm grew dangerous. The air crackled between them as he shucked his clothing.

When she moved over, he lay down beside her. Her hands caressed his chest, his sides, his hips, running over his flesh as if she couldn't get enough of him.

Dipping his head, he took her breast in his mouth. She writhed against him. He laid a hand at her waist and slipped one leg over her. She opened her own legs, letting him slide between the silky softness of her thighs.

At last, he thought hazily. *At last.*

It was the truth, he realized. He'd waited a lifetime for her to touch him like this. It was worth the wait.

Tina couldn't stop the whimpering sounds of need that escaped from her as Shane ran his hand over her stomach and caressed the thatch of curls at the apex of her legs. The pajama top had somehow climbed to her waist.

"If I touched you, you'd fly apart right in my hands," he whispered hotly. "So would I . . . if you touched me."

She heard the need and marveled that this man . . . this strong, confident man . . . needed *her.* "Shall I?" she asked. She let her fingers glide over his hips, hesitated, then reached between their tense bodies. She touched the masculine staff and found it warm and smooth, hard but not threatening.

He groaned and kissed her deeply, moving his lips restlessly over hers, his tongue thrusting in passionate play until hers answered the demand.

Against her hand, his body throbbed in wild passion that thrilled her beyond words. Slowly, he moved against her in the rhythm of life. He touched her intimately, causing every muscle in her body to tighten in shock and pleasure.

The kiss intensified as their hands brought primitive delight to their senses. He shuddered against her as she gained courage and explored his body more thoroughly. He gasped at one point and caught her hand in his.

"Enough," he whispered, trailing wet kisses along her cheek and temple. He drew both her hands above her head and held them there while he ravaged her breasts with his mouth.

"Shane, I—I . . ."

Shane raised his head and studied her face, giving them time to come down a bit. He was too close to the edge.

She opened her eyes, and he felt as if he were being drawn into those stormy depths. He realized dimly that he didn't care if he were. It was almost shocking...to want to be that deep in someone else....

He raised himself on an elbow and quickly opened the drawer of the bedside table. He didn't trust himself beyond this point. When he touched her again, he would go for the finish with her, both of them together, riding a wave of pure pleasure.

"One second," he murmured, his voice almost as hoarse as hers. He held out the packet. "Do you want to do the honors?"

Without hesitation, Tina took it from him. She realized he assumed she was much more experienced than she actually was. She removed the condom and spread it over him. When she proved a bit awkward, he helped her complete the job.

He kissed her again, long, drugging kisses, while his hands brought her back to the peak. Then he moved over her.

Slowly and carefully, he merged his body with hers. Sensation spiraled inside her. She moved, spreading her legs wider, taking him deeply into her, loving the feel of their joining.

Whatever else was wrong between them, this was right. She knew it instinctively, the way a salmon knows its river and the way to the spawning grounds. She knew...and it was right.

She moved slightly and the joining was complete, their bodies so tightly, so warmly nestled into each other that there was no empty space remaining to be filled. Happiness washed over her.

"Shane," she breathed. "Shane."

"Shh," he whispered in a deep, almost reverent tone. "I know. I know."

Looking into his eyes, she knew he, too, felt the magic. She moved her hips against him, wanting more.

"Easy," he cautioned. A smile flickered over his lips. "I want this to last."

It pleased her to know she affected him as strongly as he did her. When he began to move, the world condensed until there was just the two of them. When he slipped his hand between them to caress her intimately, it became even smaller, contracting to that point where they merged into one.

Stars seemed to spin out of control behind her tightly closed eyes. She gasped and cried out his name... again... and again.

"Yes, darling," she heard him say. "Yes. Yes. Yes."

The roaring filled her ears. She lifted toward him, needing him in ways she couldn't begin to comprehend, and he was there for her... holding her... giving her his hands, his mouth, his body, so that she was sated.

She clung to him, feeling his deep thrusts gradually slow as the powerful climax played itself out. When he was still, they lay entwined, their hearts and lungs working in unison as their senses expanded past each other to the bed, the room, the silent house that seemed to sigh in happiness at their union.

Shane lay without thinking for long, long moments, adrift in a sensual fog so thick nothing could penetrate it, except the woman nestled so snugly beneath his body. He held his weight on his arms, careful of her slenderness— this small woman whose passion had matched his own.

Caution returned slowly. He didn't welcome it.

He lifted himself from her, a new awareness washing over him. He'd wanted to see her locked in the passion he'd induced, but he'd been too caught up in it himself to observe her reactions. It was the first time he'd ever been totally lost in lovemaking.

He moved to lie beside her, his energy spent, his body slick with perspiration from their searing contact. So was hers.

Running a hand over her torso, he felt her shiver. Rising to an elbow, he gazed down at her, worried now that the burning hunger was assuaged . . . for the moment. He knew, as surely as the sun rose in the east each morning, that he'd want her again and again.

At some time during those tumultuous moments, he'd unfastened the pajama top. It opened to each side of her, damp and wrinkled from their lovemaking. Her breath rasped through her throat.

Guilt hit him. She was ill. He'd taken advantage. . . . No, she'd wanted him as much as he'd wanted her.

The strangest feeling swept over him, something like the way he felt about his nephew at times: tender, protective, loving.

He frowned grimly. He wouldn't be caught in that trap. His feelings were natural—and mutual, he realized, looking into her eyes—and were the result of that incredible climax. Who wouldn't feel tender toward a partner who shattered the world and rebuilt it with magic? It had been the same for both of them.

Pride infused him, along with a sense of triumph, as if he'd just climbed a previously unconquered mountain. Energy flowed through his muscles, and he felt reborn.

There was danger in that kind of thinking, he reminded himself ruthlessly. Sex had been known to make men do foolish things.

He ignored the warning that rang through him. Sliding from the bed, he headed for the bathroom, then turned back.

Tina saw the doubts flicker in his eyes before he smiled at her. "Do you want to join me in a quick shower? Or maybe it will be a slow one," he added with a wicked grin.

She hesitated, wanting to go with him, but not sure.

"I promise not to splash too much."

She wasn't very experienced at love play. When she'd first lived in Europe, she'd been desperately lonely and had gotten involved in a brief affair that had proven very unsatisfactory. She'd found intimacy rather embarrassing.

Strong arms slipped under her. She was lifted from the bed and carried to the bathroom. There he set her on her feet, turned on the water and adjusted its temperature. Then he turned back to her. She shivered when he removed her top and the socks.

Helping her into the shower, he washed her quickly and gently, but without a word. He seemed introspective now. She wondered what he was thinking.

He probably was worried that she was going to try to trap him into marriage in spite of his warnings. The days were long past when women expected gallantry from men, she wanted to tell him.

When he finished with her, he washed himself while she leaned against the shower wall and inhaled the steam. It opened her nose and soothed her throat, so she felt much better when he turned off the water and wrapped a towel around each of them.

He dried her hair and brushed it into shining smoothness before taking care of himself. His consideration made her want to weep. "There," he said when they were both dry.

He let her use his deodorant and powder. He gave her a new toothbrush, and they brushed their teeth side by side at the twin sinks. This felt more intimate than making love...like they were an old married couple, used to sharing.

He pulled on black sweats, the top printed with a mountain lion, its golden eyes staring out at the viewer in lordly disdain. "I should have gone to your house and gotten a gown for you," he said. "I have your key—"

"My purse!" It was the first time she'd thought of it.

"I had a deputy pick it up from the riverbank. Also your coat and shoes."

He studied her as if looking for clues to her motive for rescuing his nephew. His distrust surfacing again, she realized. Her spirits dropped several notches. "Thank you."

He shrugged her gratitude aside. "He took your coat to the cleaners. I washed your wet things. They're in the dryer." A smile flitted over his face. "They're probably done by now."

"Probably," she murmured in the same wry tone he'd used. She wasn't going to let a little thing like the most incredible experience of her life daunt her. She could be as cool as he was. "I'd like to get dressed. I need to go home. I have work to do."

"No," he said, his tone becoming low and fierce.

She was taken aback. "Really, I—"

"Stay here, at least for the weekend," he requested. "I'd feel better if I could keep an eye on you...to see that your cold doesn't take a turn for the worse."

"I see," she said slowly. If she stayed, she knew what would happen. Meeting his intent gaze, she realized she didn't want to give up the magic, not just yet. Neither did he.

In the bedroom, he opened a drawer and pulled out a blue T-shirt whose message had long faded. He gave it to her to put on. Going to the bed, he yanked off the sheets.

Turning her back to him, she let the towel drop and slipped into the T-shirt. It came to her knees. Then she watched Shane—the Mighty Macklin!—change the bed and put on fresh sheets as efficiently as a housemaid.

"If you ever need another job, I can recommend you for nursing care," she commented, trying for a light touch. She wasn't sure of the protocol between lovers.

"Thanks, I'll remember that." He smoothed the blanket, then flapped a sheet over it and tucked it in. He put another blanket at the foot of the bed. Not the one from Ronda's home, she was glad to see. The robe and moccasins had disappeared, too.

"Okay," he said, straightening and looking at her.

She hesitated. Either she insisted on going home or she stayed and . . . It was too late. They were already involved.

She went to the bed. He held the covers while she climbed in. She leaned against the thick pillows he'd fashioned for a backrest.

"There doesn't have to be sex," he said quietly, acknowledging her qualms about them. "I brought you here to rest, not to force you into a situation you'd rather not be in."

"You didn't force me," she admitted.

He observed her for a long minute. "Maybe not, but you're ill. You've had a fright, and you've been in thermal shock, not to mention the emotional one. You were vulnerable."

She thought this over. "I think you were, too."

Surprise flickered through his eyes. "I've wanted you for years," he admitted. "I realized it the moment I saw you again."

She nodded, understanding how he felt. It had been the same with her, no matter how much she'd tried to deny it. "Perhaps that's why I returned," she murmured, half to herself. "Because of that old, unfinished passion." She looked up at him, troubled. "Are we done with it now?"

"God, I wish I knew." He ran a hand through his tawny hair, mussing up the smooth effect he'd achieved by brushing. He looked as worried about them and their affair as she felt.

A noise below interrupted the moment of revelation. "Shane?" Ty called out. They heard his footsteps on the stairs.

"Damn," Shane muttered, whirling about.

It was too late. Ty stopped at the bedroom door. Tina saw his gaze take in her position in the bed, Shane standing a couple of feet away, then, finally, the wrinkled sheets on the floor.

Fury swept into his face. "You bastard," he said, crossing the room in three strides. He swung a fist at his brother's face.

Shane ducked, sidestepped the punch and grabbed Ty's wrist, twisting his arm behind him. "Cool down," he ordered.

Ty struggled, almost managing to slip from Shane's hold. Tina watched them in despair. She'd become another complication in their dealings with each other.

"Please," she said, her throat aching as she tried to raise her voice above the curses both brothers were muttering as they became locked in combat. "Oh, please! Don't!"

Shane managed to get a choke hold on Ty. "Stop it," he snarled. "You're scaring her."

Ty stopped in midcurse. Both men looked at her. Shane dropped his hold and went over to her.

"See what you've done?" he said to his brother. "You've made her cry." He pulled a tissue from the box and wiped the tears from her eyes.

"What *I've* done?" Ty scoffed. "What about you?"

"We'll talk about it downstairs." Shane shot him a warning glance that said nothing was to be discussed in her presence.

"You mustn't fight," she told them. She couldn't speak louder than a whisper after that hoarse cry.

"You're sick," Ty declared, with a strident glance at his brother. He stepped in front of Shane and sat on the side of the bed, taking her hand as he did. "Are you all right?" he asked.

She nodded, unable to speak for a moment. She squeezed his hand to show her gratitude, then tugged her hand away and pulled the sheet up to her neck, suddenly too tired to cope with the two quarrelsome men.

"If you want to go home, I'll take you," Ty promised, his jaw taking on a stubborn tilt.

Silence descended on the room. She glanced up at Shane. He watched her without a word, his face like a carved statue. She looked at Ty. He was angry and concerned. She thought she saw pity in his eyes.

She looked out the window. The sun was well above the horizon. Nine o'clock. It seemed an eternity since sunrise. "I'll stay," she said in a croaky whisper.

When she glanced at Shane, she felt seared by the flames that danced in his eyes for a second; then he spoke coolly to his brother. "If you can tear yourself away, we'll talk downstairs. Tina needs to rest." He calmly gathered the sheets and towels.

Ty's mouth tightened. He turned to her.

"Please, go on. I'm fine. Truly."

"All right, but if you ever need me . . ." He cast a hard glance at his brother. "I'll never be able to repay you for saving my son. He's the one thing that makes life worth living nowadays," he told her in a low, tortured voice.

Her heart went out to him. "He's a fine boy, brave and . . ." To her consternation, her eyes filled with tears again. She was turning into a drippy faucet.

"Call me," Ty said. "Anytime you need me, just call."

"I will." She dabbed at her eyes with the sheet.

Shane snorted from the door, where he waited for the scene to be over. Ty got up and walked out of the bedroom, while Shane lingered for another moment. He looked at her without smiling, his gaze filled with thoughts she couldn't read, but so penetrating she felt he was trying to see into her soul. Then he followed Ty down the steps.

She relaxed against the pillows, her heart sounding loud in her ears. She wasn't sure of anything anymore. All her logical reasons for returning to Oregon seemed a lie, yet she couldn't have returned just for . . . for *this*.

Gazing around the bedroom, she fought an inner panic. She wouldn't be anyone's kept woman. Not that she was, she assured herself. She had her own home and money enough to live on for a few years. She was still her own person. But she had a sense of her life becoming hopelessly entangled with the Macklin family.

"What are you going to do about her?"

Shane studied his brother, refraining from telling him it was none of his business. Ty obviously didn't see it that way. He had developed a protective-big-brother attitude toward Tina.

"We'll have to work it out," he said. "We haven't talked—"

"I noticed." Ty cast an enraged glance at the washer, where the used sheets and towels swished around in soapy water.

Shane removed Tina's clothes from the dryer and neatly folded them. Her underwear was pale green, the color of sea foam. It was sheer and dainty, reminding him of the delicate curves of her body. In spite of her fragile stature, she'd held her own with him, answering hunger with hunger, matching need with need.

A sensual pang bit into him. It had been the experience of a lifetime . . . hot and wild and incredibly arousing, as wonderful as he'd somehow known it would be. Nothing and no one could make him give her up. Except the lady herself.

It would kill him if she said no. . . .

"If you're trying to run her off like you did before, I don't think it will work this time," Ty informed him.

"How did you—" Shane stopped, but it was too late.

"How did I know? Emma Tall lives right across the river from us and next to the Snyder place. When Anne said Tina had left, I had a talk with Miss Em. I figured if anyone knew anything, she would. And she did, Big Brother. Did it make you feel like a hero to scare a young girl into running away by nearly raping her?"

"It didn't go that far," Shane muttered. He touched the tiny scars on his lower lip.

"I know how you got those." Ty grinned suddenly. "I think you've met your match this time, Brother. I can't tell you how much that pleases me. You'd better watch it, or you'll be housebroken in no time."

With a harsh laugh, he walked out, leaving Shane standing in the kitchen.

Shane looked at the female clothing in his hands and uttered a curse on brothers, small towns and gossiping neighbors, including the geezers at the barber shop. They were going to make his life hell when word got out, as it invariably would, about the sheriff and the town's resident celebrity.

"Just one more shot." Clint Adams moved to another angle, bent one knee and snapped the photo.

Tina blinked as the flashbulb went off. Clint had taken several pictures of her on the sofa in the living room of the Macklin home. She had insisted on getting up and dressing when the media deluge began. One television crew had already been there.

"So when nobody was home at Shane's house, you walked on up the road to Ty's place, carrying Jonathan, right?" Dolly asked.

The newspaperwoman sat opposite Tina, her leg propped on a footstool while she went over her notes for the second time. She and her husband had decided to publish a Sunday edition. They didn't want the local paper to be scooped by the "big city" papers in Medford and Ashland.

"Yes, that's right," Tina answered in a barely audible voice.

"Then...how did you get back here?" Dolly wanted to know.

"When she insisted she was fine and refused to go to the hospital, I brought her here to keep an eye on her," Shane answered tersely.

Dolly beamed with delight. "What a wonderful story— Sheriff Plays Nursemaid to Local Heroine!"

Shane grimaced good-naturedly. "You have the story. Tina needs to rest now."

Dolly put her notes away while her husband packed up their gear. "Maybe you'll be well enough to do A Day in the Life of the Sheriff for next week. That would be the perfect follow-up to this story.'' She smiled happily at the idea.

''Well, maybe,'' Tina temporized.

Shane escorted them outside and helped Dolly into the car. They'd barely gotten out of the drive when the news crew of another TV station pulled in and spilled out of a van.

Tina heard Shane refuse admittance to the brash young reporter who was trying to push his way into the house. ''How would you like to be arrested for breaking and entering,'' he asked in a dangerous tone.

''Who are you?'' the reporter demanded.

''I'm the sheriff, and this is my house,'' Shane explained, his tone that of a grizzly about to attack.

Tina sighed wearily and went to the door. ''It's okay,'' she murmured. ''I'll talk to them.''

Shane stepped aside and let the reporter and cameraman into the house. He made sure she was comfortable on the sofa, a cup of hot lemon tea by her side, before the interview began.

''How did you happen to see the boy fall in?'' the reporter asked, while the cameraman beamed a spotlight at her.

But her voice had gone. Nothing came out but a wheeze of sound. Shane answered most of the questions for her, since he'd heard the story three times that morning.

When the reporter wanted her to return to the river and point out the spot where she'd first noticed Jonathan, Shane put his foot down. In less than twenty minutes, the crew had its interview and were out of the house.

Tina closed her eyes and leaned her head back on the sofa. She ached all over. She heard the door close firmly and the lock snick into place. Then Shane returned.

Opening her eyes, she gazed into his. He bent and scooped her into his arms. "Insolent pup," he growled. "Next thing, he'd be wanting a reenactment of the whole damned scene."

She looped her arms around his neck and laid her head on his shoulder. Against her breasts, she could feel the steady pounding of his heart. Her weariness seemed to decrease as her own heart picked up its tempo.

In the bedroom, he set her on her feet. His hands went to the buttons of her blouse. Before she thought, her hands covered his, stopping him.

They looked at each other for a long minute.

She dropped her hands, allowing him to continue. She didn't know why she'd had a sudden attack of modesty. He'd done much more than undress her in the past twelve hours.

Heat ran along her skin as she recalled his hands on her, rough with passion but gentle . . . so gentle.

"I feel the same," he said.

"How do you know . . ." The words trailed away when she met his eyes. She thought perhaps he did know how she felt.

He deftly removed her clothing. "T-shirt or pajama top?" he asked. Both were clean and neatly folded on one of the chairs.

"The T-shirt, please." She held her arms up while he slipped it over her head. "Thank you."

When she was in bed, he sat beside her and held her hand. A frisson slithered down her back. She wondered if he would lie down with her. When he looked at her . . .

"Rest now," he advised, smoothing her hair back from her face. "I need to answer some messages from the dispatcher, then maybe I'll join you for a nap. Okay?"

His concern made her feel fragile inside, as if she might break at a sharp word or look. She nodded, then let him pull the covers up to her chin. She closed her eyes, infinitely weary, and felt him move away. When he left the room, she dropped the facade of calm that had carried her through the morning.

The future loomed dark and uncertain before her. In giving in to the passion, she seemed to have lost her way in life. She was no longer sure what she should do.

Leave? That was a possibility.

An ache vibrated through her chest. She didn't want to leave yet. There was still so much to discover between her and Shane.

Although she tried to suppress them, little bubbles of hope kept surfacing within her. She swallowed, causing her throat to hurt. But it was nothing compared to the pain in her heart as she admitted the whole truth—she was totally, hopelessly in love with Shane Macklin.

Chapter Ten

Tina woke to the sound of Shane's voice. He was on the telephone, a frown on his face. When he hung up, he glanced at her and saw she was awake. He turned the lamp on. "I have to go out," he said. "Do you need anything before I go?"

"No, I'm fine. Is it an emergency?" Her voice was audible, but she still sounded like a foghorn.

He nodded. "A robbery at a gas station over by the highway."

"Was anyone hurt?"

"No, just scared." He pulled on a pair of boots, then fastened the black belt with the lethal-looking weapon stuck in the holster. He checked his gun with quick, efficient movements and was ready to leave in a matter of minutes. "You look rested."

"I feel much better." She smiled to show him.

He came over to the bed. "We haven't talked."

"A-about what?" She hated the telltale break in her voice.

"Us. About what happened . . . and where we go from here," he said bluntly. "I haven't the time now, but later, when I get back, we'll figure it out." He sat beside her, his gaze questioning.

She saw the doubts in his eyes and felt her own wariness return. Recalling his warning, she managed a sardonic smile. "That's all right. I remember the rules."

He frowned. "What rules?"

"Yours. One, you don't play games," she recounted. "And two, don't expect anything permanent in an involvement with you, or something like that. I agree completely."

"Do you?" he inquired, giving her a narrow-eyed scrutiny that made him look dangerous.

"Of course. Actually, neither of us has time for a serious relationship. You have important duties, and I have a book to finish. I think I might travel after that."

Shane frowned. He didn't like having his words tossed back in his face, especially by her. "What about your job at the newspaper?"

"That's temporary. I'm helping out until Dolly is well."

He watched her for a minute. She wore that defiant little smile that hid her emotions so well, and he had no time to delve beneath the surface. He had work to do and a responsibility to the citizens of the county to restore law and order. Personal problems would have to wait their turn.

"You'd better go," she reminded him.

She looked so calm and cool there in his bed wearing his T-shirt, yet he'd seen her tremble with aftershock, he'd seen her weep, he'd held her while passion burned them both to a cinder. Someday he'd discover what thoughts and emotions roiled under that unruffled manner. But not today.

"Do I get a goodbye kiss before I venture into the cold, cruel world?" he asked.

He didn't wait for an answer, but bent to her and took the kiss before she could refuse. He felt her hesitate, then her mouth opened beneath his. His body surged with need as she responded. He ran his hands over her in a hungry caress.

"I'll be home as soon as I can," he murmured when he could take no more of the kiss without taking everything.

"Be careful," she said, releasing him.

He nodded, grabbed his hat and coat and headed outside. It gave him an odd sensation inside his chest to know she was worried about him. He started the truck and drove down the driveway. Glancing up at the lighted window in his bedroom before he turned onto the road, he felt a flood of warmth hit him.

She'd be there when he returned, he realized, waiting for him. That was something to look forward to. He'd lived alone so long he'd forgotten what it felt like to have someone waiting, just for him, at the end of the day. They'd talk and sort things out then.

Tina snuggled in the warm bed, Shane's pillow hugged against her so she could inhale his scent with each breath. She watched the sky darken into twilight. She'd slept most of the afternoon. Now she was restless, wanting him to return.

Heat radiated from deep inside her. With a start, she realized she was happy. If she hadn't been so miserable from the cold, she'd have jumped up and danced around the room like one of those whirling dervishes she'd read of but never seen.

She tossed the covers aside and sat up against the pillows. She didn't want to talk. She wanted him to make love to her again.

She sighed deeply. There was more than physical attraction between them. She was certain of it. No one could make love as they had and not be affected by the depths of it. She wanted to see where that shattering intimacy would take them....

Downstairs, a door slammed. Tina glanced at the clock, her heart beating wildly. He'd been gone only an hour.

But it wasn't his step on the stair. It was too light. "Mrs. Perkins?" she called.

"No." Ronda appeared in the doorway.

Ty's wife was dressed exquisitely in black leather pants and a white silk blouse that dipped low to show her generous cleavage. The lacy bra she wore was alternately visible and invisible through the thin silk as she moved. A sequined belt emphasized her small waist and flaring hips.

"Oh," Tina said, startled. Alarm speared through her. For no apparent reason, she felt threatened by the woman.

Ronda put her hands on her hips and gave Tina a look of utter disdain. "Well, I guess the gossips are right for once. I heard you were here...that you'd been here all night." Her lips lifted in a cruel smile.

"Yes," Tina said. She could hardly deny the story, since she'd sat through three interviews in the house that day. "Shane was kind enough to take care of me after the accident."

Her own smile was carefully neutral. She had no quarrel with Shane's sister-in-law. She'd do her best not to invoke one.

"Kind?" The smile turned to mocking laughter as Ronda advanced further into the room. "Yes, Shane is kind. When I begged him to save my marriage from a home wrecker, he said he would. He swore he would stop you from seeing Ty.''

Tina couldn't speak. She wanted to deny the charge, but all Shane's earlier warnings for her to stay away came flooding back.

No, she didn't believe Ronda. These were the spiteful words of a spiteful woman. Not even Shane would go that far....

He might. He'd told her he would think of something if she didn't tell Ty to stop coming by. Apparently he didn't know that she had done as he requested.

All the warm anticipation seeped out of her, leaving her empty and cold as she realized exactly how making love to her would put a barrier between her and his brother. By claiming her as his woman, Shane had built a wall around her so solid that no man in the community would dare broach it.

She smoothed the sheet over her legs, then drew her knees to her chest, wrapping her arms around them. She was drawing inward, she realized—closing herself off from hurt as she had in the past.

Ronda seemed to think Tina's silence was a victory for her. One perfectly formed eyebrow rose haughtily. ''I admit I never thought he'd go to such drastic measures.''

''And very pleasant measures they were,'' Tina commented with a droll grin, as if she found the conversation quite amusing.

Red flags of fury highlighted Ronda's face.

Score one for my side, Tina thought. The blonde was one of those women who had to have all men in her domain at her feet. To have Shane even temporarily involved with someone else, even for a cause she endorsed, enraged her possessive nature.

"You won't hold him for long," Ronda declared with a venomous glare. "His last affair lasted little more than a year."

"Just long enough," Tina declared. "A year is all I intend to stay in this charming little…town." Her pause was calculated to offend, as if she were censoring her real opinion of the town and its residents. She changed the subject. "How is Jonathan?"

Ronda's eyes, thick with mascara, narrowed sharply. "Stay away from my son. I don't know what happened, but I don't believe you tried to save him. He's an excellent swimmer."

"I would never harm a child," Tina said, refusing to be daunted by the other woman's suspicions.

She didn't know why, but she knew Shane's sister-in-law was a very real enemy. She wondered what she'd done to earn such hatred from a person she didn't know.

"The stupid doctors are running more tests," Ronda finally replied. She walked over to the door. "They're after the Macklin money…just like you. If you think Shane will ever marry you, you'd better think again. He's not a marrying man."

With that barb, she walked out. A minute later, Tina heard the door slam, then the sound of a motor cranking. She watched out the window as a sleek luxury car headed for the house a quarter mile up the road, then she drew a shaky breath.

She could see the roof of her snug brick house across the river. *It's past midnight, Cinderella,* she reminded herself with cynical humor. *No use hanging around waiting for the prince.*

She rose and dressed in the slacks and blouse she'd worn so blithely to work on Friday. Her shoes were in the closet, dry and polished to a high shine, but there were no stockings. They'd been ruined by the rocks in the river. Her coat was at the cleaners, she recalled.

She made up the bed and put the T-shirt in the bathroom hamper. Picking up her purse, she went through it. Her keys were inside. She turned out the lamp by the bed, casting the room into deep shadows.

It was almost dark. She'd have to hurry.

Borrowing a warm hunting jacket of Shane's she went into the garage. She hit the button that opened the garage door. Hitting it again, she ducked and rushed out before the door could come down on top of her.

On the fifteen-minute walk to the bridge, she had time to think about Ronda's statements and accusations.

She couldn't bring herself to believe Shane had made love to her just to stop any friendship between her and his brother, yet...

It was a possibility. There was an undeniable attraction between her and Shane. That, compounded by his very protective attitude toward his family and the aftermath of worry about his nephew, could have overcome his scruples.

He also seemed convinced that she was a troublemaker, if not an out-and-out fortune hunter. From what Mrs. Perkins had told her, she knew his stepmother had made him suspicious of women, but why did he assume she was cast in the same mold?

She stopped on the bridge and watched the rush of water, which looked black and dangerous in the dark of evening. The devil-may-care facade she'd kept up in front of Ronda dissolved. Depression hit her. She shook it off. She'd learned long ago not to wish things were different. They weren't.

For long minutes, she stood there. It seemed as if the river carried her dreams with it... right out to sea. When she continued her journey, all her shields were in place. She crossed the bridge and turned up the street that ran along the woods by the river.

The house was dark when she arrived, but it was warm. She was glad to be home. She felt safer there. . . .

She hung Shane's coat on the hall highboy and went to the kitchen, stopping to turn on the lights as she did. She made hot tea and a sandwich, then took them with her into the office.

Sitting at the familiar desk, she ate her solitary meal. The summer she'd visited Anne, she'd read randomly through the books of poetry on the shelves. Spying a tome with a piece of paper sticking in it as a bookmark, she retrieved it, returned to the chair and opened it to the marked page.

The passage was one of Wordsworth's poems—his "Ode." She skimmed its stanzas. Closing the book, she reflected on two lines that seemed to have been written for her: "Though nothing can bring back the hour/ Of splendor in the grass, of glory in the flower."

Well, she'd had her hour. She hugged the book to her chest as a tremor rippled through her. Like the poet, she refused to grieve for what was past. But, she admitted, it was hard not to.

Once, all her dreams had been of Shane. She'd gotten over them. She'd get over this, too. If he came by, she'd tell him she'd decided not to see any of the Macklin men. Having made this decision, she read until the clock struck eleven.

Idly, she picked up the piece of paper that had been Anne's bookmark and unfolded it. It was a note from Anne.

My dear Tina,

I have often thought that poetry was the music of the lonely soul. I noticed that you chose poetry to read when you were quiet and introspective, thus I can guess at your mood now. There isn't anything I can do for your loneliness except wish you a true and lasting love. Be patient. I think it will come to you.

In the meantime, a treasure hunt will lift your spirits. Here is the code: 32,23,20. When you find the treasure, remember this: it is a gift from my heart to yours, a connection to the future through you and your children as it was a connection to my past through my mother and hers. Enjoy it as I have.

Tina closed her eyes and waited for the painful surge of emotion to subside. The letter sounded so final. Anne, unafraid to face anything, must have known the end was near.

Glancing again at the number, she realized a possibility. They were surely the—

The chime of the doorbell stopped her speculation. She stuck the note in the book and left it on the desk. The bell dinged again, impatiently. Her heart started kicking. There was only one person it could be.

She turned on the porch light and peered through the peephole. Yes, it was Shane. She opened the door.

He glared at her, pushed the door open farther and came inside. "Damn, it's getting cold again. I hope the bridges don't ice over." He hung his hat and coat on the highboy next to his green hunting jacket. "Why did you leave?" he asked, swinging around to face her. He looked grim.

"I was feeling better, so I thought I'd come home." She'd had that answer ready for the past hour.

"Got any coffee?" He caught her hand and escorted her into the big, homey kitchen.

"I can make some," she said wryly. *Keep it light.*

"Do that. I'm frozen. We had to track one of the holdup men through the woods." He chuckled. "You should have seen it—a real chase scene, just like in the movies. He abandoned his car on a washed-out country road and tried to make it on foot. We caught up with him about a mile out and brought him in."

"He didn't give you any trouble?" She fixed a sandwich after she put the coffee on. She would ease into telling him not to come back, that she didn't have time to see him....

"No. How did you get home?" he asked, suddenly looking like a tough lawman determined to ferret out the truth.

"I, uh, walked."

"Why?"

"Well, it wasn't all that far."

"I meant, why didn't you wait until I got back, so we could talk about it? You were supposed to stay the weekend."

"I didn't agree to that." She spoke calmly, though her heart was beating at a frenzied rate. She had no reason to be nervous, she chided herself. She'd done nothing wrong.

"Dammit!"

The explosive curse startled her. She dropped the knife she was using to spread mayonnaise on the whole-wheat bread. He crossed the room in three quick strides and took her by the shoulders. She stared, expecting him to shake her.

"Don't look so scared," he muttered. "I'm not going to beat you with a rubber hose... yet. Tell me why you decided to run off in the dark of night without a word."

She tried to think of something plausible, something that he would believe.

"Did Ronda come over?" he asked softly, changing tactics.

She glanced away, then back, but it was too late. She'd already given herself away. If she denied it now, he'd know she was lying. "Yes. She said Jonathan was having more tests. Is he ill from the dip in the river?"

The anger left him like a dust devil settling, leaving no trace in the air. His eyes darkened, but his hold on her eased. "No." He let one hand fall to her waist while the other slipped behind her neck. He pulled her to him, surprising her, and laid his cheek on top of her head. "They think he may have leukemia."

"Oh, Shane." She wrapped her arms around his waist and hugged him hard, feeling his pain as if it were her own. "I'm so sorry."

After that, there was nothing to say. She held him, offering him the comfort of her arms, and postponed telling him of her decision not to see him again.

When he shifted, she eased from his arms and picked up the knife. "Go sit down. I'll have your food in a minute."

He nodded, his face so grim and weary it made her want to weep for him. She served the tuna-salad sandwich with sliced fresh vegetables and corn chips. When the coffee was ready, she poured two mugs and joined him at the table.

The outdoor lights at his house were on, but she couldn't see any lights on in the house. "Did you go home?" she asked.

"Yes."

"You didn't turn any lights on."

Shane glanced out the window and studied the dark outline of his roof among the pines. He looked at her. "I didn't need any. No one was there."

He'd been eager to return home, to see her, he admitted to himself. Not that he'd tell her such a thing. The power she held over him was already troubling. When he'd turned in the drive, he'd looked up at the bedroom window, expecting to see a light there.

The entire house had been dark. He'd stopped in front and gone in and found ... nothing. No lights, no warmth, no welcome.

And no small, incredibly sexy woman in his bed, waiting for him with her tempting smile and her stormy eyes that saw so much and disclosed so little.

The sensation he'd experienced had been like a rabbit punch to the ribs, quick and painful and possibly lethal.

He'd slammed the door, climbed in the truck and headed over to her house, where the lights gleamed softly from the windows.

It occurred to him that he'd always liked visiting here when Anne had been alive, and now, with Tina. His own house had always been just that—a house, a place to stay when he had nowhere else to go.

Until today. Then he'd been eager to get back.

But it wasn't the house itself that had attracted him, he finally realized. It was the person in it.

He watched his hostess while he ate the food she'd prepared for him. Everything tasted good, and he ate hungrily, aware of other hungers that weren't yet satisfied. Warmth seeped deep into him, thawing a spot that had been frozen for a long time.

Danger, some sixth sense warned him.

Maybe, but what better way to keep an eye on her? If they were lovers, no other males would come around. She'd be marked as his. A lightness entered his soul, and for the briefest moment, he felt something akin to happiness.

He frowned. He wouldn't be caught in her spell. His motives were simple. By playing the ardent lover, he'd be protecting his family. God knew, he had enough to worry about there. His heart clenched painfully as he thought of his nephew. He'd give his life for the boy....

A small, delicate hand touched his forehead. "You look so fierce," she said.

"Sorry, I was thinking." He smiled at her. Finished with the meal, he captured her hand in his. Flames licked inside him. He wanted to grab her and rush to the bedroom. There, he would strip the hindering clothes from them and bury himself in her until he forgot everything but the bliss of that joining.

He lifted her hand and kissed the back of it, wryly amused at his own wild desires. A man had to show some finesse. Maybe a wife would understand such needs, but an independent woman who kept her thoughts and dreams as carefully hidden as this one did would have to be wooed more gently.

She stood and came to him. He felt a jolt of pleased surprise when she pulled his head against her breasts. Her lips caressed his hair as she bent over him, her hands moving over his shoulders, massaging away the tension of the chase and other worries.

"Come to bed," she whispered.

He knew he should express a token resistance just to prove that he could. He didn't. Instead, he wrapped his arms around her hips and stood, holding her high in the air.

She smiled at him, and her face was filled with sympathy. A fierceness washed over him. He wanted more than that from her.

Tina was completely aware of Shane in every part of her. Her body was languid, soft, warm...ready for his caresses. He carried her swiftly to the bedroom. With great care, he set her on the rug beside the old-fashioned four-poster.

When he started on his buttons, she undressed, too. They worked in unison, each piece of clothing floating away so that they revealed themselves to each other as if their actions were choreographed. The last items fell to the floor. He gazed at her and let her see the hunger.

His body was ready, hard and erect, and hers answered in its own way, becoming soft and welcoming. However, there was more than physical desire between them, wonderful as that was. In the other room, she'd sensed a need in him, one that was strong, elemental and primitive, that spoke to her soul. That was what she'd answered by taking him to her breast.

She wondered if he had an empty place inside that only she could fill. That was the way it had been for her when they'd made love—fulfillment so sweet, it had stolen her breath away.

A shudder went through him. He moved swiftly, tossing the covers into a careless heap at the foot of the bed, then lifting her onto the high mattress. He stood there, looking down at her, his face pensive, almost moody.

"This scares me," he said in a low, husky voice.

"What?" She could hardly speak above the drumbeats of her heart, which seemed to be lodged in her throat.

"Wanting you. It makes a man...vulnerable."

"It does the same to a woman."

"Does it?" He lay down beside her, leaning over her, his weight on one arm. He placed his hand on her abdomen and splayed his fingers wide. The tip of his thumb and little finger almost spanned the distance between her hipbones.

His confession made her want to open her heart to him. "I've often wondered..." She stopped, unsure of exposing herself this much to him. What if he laughed at her idle fantasy?

"What?" He moved his hand upward until he touched the bottom side of her breast. Her breath became jerky.

"If things would have been different between us if we'd met before—before other things got in the way." She traced the line of his eyebrows, then ran her fingers into his hair.

He lost his moody introspection and stared intently into her eyes as if determined to read her every thought. "When I was still a wide-eyed romantic?" He laughed. "I was never that."

"Me, neither," she said, closing the lid on any further confidences. Life had never let her indulge in dreams for very long. It snatched them away almost as soon as they formed.

He ran a finger lightly over her mouth. "You have the most kissable mouth. The first time we kissed, your mouth trembled under mine. And then you opened your lips and kissed me back. I've never forgotten how exciting that was."

"Before I remembered you were my enemy," she whispered through an aching throat, wanting his kiss now.

"Am I your enemy now?" He bent nearer, his lips but a breath from hers. He waited for her answer.

"Sometimes..."

"No," he growled, denying it.

His mouth took hers. For a second, she felt only the demand and none of the gentleness.

"Kiss me," he ordered. "Dammit, you've stolen my soul, my dreams and my every waking moment, now give me something back."

She opened her lips to him and allowed the tactile plunder of his tongue against hers. But love and desire and a strange, aching pity swirled into one undefined mix of hunger and need that matched his. Wrapping her arms and legs around him, she molded herself to his broad frame and let him reach inside to the very depths.

He kissed her eyes, her nose, her ears, her chin, returned again and again to her lips, and then, with his mouth, he taught her new ways to be intimate.

She moaned when he moved away from her, down to her breasts, which throbbed from his caresses. He rolled his tongue over the sensitive tip, around and around, until she writhed against him.

"Shane," she gasped, loving the wild things his touch did to her. "Oh, love, yes..."

He suckled and nipped until she could stand it no more, then he moved down her abdomen. He paused at her navel and thrust seductively into it. She hadn't realized the erotic potential there until he showed her.

When he slipped between her thighs, she was even less prepared for the overpowering sensations that burst through her. She closed her eyes tightly and clutched the sheet, her movements beyond her control now. She was entirely his.

When the world was in danger of flying apart, he raised his head. His eyes seared over her, twin flames of passionate blue, so intense she was almost frightened.

He gathered her close, cradling her against his heaving chest. "When you respond like that, it drives me to the edge. One touch and I'd explode. I wouldn't even have to be in you."

"It's you," she protested. "You—you make the world go away so that there's only you...me...and this moment."

She burrowed against him, loving the caress of his chest hair against her breasts, the rougher feel of his body against her smoothness. Spreading her legs, she trapped his hard staff between her thighs and moved slightly against him.

He caught her hips in his hands and stilled her soft thrusts. "Don't rub against me like that," he murmured in a hoarse whisper. "It arouses me beyond endurance."

"I'm glad," she said simply. "Because that's the way you make me feel."

He hugged her to him in a harsh embrace. She responded just as fiercely, needing him in ways she couldn't describe.

"Wait," he said at last, raising his mouth from its devastation of hers. "We have to... take care of things." He gasped for breath and pulled out of her arms.

I wouldn't care if we had a baby. But she didn't say the words aloud. They revealed too much....

She waited while he fumbled through his pockets, then smiled at the string of curses he muttered when he couldn't at once find what he needed. Finally, he returned to her side.

He quickly prepared himself. "I wouldn't be able to take those nervous, fluttery touches from you tonight," he said in apology.

"Shall I get on top?" she asked. She wanted to pleasure him as he'd done for her.

"Only if you don't move," he grumbled. But he rolled onto his back and, putting his hands on her waist, lifted her onto him.

They came together easily, naturally, she found. He gasped and held her still.

"It's been years since I've felt like this...if ever," he told her. "The first time we kissed, we didn't get this far. Yesterday we went too fast. Today I want it to last."

She lay over him. He seemed to take her weight easily. With a new confidence, she took his lower lip between her teeth. He held his breath. She ran her tongue back and forth over the captured lip, careful of her hold. His breath fanned over her mouth in a throaty chuckle.

A reckless passion invaded her, and her spirit soared as she realized she could excite him as much as he did her. It was a wild, heady sensation. Yet it was coupled with a tenderness of feeling so profound that she was as acutely conscious of his needs as she was of her own.

"Shane," she whispered as emotion and passion melded.

His mouth took the soft plea from her. He parted her lips and gave her his tongue, while his hands took her breasts. She uttered a wild, smothered cry and surged recklessly against him.

"Don't, love," he cautioned. "Too late."

He grasped her hips and moved her in rhythm with him. He showed her how to slide her body against his so that she felt the intense pleasure. She closed her eyes and welcomed the final plunge as the pulsating climax took over her senses. Inside her, his body responded in tune to hers.

They went over the edge together.

When she collapsed onto him, he held her close and stroked her back until she quit trembling. Then he turned so that she rested beside him. They were quiet for a long time.

Finally, he kissed her cheek. "It's hard to believe a frame of such delicate proportions can hold that much passion. You're the answer to every fantasy I've ever had."

She was too spent to reply. Instead, she snuggled close and planted a kiss on his damp chest. The hair tickled her nose. She rubbed the tickle away, laid her cheek against him and slid gently down toward sleep.

This might be a fantasy, but she wanted it to last....

Chapter Eleven

Tina woke to a kiss. When she opened her eyes, Shane stood beside the bed. "Wake up, sleepyhead. I've got to go to work."

Disappointment wafted over her. "Are you leaving now?" She glanced at the clock. It was six-thirty.

"No. Breakfast is ready. If you want to eat with me," he added, a note of uncertainty in his husky baritone.

She smiled, feeling tender toward him. "Yes." She pushed the covers back and realized she wore no pajamas. Heat climbed in her face. "I, uh, need to dress."

He laughed. "I like you as you are. Hurry. The toast is getting cold."

When he left, she dashed for the bathroom and washed up, then yanked on her cranberry velour slacks and top. After pulling a comb through her tangles, she rushed to the kitchen. Shane was at the table, waiting for her.

She took her seat. When she started eating, he did, too. He'd prepared hot oatmeal again, which felt good on her healing throat.

"You sound better."

"I think the worst is over." She looked out the window, unable to stand his concerned regard without melting right at his feet. "But the weather doesn't seem to be improving. It looks like more rain is coming."

"Yeah." He studied the clouds. "The creeks are close to flood level all over the county. There will probably be some washouts along the gravel roads, plus a mud slide or two...and a few wrecks to liven things up." He recounted the expected disasters with stoic humor.

She grinned at him in sympathy. Finished with the meal, she pushed the dishes aside and sipped the hot coffee.

"Here, you haven't seen the paper yet." He handed her the front page of the *Riverton Daily News*.

Her picture figured prominently on the front page. Another showed the river splashing over the boulders behind her house. A picture of Jonathan and his father fishing along the river at a happier time also accompanied the piece.

"Very touching," she said when she finished reading.

Dolly had used every known trick to dramatize the event so that Tina sounded like a heroine of Olympic proportions. The story cited two authorities on the temperature and velocity of the river, and the danger of being battered against the rocks or swept down the gorge. The effects of hypothermia were explained, making it seem like a miracle that Tina had managed to walk a half mile in the near-freezing wind after courageously fighting her way through the water, all the while carrying the boy.

Last but not least, there was a revealing shot of Shane refilling her cup of hot lemon tea when her voice gave out during the interview. The caption under the photo read "Sheriff Macklin plays nursemaid to heroine."

Tina felt heat pool deep within her. The way he was looking at her... His eyes... Surely anyone looking at the photograph would know they were lovers.

"Dolly was determined to get the nursemaid quip into the story, wasn't she?" Shane smiled good-naturedly.

Tina let out an uneasy sigh. She thought the feisty newswoman had just made life a little more unpleasant for her. When Shane's sister-in-law read the article, she'd be furious.

"Rather domestic, isn't it?" He tapped the photo, his words echoing her worries about the homey little scene.

"Yes."

He touched her temple with his fingertips, drawing her gaze to his. "Does it bother you?"

"What?" She was acutely aware of his fingers trailing down her cheek, then touching her earlobe.

"That people know about us... that we're lovers."

"I don't know," she answered truthfully.

The moment hung suspended between them while he probed her eyes, searching and questioning. She didn't know what he was looking for, but she felt his reservation concerning her as if it were a blow to the heart.

He released her and sighed, his expression thoughtful. "I need to check on a few things today. Do you feel up to taking a ride? I thought we'd stop for lunch at the ski lodge."

She weighed spending the day alone in the house to being with him. Being with him won. "I'll go."

"Wear comfortable clothes and boots."

When they left an hour later, she saw her neighbors, the Talls, backing out of the adjacent drive. They ate breakfast out on Sundays. During the week, Mr. Tall opened the hardware store at seven and his wife usually went down around nine, when she finished with her housework, Tina had learned.

It must be nice to work with your mate, she thought. But then, it would be nice to come home after a hard day and have that special someone there.

Her body warmed as she remembered Shane's arrival last night. The bliss of being in his arms, of knowing he'd wanted her enough to come to her house, revived old dreams that she'd locked away years ago.

A foolish thing to let happen. When the passion was played out between them, she'd leave Riverton. Next time, she'd stay away.

"Not as bad as I'd feared," Shane remarked.

She came out of her reverie and attended to the present. They were at the junction of the Rogue River and one of the many creeks that ran into it. The creek was full right to the top of its banks, the water frothy and brown with silt.

He put the truck in gear and drove along a narrow, paved road. They wound their way up the mountain. The snow under the trees became thicker as they went higher.

Approaching a narrow bend, they came upon a scattering of rocks over the road. Shane turned on the flashing lights of the patrol truck and stopped.

"Dangerous place here," he commented. "There has already been some slippage." He indicated the fallen rocks.

Tina leaned forward and peered at the high bank next to the road. The rock was fractured into irregular pieces, from pea gravel to boulders. The land seemed to tilt in every direction and looked unstable even to her untrained eyes.

"Do you think there will be more?"

"Maybe." He looked worried. "If we have a lot of rain or a fast warming spell that melts the snow, it could cause problems."

"I see."

"I'll have to call the road department." He picked up the phone and dialed.

She listened while he talked to the supervisor in charge of county roads. The man informed Shane a truck had gone through a guardrail and down an embankment. He'd put a crew on it, but it would take two days minimum to repair. A deputy sheriff was on the scene.

Shane told his deputy to route a detour around the area and asked the supervisor to get the job done in one day, if possible.

"Will do," the two men replied and rang off.

"I didn't realize your job entailed so many tasks," she said.

He grinned. "Sometimes I think I'm dogcatcher, nanny and the nursemaid to the entire county."

She laughed. His laughter joined hers. She realized it was the first time they'd ever laughed together. "It's your nature," she told him. "You take responsibility for others."

"The big-brother syndrome?" he mused. "Maybe. You feel like moving some rocks?"

She got out of the truck with him and together they tossed the largest stones off the roadway.

With a push broom, he cleared the rest. "There. That's safe enough for now. A couple of young guys who work for a logging outfit take these curves at max speed. Maybe they won't spin out and lose it on this one."

They returned to the main road and surveyed several other side roads off it. He seemed to know everyone in the county and who lived on what road. He kept her amused with stories about the local residents while she observed him at his work. It was after one when they stopped for lunch at the posh ski resort.

Up there on the mountain there were no signs of spring. Snow still covered the ground in solid white. Skiers zipped along the trails through the woods like brightly plumed, exotic birds.

"Do you ski?" he asked.

"Yes. I learned in France." She shaded her eyes with one hand as she watched a group ski down to the chair lift. "I've never been skiing in the States."

"We'll have to fix that. When you're well, we'll come up during the week one day. The slopes are less crowded then."

"That sounds like fun."

It made her feel odd to be planning an event in the future for them. She felt that each day they were together was on its own, a time out of time that might not come again.

Shane took her hand to steady her as they walked over the snowy path to the lodge steps. Inside, the air was warm. She and Shane pulled off their jackets and went up to the restaurant on the second floor. Rafe Barrett was at a table by the window.

He stood and motioned them over. "Join me for lunch," he invited. "Genny will be here soon. She's translating a book by some French writer."

They were soon settled. When Genny arrived, they ordered, then talked about the ski season.

"With the late snows, the season should go right into May," Rafe explained.

"Unless we have a really warm spell," Genny added. "How are you doing on your book?"

"Great, so far," Tina answered. "I'm getting my notes in order and using the computer to set up a cross-reference file."

"How did anyone ever get any work done before computers?" Genny exclaimed.

"Looks like our women have gone high tech on us," Rafe said in an amused tone to Shane.

Tina froze at the casual mention of "our women." She glanced at Shane to gauge his reaction. He seemed totally relaxed. One arm rested on the back of her chair. He idly plucked at a strand of her hair and smoothed his fingers down it.

"Modern times," Shane said regretfully. "Tina only made me a sandwich for supper, while *I* fixed a hot breakfast for her."

She could have curled up in embarrassment. Nothing like broadcasting their involvement, she thought hotly. Her eyes met Genny's across the table. To her surprise, the other woman beamed in approval.

"Yeah, Genny makes me cook even when we have guests. Of course, I am much better than she is in the kitchen," Rafe said with no trace of modesty, while his wife huffed.

"Liar," she snarled, nuzzling him with her nose, then biting him on the neck.

Shane rubbed the tiny twin scars on his lip. "Watch out," he warned his friend. "Women have been known to bite."

"Hmm, methinks there's a story here," Rafe deduced.

"No, there isn't," Tina quickly put in.

Everyone laughed, while she turned beet red at giving herself away. Shane tugged at her hair. "Eat up. We have a couple more chores to do today."

They discussed the conditions of the roads, the water levels in the creeks, the account of Tina's rescue of Jonathan. When Genny asked, Shane admitted things didn't look good for the boy, but he didn't go into details.

Tina kept quiet, her compassion for both Macklins a vague ache inside. Like yesterday, she wanted to clasp Shane in her arms and comfort him. She didn't think he'd gotten much of that in his adult life.

People needed someone special to share things with, she thought, looking at the affection between Rafe and his wife. They were discussing the wildlife hikes Genny led through the woods twice a week and how popular they were with the visitors.

When they finished, Shane insisted on paying for their share of the bill. "I have to maintain my integrity," he explained.

Rafe scoffed. "You're the only totally honest cop I've ever known."

"Oh, I can be had," Shane quipped, standing and moving his chair so Tina could get out. "You just have to know the price." His gaze on her indicated she was it.

Ignoring him, she said goodbye and told the Barretts that she'd enjoyed the lunch. In spite of its disconcerting moments, she added mentally. Shane seemed determined to claim her as his.

Her heart stopped, skipped a beat, then raced like mad. Was he . . . could he be falling in love, too?

A delirious joy leapt over her like electric tingles. If they were both in love, the possibilities were endless. Love could conquer anything!

Spoken like a true romantic, she chided. Though she longed to tell him of her love, she didn't. Caution learned long ago kept her silent. She was afraid to expose her heart so completely to him, she realized. If he didn't love her...

"Ready?"

She looked up into his eyes and nodded.

"Let's have lunch later this week," Genny invited Tina. "Come join me on Thursday. Rafe will be out, and we can do girl talk without the men bothering us."

"I'd like that," Tina said. She felt she and Genny were destined to be friends. She'd like to get to know Gabe's wife, too. She'd have the two of them to her place one day soon, she decided.

And Adrianna, her attorney's wife, too. Friends were nice things to have, and she missed her best friend, who was still in Italy, teaching English as a second language.

Saying goodbye once more to the Barretts, she and Shane left the stone, wood and glass lodge, with its view of the mountains and of the town snuggled into a bend of the river.

"You're quiet," he said, driving down the snowbank-lined road.

"Just thinking," she murmured. "Your friends make a lovely couple. I like them."

"You and Genny get along well."

"Yes."

"Does this mean you might change your mind and stay in the area after you finish your book?"

She looked at the question from every angle, but she couldn't tell from it or his inflection if he wanted that or not. "I might," she said noncommittally. "Would you mind?"

He stopped at the main road and looked at her, his gaze dark and unreadable. "As you once pointed out—it's a free country," he finally said. He checked for traffic and pulled onto the road.

They were both being cautious, she realized. With good reason. They'd learned it the hard way—he because of his stepmother and, perhaps, her; she because she'd learned early that people could be cruel, even though the circumstances of her birth had been no fault of hers.

They arrived back in town in late afternoon.

"I need to stop by the office a minute. Would you like the twenty-five-cent tour?"

"Sure. I've always wondered what a sheriff's office looked like," she quipped, matching the light mood she'd maintained all afternoon.

He checked with the dispatcher and with the sergeant at the main desk, discussed some items with them, then gave her a quick run-through of the building, which was busy even on Sunday. She was aware of the speculation behind the polite greetings of the law officers she met.

Shane's office was on the second floor, in a corner room that overlooked the town center and had a terrific view of the river a block away.

"Wow," she commented. "Windows on two walls. That puts you way up on the ladder of success."

"Does it?" He didn't seem interested.

Well, when one had always had money and position, the perks probably seemed one's normal due. "According to all the business magazines."

"Come here," he murmured. He sat on the side of his desk and opened his arms to her.

She went to him.

He enclosed her in a warm hug. "I've wanted to hold you all day. At lunch I could hardly concentrate on the conversation, I was so aware of you beside me."

She beamed a smile of pure happiness at him, surprised and pleased at this revelation.

He opened his legs and pulled her closer. She felt as if his entire body embraced hers. She let herself snuggle to her heart's content. Just to be held by him was wonderful. To make love was simply mind-blowing.

Feelings rose in her, so strong her body felt too small to contain all of them. Tonight, she thought hazily, tonight she'd tell him of her love.

His lips drifted over her forehead in the gentlest of kisses. She closed her eyes and sighed.

"I need to go down to the hospital in Medford and check on Jonathan. Do you feel like coming?"

"Do you think I should? I mean, with my cold?" She leaned her head back and looked at him anxiously.

"Would you mind staying in the waiting room? He probably can't have anyone but immediate family in to see him."

"Oh, of course. No, I don't mind waiting."

He rubbed the back of his knuckles over her cheek. She turned his hand and pressed his palm to her lips.

"I could take you home, if you're too tired. You sound so much better, I forget you've been ill as well as dunked in an icy river in the past two days."

"I'd rather stay with you."

She felt his chest rise in a deeply drawn breath. It gave her a fluttery feeling inside to know how he wanted her with him.

During the short drive down Interstate 5, she watched the scenery whip past. Neither of them spoke much. A worried frown slashed a deep groove between his eyes. She knew his thoughts were on his nephew.

He stopped at a shopping center. "What do you think a kid would like?" he asked, leading the way to the toy department of a large department store.

Tina was enchanted with this vision of Shane. She watched him try out different items with the concentration of a scientist conducting a vital experiment. Finally, she suggested a couple of storybooks, a coloring book with a marker pen set or a monkey that could do loops between two sticks when manipulated by strings.

He agreed and purchased everything she mentioned.

"I can see what kind of parent you'd be," she told him on the way to the truck.

"What kind?" he demanded, giving her a threatening glance.

"Indulgent."

"If you mean I'd spoil the kids, you're probably right." He grinned. After putting the package in the back, he opened the door and helped her step up into the truck. "I'd probably spoil my wife, too," he murmured.

Her heart nearly beat its way out of her chest.

He slammed the door, walked around the front of the vehicle and climbed in his side. The sultry teasing left his face, and she knew his thoughts were on more serious matters. Her heart returned to its normal rate, and she, too, turned grave.

At the hospital, she settled on the vinyl sofa in the waiting room while Shane went to visit, his presents in hand. She picked up a magazine and began reading an article on parental discipline.

When she finished, she put it down and stared out the window at the gray clouds forming over the mountain peaks. The sun had broken through that afternoon, but now the sky looked threatening again. She sighed worriedly. Shane had enough on his mind.

When he reappeared, she stood, ready to leave.

"Jonathan wants to see you," he said. "Would you mind?"

"Of course not." She followed him down the corridor.

Jonathan was in a private room. His gifts from Shane were piled at the foot of his bed. When he saw Tina, he held out his arms. She went to him and received a big hug. She hugged him back, choked up with emotion.

"Dad said I was to thank you for saving my life," he told her. "Thank you."

"It was my pleasure," she said sincerely.

"Did you see our pictures in the paper?"

"Yes. Dolly wrote a nice article to go with it."

"Yeah. Dad read it to me. I liked the part where they told about me and him catching a big fish right where I fell in. If Dad had been there, you'd have had to save him, too."

"I'm sure he could have gotten out without help," she assured her young friend.

"Look at this neat monkey Uncle Shane gave me. It works like this." He showed her how to make the monkey turn a flip. "Now you can try it," he offered generously.

For several minutes, she stood by the bed and played with Jonathan. They both giggled when she flipped the monkey backwards by accident. They were still laughing when the door was pushed open from its half-closed position and Ronda entered the room.

The other woman's mouth tightened when she saw Tina with her son. Tina determinedly kept the smile on her face. "Hello," she said. "Jonathan is teaching me how this thing works. He's a good instructor, but I'm a slow student."

"She made it go backwards, Mom," he explained, giggling again.

"Who let you in?" Ronda demanded sharply, glaring at Tina. Jonathan's laughter disappeared.

"I did," Shane announced.

Ronda peered around the door, which had hid him from her view. "Oh, Shane, I didn't see you." Her voice was a purr. "I'm surprised the doctor let an outsider visit. He's been so strict."

"Jonathan wanted to see her. I didn't think it would hurt."

"Of course. I wanted to thank you for helping Jonathan," she said graciously.

Shane made a little sound, rather like a snort. Both women waited for him to speak. When he didn't, Tina picked up her purse from the bed, smiled brightly at Jonathan and announced she'd wait down the hall for Shane. She headed out.

In the waiting room, she breathed a sigh of relief. Ronda's dislike was so puzzling. Tina didn't believe the lovely blonde was jealous of her and Ty. That left her and Shane.

Did Ronda regret marrying the younger brother and wish she'd waited for the older one?

Not a very pretty triangle, if true. It could turn the two brothers bitterly against each other. However, Shane showed no more than brotherly interest in his sister-in-law.

Tina hugged herself as a shiver chased over her. Whatever was between her and Shane, it was no one's business but theirs. If Ronda butted in, Shane wouldn't mince words telling her to butt out.

Leaning against the windowsill, she watched the traffic rush along the street. It seemed busy for late Sunday afternoon. Her thoughts drifted, and she pondered over the day with Shane.

He had paraded her all over the county that morning and afternoon. Had he simply wanted her company, or was he marking her off-limits to the rest of the males in town, telling them they were a couple? It didn't sound so bad . . . to belong to each other.

When he returned to the waiting room, he stopped behind her, his chest touching her back. She sensed his worry and slipped her hand into his, quietly offering the comfort of her touch. They stood there for several minutes without speaking.

"It's time to go." He kept her hand in his as they walked outside. "Jonathan looked lively, didn't he?" he asked once they were on their way.

"Yes, he did." She spoke as reassuringly as she could.

"It would kill Ty..." He stopped and took a long breath. "Shall we go out for dinner? It's almost six."

"It looks like rain. I think I'd rather go home."

"Yes, of course. You must be tired. I've kept you out all day." He laid a hand on the back of her neck and massaged gently.

The rain had started by the time they arrived at her house. They dashed up the sidewalk and onto the porch through a fine mist that shifted like veils in the air. She quickly unlocked the door, and they went inside to the warmth.

"I love this house. It seems to welcome me each time I return," she said when they paused to hang up their coats.

He pulled her to him. "I used to think that, but now I know the truth."

"What?" she demanded, smiling up at him.

"It's the person who lives here." He kissed her.

The kiss heated her blood and warmed her clear down to her toes. She strained upward, reaching for him. He lifted her and guided her legs around his waist, then linked his hands under her bottom.

"I've never made love standing up, have you?"

She shook her head.

He chuckled seductively. "Let's see, we've done it with me on top and with you on top." He whispered several scandalous suggestions in her ear until she was blushing and laughing helplessly.

"No one could do that," she said at one point.

"But it would be interesting to try." He lifted her until he could nibble at her breast.

"Dinner," she gasped. "We haven't had dinner."

He let her slide down him, but continued holding her while he walked down the hall to the kitchen. "Okay, dinner," he agreed. "My mom always insisted dessert was last, so I guess I'll wait."

She pushed out of his arms and went to the refrigerator, smoothing her hair and clothing into a semblance of order. She couldn't keep a smile from blooming on her face.

There were serious problems in the world—and in Riverton— but when she and Shane were alone like this, it was possible to leave the worries outside the door for a little while and just be happy together. That was what love was all about.

Oh, yes.

"Chinese?" she asked.

"What?"

She saw his mind wasn't on food. "Stir-fry veggies with popcorn shrimp?"

"That'll be fine." His gaze was hot, so hot, as he watched her, those hungry flames burning deep in his eyes. They licked at her soul and her self-control.

Tonight she'd tell him of her love. She knew now she'd always loved him . . . and that love was the reason she'd returned. Anne must have known. . . .

Oh, Anne, thank you!

The meal was easy and quick. After she put instant rice in the microwave oven, she dumped frozen vegetables, already sliced, into a skillet, added low-salt soy sauce, one tablespoon each of sesame-seed oil and slivered almonds, and finally tossed in a handful of popcorn shrimp. Last, she sprinkled in garlic powder and pepper, stirred until the mixture was steaming, then served it over the rice.

"Very impressive," he said when she handed him a plate.

With wine and rolls, the meal was plenty for them. They ate, their eyes often meeting across the table. Hers would skitter away as the emotions became too much.

He laughed once and chucked her under her chin. "You make life new and exciting," he murmured, which touched her deeply. "And making love a wonder...."

He let his voice trail off seductively. Eddies of lightning flashed along her skin, burning her alive and leaving her feeling gloriously, foolishly happy.

Tonight...

They ate, then cleaned the kitchen together. Together they drifted down the hall. She paused at the living-room door. He took her hand and guided her into the bedroom. Smiling, she went with him, completely willing.

"The treasure is in here," he murmured.

"Oh, I just remembered. I found some numbers. I think they're a combination. Did Anne ever mention a safe to you?"

"No, I don't think so."

Tina went past him into the sitting room. He followed. She picked up the note and read the numbers.

"Hmm," he said. "Perhaps a wall safe. Have you looked?"

She shook her head.

He glanced around the room, then went to a small picture on a side wall. Nothing. He checked another. Nothing. There was an unused fireplace in the room. A huge mirror held pride of place over it. He tugged at it, then ran his fingers along one edge.

"Eureka," he said.

The mirror swung open. Tina gasped.

"See if the numbers work."

She flicked the knob on the safe in a standard pattern, clockwise first, then back past the first number to the second, then clockwise again for the third. She grasped the handle and turned. The safe opened.

She peered inside and spied two large hinged boxes. They reminded her of jewelry boxes. She pulled one out and opened it.

"It is," she said, stunned. "It is jewelry."

The pieces were obviously heirloom quality. There were rings, pendants, earrings, bracelets—all set with the most exquisite rubies, diamonds, emeralds and other gems she couldn't identify.

"Well," Shane said in a coolly amused voice. "Looks like you hit pay dirt after all."

"What?" She frowned as she turned to stare at him. She saw the cynical amusement in his smile . . . and the suspicious assessment in his eyes. "What do you mean?" she asked levelly.

He touched a pair of earrings made of diamonds and rubies. "You might not have known about Anne's niece, but you had to have known about the jewels. They were family heirlooms. Anne wore them often. Ronda wondered what had happened to them."

His distrust hovered in the air between them. Tina thought of showing him the letter. It would have dispelled the doubts.

For the moment. Until the next time something questionable came up about her.

A shiver cascaded through her. This time she couldn't put on her words-can-never-hurt-me facade. This time she couldn't smile and pretend it didn't hurt.

"Get out," she said. "Damn you, get out of my house. I never want to see you again...ever!"

Long after the front door slammed behind him, she stood there, shaking and furious—with Anne for not explaining why she would leave a fortune in a wall safe, with him for his suspicions and doubts, and most of all with herself for believing that desire was love and love would make everything right.

Chapter Twelve

Jack Norton lifted a necklace. Its gems gleamed in the lights of the attorney's office. He whistled in admiration.

"They were in a wall safe in the sitting room, the room she used for an office," Tina explained, still not able to believe it. "Could she have forgotten about them? Was she senile at the end?"

Jack gave Tina a sharp glance, then put the necklace back in the hinged velvet box. "No. Anne Snyder had one of the best minds I've ever encountered, right up until the day she died."

"Then why did she leave a fortune in the house?" Tina asked.

"A gift to you, as her letter explained."

She frowned at the lawyer. He was no help at all.

"What are you going to do with them?" He stacked one box on top of the other and pushed them across his desk to her.

She looked at him in exasperation. "Do with them? Why, give them back, of course."

He listed his eyebrows in a quizzical manner. "To whom?"

"Her niece." Tina looked down at her clenched hands and forced herself to relax. She sat back in the comfortable chair and took a deep breath. "I'll give them to Ronda Macklin."

Jack shook his head. "The will stated you were to get the contents of the house."

"But...she didn't leave her niece anything."

He shrugged.

A tense silence filled the room. "Why?" Tina asked at last. "Why would she leave me so much and nothing for her blood kin?"

"You were her goddaughter. Besides, she left Jonathan a trust fund. Her will was very specific, I might add. My father wrote it. He didn't leave any loopholes, I can assure you." He grinned. "There was also a penalty if anyone tried to break the will."

"Anne fixed it so that her niece couldn't contest it?"

"That's right."

"But how? What did Ronda have to lose?" Tina stared at the lawyer, who in turn observed her closely. "There's a mystery here. I'm going to find out what it is."

"Are you?" He leaned forward. "Do you really want to know?"

Fear clutched her by the throat at his portentous words. "Yes." She nodded decisively. "I want to know."

"Anne said you were smart, inquisitive and courageous," he told her with a smile. He stood and went to a locked file.

When he started opening it, Tina's heart gave a gigantic leap. She wasn't sure she wanted to solve this mystery, after all.

"There's only one mystery in my life," she said slowly. "Does this concern my parentage?"

She couldn't bring herself to ask if Anne knew something about her father. All the older woman had ever admitted was that she'd promised Tina's grandmother—an "old and dear friend"—that she would keep an eye on her grandchild.

"I declared myself your godmother," Anne had explained.

Tina swallowed as Jack sorted through file folders and withdrew one. He removed a letter and brought it to Tina.

She took it with trepidation. The letter was sealed and addressed to her. She looked at Jack, puzzled.

"Anne said there was information in here that could hurt you," he said gently. "She said that if you ever asked, I was to give it to you, but if you didn't seem interested in knowing, then I was to destroy it after a certain length of time."

Tina nodded, but her mind was awhirl with confusion.

"Why don't you use my conference room?" he suggested. "You'll have privacy there. When you're ready to talk, we will."

She stood and went into the adjoining room. He closed the door behind her. She noted there were coffee and cups on an oak credenza, along with a box of tissues.

The crying room? she wondered, and determined not to cry no matter what information the letter contained. She lifted her chin, took a seat and slit open the letter.

My dearest Tina,
You have come seeking the truth, and I know you are

strong enough to take it. I hope you're also strong enough to forgive.

I know who your father was. My nephew fell in love with your mother the year he graduated from Harvard. Like you, she was lovely, intelligent and a joy. But he had a very deep sense of family responsibility.

Our family started the first bank in the valley. Associated with that is a certain pioneer pride. Sometimes such pride may cause a person to do foolish things.

The bank was in difficulties, you see. It needed an infusion of money to keep it going during a difficult period. My nephew was the key. He was engaged to a woman from a very wealthy family that had agreed to invest in the bank. Then he met your mother, fresh and young and full of life when his life was in a rut of duty and responsibility.

He made a terrible mistake, one he regretted his entire life, I can assure you. He chose duty over love. He chose the bank over your mother and you. Yes, he knew about you. Your mother left town, and my nephew spent his life trying to be a good husband and father to his wife and daughter. But it was a hard life for him. I pray you will understand and forgive.

You are my niece, my dearly beloved kin. You never received your due from your father. He tried to find you after his first heart attack, not to make amends—he knew he could never make up for what he had denied you—but because he'd never forgotten his first—his only—love and the child they'd conceived. He wanted to give you half of his wealth to insure that if you had dreams, you might be free to pursue them as he felt he could not himself all those years ago. But it was too late. He died before he could trace you.

I didn't learn all this until he was on his deathbed. After he died, I took up the search and found you. I want you to have what little in life I have accumulated, including the family jewels I inherited. You mustn't feel you have to give them up. They rightfully belong to you. My nephew's family received their share from his father, who was my brother.

May your days be filled with love and peace, my dearest niece. (It feels so wonderful to be able to say those words.) I hope you achieve all the wishes of your heart.

> With love,
> Aunt Anne

When Tina finished, she held the letter against her chest and stared out the windows at the mountains for long, long minutes, too stunned to think.

She read it again.

Her father was Anne's nephew, John Franklin Snyder. That meant Ronda was ... oh, God, her half sister!

And *she* was aunt to Jonathan, Shane's nephew!

She wanted to laugh or cry hysterically, but she'd learned long ago to control her emotions and show nothing to the world.

Later, she knew, it would catch up with her, when she was alone and no one could see. Then she'd tremble until the emotions were spent. She read the letter through once more, then folded it and put it in her purse. She stood and left the room.

Jack was on the telephone when she returned to his office. He finished and hung up. "Any questions?" he asked.

She shook her head. "It all becomes clear," she intoned with a faint smile. "Hard to believe, but clear."

"Anne was so afraid of hurting you."

"She didn't. I'm glad to know. I assume you know what was in the letter?"

"Not exactly, but I saw a picture of Anne's mother once. You look very much like her. I put two and two together. John Snyder was my father's friend." Jack glanced at her.

"He was my father."

"I thought so."

She sighed. "I don't know where to go from here. Home, I suppose, to think things over . . . figure out what I'll do."

"Some advice?" he asked. When she nodded, he said, "Don't do anything. Leave things the way they are."

"Keep the jewels and the house?"

"Yes. They're yours."

"I don't know." She rubbed her forehead as weariness descended. There were too many things to think about. "I'm not sure what's right. . . ."

"Well, one thing's for sure—Ronda doesn't lack for material possessions," he said dryly. "Let things stand, at least for now. Stay for the year as you'd planned. Anne deserves that much. She thought the world of you."

Tina fought the press of tears. "I know. I loved her, too." She rose. "Well, thanks for seeing me on such short notice. I didn't know who else to call about the situation."

"I'm sure Shane would advise you to do the same," the attorney told her with a smile.

It seemed everyone in Medford, as well as Riverton, knew of her involvement with Shane.

"By the way, I think you should get those jewel cases into a safety deposit box right away. Don't leave them at the house."

"I will. Thank you for your help." She folded the letter and put it in her purse along with the jewel cases.

He laid Anne's folder on his desk. "This can go into the archives as a closed file," he said with obvious satisfaction.

On the way home—after putting the jewels in the bank as advised—she thought over his words. It might be a closed file for him, but Anne's letter had opened up serious questions for her.

She'd been uncertain about her rights to keep the house when she'd learned there was a living relative. With the discovery of the jewels, she'd been positive she should return everything. But now...well, she just didn't know.

John Franklin Snyder. Bettina J. Snyder. A rush of disloyalty toward her adoptive father came over her. He was the father of her heart, but to know her real father—her biological father—and to know she had relatives...

Anne, her aunt! It was almost more than she could take in. However, she also had Ronda as a half sister. She grimaced.

Her half sister in Portland was wonderful. Tina had been present when Lucy was born and felt a special love for her little sister, who was now eighteen and a freshman in college.

A horn beeped impatiently behind her. She jumped, then realized the light had turned green. She went through the intersection and stopped at the second traffic light.

Her gaze went to the sheriff's office. To her consternation, Shane came out just then. He was talking to another officer. Maybe he wouldn't see her.

No such luck. He walked to his truck and glanced toward the vehicles at the light. His eyes met hers.

For an eternity, they gazed at each other. Neither smiled. The same horn sounded again. Tina looked at the light. She tromped on the pedal and drove off.

In another minute, she was home. She went into the sun room from the garage, hung up her coat in the hall, then went to the kitchen. She made coffee, more as a reflex than because she wanted any.

When she sat at the table, cup in hand, she watched the river for a long time, her mind carefully blank. She closed her eyes as a picture of Shane came to her. She wanted to go to him, thrust the letter under his nose and say, "See, I belong here as much as you, as much as anyone. I have a right to an inheritance."

"I have a right," she murmured aloud. But it was one she'd never tell anyone about, she realized. What would be the use? It would only stir up old gossip better left buried.

She wondered if she should call her mother and tell her. But her mother already knew the circumstances of her birth. It might hurt too much to have the past opened again.

Tina remembered how poor they had been, how hard her mother had struggled to learn shorthand at night school so she could move up to secretary from clerk-typist. Finally, she'd gotten a degree in business and had gone into personnel management.

She and her mother had been close during those years of struggle. Never had her mother made her feel she was an unwanted child. Then there had been her wonderful stepfather, who'd claimed her along with her mother.

Ronda had been brought up in wealth, but what had life been like for her in a loveless household?

Tina couldn't help but think she'd had the better deal. For now, she decided, she'd accept Anne's gifts for what they were—symbols of the deep affection and kindness the older woman had felt toward her. The rest of the past would stay closed, just like Jack Norton's file.

She sighed and went to call Dolly at the newspaper office, to tell her she would be well enough to work the next day.

"Well, you're looking better than you did Friday, in spite of your dip in the river," Dolly greeted her on Tuesday morning when she arrived at the office, ready for work.

Tina breathed in the scent of stale coffee, musty paper and dusty equipment. It felt like home. She thought she might talk to Dolly and Clint about a permanent job. Perhaps a part-time position while she worked on her book.

"It's good to be back," she said, patting at a yawn. "What's on the agenda today?"

"A day in the life of Sheriff Macklin," Dolly reminded her. "The follow-up to the rescue story, remember? Be sure and get an update on Jonathan. He's still in the hospital. Did he catch pneumonia or something?"

Tina realized the community at large didn't know of the boy's illness. Shane had told her, but no one else. "No. I'll check it out," she said. She wouldn't betray his confidence. If the family wanted the news known, they'd have to tell it.

One thing she knew how to be—a professional. No matter how she'd felt, she'd covered her news stories the best she could...no matter how she might react afterward. She'd do the same here.

Going to her desk, she settled at it and picked up the phone. "This is Tina Henderson at the *Daily News*. I'd like to speak to Sheriff Macklin, please."

"I'll transfer you to his office."

"Thank you." She clenched the telephone in a panicky grip. She hadn't expected him to be in.

"Macklin," he said in a throaty baritone growl.

"Shane, this is Tina. Dolly has asked me to do a story on you as sheriff. I'd like to follow you around this week—"

"I'm doing mostly paperwork. It isn't very exciting."

"Oh. Are you refusing then?"

There was a lengthy pause.

"Of course not," he said. "The sheriff's office is always glad to cooperate with the media. Tell me what you want to do." He had changed to the smooth politician.

"How about lunch? My treat. I'll interview you on background—how you got to be sheriff and all that."

"I was appointed by the county commission."

"I'll get it all down at lunch. Shall we meet at...." She didn't want to go to the tea shop or the ski lodge, where they might be joined by friends. "Land's End down by the river?"

"Fine. What time?"

"One-thirty, after the crowd thins out?"

"Good. I'll see you then." He hung up.

Tina replaced the receiver and huffed a sigh of relief. She could handle this, she assured her quaking heart. What did it matter what the Mighty Macklin thought of her? She was strong. She was tough. She could do it.

She wished she didn't have to.

He was late. Tina looked at her watch. If he stood her up... No, there he was, coming down the street. Like her, he'd opted to walk the short block to the posh river restaurant. It was so pleasant out, a person didn't need a coat. The spring day was warm with sunshine, the air clear after the recent rains.

As she'd expected, the dining room was filled mostly with tourists and businessmen on expense accounts. This should be on the paper's account, but she'd decided she would absorb the cost, since she'd chosen the most expensive place in town.

She watched him come closer, his long, confident stride covering the ground effortlessly. He wore a formidable frown.

A dart of pain arced through her. She ignored it. She wasn't going to let Shane's opinion bother her. Lifting her chin, she prepared to meet him...her lover, her enemy...with equanimity.

He spotted her by the window. When he entered the restaurant, he came immediately to the table. She smiled coolly when his eyes met hers. His narrowed slightly, then relaxed.

"Sorry, I got tied up at the last minute," he said.

"No problem."

He took the chair opposite her and laid his hat on the one next to him. She noticed he hadn't worn his gun or two-way radio. Only a pager was clipped to his belt.

They studied the menus, then ordered. When he chose coffee, she did the same, although she thought of ordering a bottle of wine to see if she couldn't get him to loosen up and talk freely.

Ha, that would be the day! Shane would say exactly what he wanted her to know—no more, no less.

"Fire away," he invited when they were alone. His tone was neutral, but she detected the underlying anger. He was convinced beyond a shadow of a doubt that she was a fortune hunter who'd managed the ultimate scam.

"What made you decide to seek the office of sheriff?" she asked, getting her notebook out. She put a tiny tape recorder on the table between them. "Do you mind the recorder?" she inquired automatically. No one ever did.

"Yes."

She was taken aback. She met his hard gaze with a glare of her own. He didn't blink. She gritted her teeth, shut the machine off and stuck it back in her purse. "The sheriff's office," she said to remind him of the question.

"I didn't seek it. They came to me."

"Who?" she asked.

"The county commission."

"What were their reasons?"

"They said I was known for my integrity."

"Are you?" She leveled a challenging glance at him. "Do you consider yourself an honorable person?"

His chest lifted in a slow, deliberate breath, as if he wanted her to know he was controlling his temper with an effort. "Yes."

"A lawman of few words," she mocked.

One way to break a difficult interview open was to make the person angry. Another was to ask an easy question that had nothing to do with the topic at hand. Barbara Walters's tactic was to ask, "What's your favorite color?" Tina liked to go for anger.

He raised one dark eyebrow. A sardonic smile appeared at the corners of his mouth. He didn't reply.

The stubbornness that had gotten her through more than one tough situation in life reared its head. She was going to get information from him or die trying.

"What's the hardest part of your job?"

His smile widened. "Dealing with the press."

She glanced at her notepad. "Touché," she said softly. She'd heard complaints about the press from those in the public eye on many other occasions.

He inclined his head, acknowledging her concession of a point to him in their ongoing battle.

All's fair in... She broke off the thought without completing it. There was no love between them.

She continued to look at him, captured by the deep blue of his eyes, the hard, sculptured planes of his face, the softer cast of his lips. She wished things could be different....

So did the rest of the world, she mocked.

His expression subtly altered, becoming introspective as he studied her. She saw the hunger deep inside him, a longing that matched hers, she realized. It came to her that he was a lonely man in spite of having family and friends all around him.

Everyone needed someone special, even the Mighty Macklin.

"Why haven't you married?" she asked.

He blinked. She'd taken him by surprise with that question. Score one for my side, she thought, briefly triumphant.

"No one ever asked me."

She bit back the anger. He was determined not to give her a damned thing she could use. "Why did you take the job of sheriff?"

He became serious. "I felt an obligation to the town. The former sheriff had been indicted for graft, along with malfeasance, misfeasance and nonfeasance of office. He'd given his friends jobs in high places. He was blackmailing one of the commissioners. The town needed cleaning up."

"Ah, yes," she murmured, "The Mighty Macklin to the rescue."

He stood. "I don't have time to take a lot of crap right now. Unlike my predecessor, I try to do the job. If you want to see what I do, then come to the office at seven in the morning and we'll start. You can spend the entire day learning the sheriff's duties.'' He picked up his hat and walked out.

Tina sat there, silently furious . . . with him and with herself. She had been baiting him, she admitted, but on a personal level rather than a professional one. She could do better.

She smiled grimly. When the story was finished, she'd tell him she'd been walked out on by heads of states. It didn't bother her at all. She dropped enough money on the table to pay for the two uneaten meals and headed back to the office. She'd do some digging in the old files.

Tina saw there was one other person in the tea shop when she stopped by late that evening, ravenous after having had no lunch or dinner. "Hello, Mrs. Tall,'' she said after speaking to Bess.

Mrs. Tall looked delighted to see her. "Come join me,'' she invited, moving her knitting from the other chair at her table.

Tina walked over slowly. She didn't want to hurt her nosy neighbor's feelings, but she didn't feel like talking.

"Isn't the sunshine nice? My hip bothers me in rainy weather, so it's good to see the sun.'' Mrs. Tall's chatter filled the silence while Tina took the chair.

"Yes,'' she agreed. She ordered a sandwich and helped herself to French roast coffee.

When the shop owner answered the telephone in an office off the main room, Mrs. Tall confided, "Bess is doing right well here. Surprised us all, she did. She just opened the tea shop without asking anyone how to do it. Her husband probably turned over in his grave more than once, watching her spend their life savings that way.''

"Would you like your coffee warmed?" Tina asked politely. When Mrs. Tall nodded, she refilled the cup and returned the pot to the counter. "Do you take anything in yours?"

"Just a little sugar," the woman said. "I've learned to do without cream since it's supposed to be bad for a person. My father had cream, *real* cream, with his coffee every day of his life, and he ate two eggs and sausage for breakfast every morning. Lived to be ninety-three, he did."

"Makes you wonder if we're living right, doesn't it?" Tina said in sympathy. She joined the older woman at the table, and laid several packages of sugar in the middle.

"It does," Mrs. Tall agreed. Her soft, fluffy white curls bounced up and down as she nodded. "That was a good piece you did on the school administration staff decorating their offices with money that was supposed to buy textbooks. Huh, ten thousand dollars for a bronze horse! Mighty fancy decorations for a small town, it seems to me. How did you happen to catch on to it?"

"I recognized the name of the artist and knew the prices he gets for his pieces," Tina explained patiently. "I'm working on a story about Shane Macklin now. 'A Day in the Life of the Sheriff' is what it'll be called. Tomorrow I'll spend the day with him."

"That sounds nice."

"Right now I'm gathering information about him. I saw in the old newspaper files that he was president of his class in high school and in college."

"Yes, I believe he was. He was good in sports, too. We used to never miss a game until my arthritis got to acting up. I can't sit on those hard benches anymore, don't you see?"

Tina nodded in sympathy. Bess brought her sandwich, then bustled off to put a batch of cinnamon rolls in the oven.

After a moment of silence, Mrs. Tall started talking again. She related incidents of Shane's past. He'd fallen in the river once when he was a kid, she said.

Like uncle, like nephew, Tina thought with a tenderness she didn't want to feel. She would use the information in her article.

"That stepmother." Mrs. Tall shook her head in disgust. She ate the rest of her pastry. "Well, there's no fool like an old fool, they say. I guess it proved true for Johnny Macklin. I thought he had better sense."

She related the gossip about the stepmother and her demands on the family. Tina felt slightly guilty for gathering old gossip on Shane, but defended it as being part of her job.

"I saw her myself, hanging onto Shane and trying to kiss him one day down by the pear-sorting shed. Poor boy, he couldn't get away fast enough." Mrs. Tall grinned, reminding Tina of a jolly old elf with a mischievous bent. "Not the way it was with you two that day over by the river...the summer you stayed with Anne," she added, as if Tina might have forgotten.

Tina hadn't realized anyone had seen them. Heat flowed up her neck to her ears. "Oh," she said faintly.

"I'm glad you're getting back together again. I don't think he ever forgot you. Although," Mrs. Tall added truthfully, "I did think there was a woman over in Medford who was going to get him to the altar, but they broke up two or three years ago."

"He's had no serious relationships since then?"

Mrs. Tall shook her head. "He hasn't time, what with taking care of the town and refereeing the fights between his brother and that Snyder girl from Medford. Uppity, she is, don't you know?''

"Umm," Tina said noncommittally.

"Isn't it terrible about the boy?''

"Jonathan?''

"That's right. Milly Smith over at the hospital says he's real sick. Leukemia, it is. The doctors don't give him more than six months.''

Tina gasped. "Are you sure?''

"Yes, some fancy doctor gave the word yesterday, according to Milly. She's head of the children's ward, so she would know.''

Tina set her coffee cup down. She'd been so awful to Shane at lunch. She remembered how grieved he'd been the other night at her house, when he'd told her they suspected the disease. She'd held him against her breast, wanting to comfort him.

She wanted to hold him now. She wanted to be held. Jonathan was her nephew, too, a bright, laughing child with the confidence of spirit that his uncle had. The world would be a lesser place if that spirit were snuffed out.

Mrs. Tall continued to talk, relating tales of other tragedies concerning children that had happened over the years in the area.

Tina hardly listened. She was restless. She needed to walk and think. Staring out the window, she felt pity for Shane and Ty, and for Ronda. For all their money, life hadn't been particularly happy for any of them, it seemed, and now this....

It was another thirty minutes before Mrs. Tall left. She was going to the store to stay with her husband while he closed up.

Tina paid for her meal, slipped into her jacket and headed for the river park. She walked along the trail, her thoughts and emotions in turmoil.

There was a terrible compulsion inside her, a desire to go to Shane and apologize. And, she admitted, she simply wanted to be there for him if he needed someone.

Upon nearing her place a bit later, she saw his truck on the drive to his house. The house itself was dark.

By contrast, her house—where a lamp came on automatically at dusk—looked bright and welcoming in the deepening twilight. She leapt over the fence and went to one of the boulders that lined the river. She sat there and watched the last golden light fade from the sunset.

When she glanced across the river, she started. A tall masculine figure stood on the other side.

His eyes met hers, and for a moment she saw the stark need in him. Then it was gone. He turned and walked up the knoll to his large, empty house.

She sat there until the night wind chilled her, forcing her to go inside. If he'd come to her, she wouldn't have refused to take him in.

Chapter Thirteen

To Tina's surprise, Shane wasn't in uniform when she arrived at his office promptly at seven. In fact, he looked very much the successful tycoon in a blue pin-striped suit.

"I'll be with you in a minute," he said. "There's coffee and bagels on the table. Help yourself."

He picked up the telephone, punched a button where a call was on hold and spoke for several minutes to the mayor of Medford about a patrol for an upcoming event at the county fairgrounds.

"I can put on five extra men if you can pick up the cost," he told the man.

Tina prepared a cup of coffee, then sat quietly as Shane and the mayor worked out the details of their problem. She noted that the lines on Shane's face seemed deeper. He looked tired.

She pulled her gaze away and hardened her heart. She wouldn't be swayed by pity. She, too, was worried about Jonathan.

Blowing gently at the steam rising from the coffee, she marveled again at her own kinship to the child. It wasn't until she'd learned about her father's family that she realized how much she'd missed that connection to her past.

She glanced at Shane, then away, as he concluded his conversation with the mayor. "Ready?" he asked, standing.

"Yes. For what?" She rose, notepad and pen in hand.

"Staff meeting. After that, the schedule for next month, then we go to the resort for the Chamber of Commerce luncheon."

"A busy day," she remarked wryly. She glanced down at her outfit. She wore black slacks with a gold silk blouse and a gold cardigan. Her black loafers were rather informal.

"You look okay," Shane assured her.

His gaze slid over her like a heat wave. She felt flushed and nervous all at once. "Good."

She sat through the meeting, faithfully jotting down the problems and noting Shane's efficient handling of details. What surprised her was his skill with the staff who reported to him.

He was patient, understanding and very clear in what he expected from each individual. He treated failure as a problem to be solved, not as a chance to place blame. She was impressed.

Later, when she sat through the review of the next month's schedule, she noted he made sure each request for specific time off by his deputies was honored.

While he was on the telephone, returning calls before they went to lunch, her mind drifted into its own musing.

She wondered why he gave everyone but her the benefit of the doubt. He'd been wonderfully understanding of his staff. Why did he regard her every move with suspicion?

"Ready for lunch?" he asked, putting the phone down.

She focused on the present. "Yes."

"Are you getting enough information?" He held the door open for her. They went out to the patrol truck.

"Yes." She settled in the seat while he closed the door and went around to his side. In a minute, they were on the road to the ski lodge. "You're very good with the people under your command," she commented.

"Am I?" He sounded skeptical.

"Yes."

They rode in silence for a while. It wasn't until they were pulling into the resort parking lot that he spoke again. "You're different today. Quieter."

He turned the engine off, removed the keys, then studied her for a long minute. She looked at him without speaking.

"I expected anger and that little mocking smile you wear when you're hurt, but instead you've become...quiet. It's unnerving." He shook his head, then gave a snort of laughter. "I've been trying to figure you out since you returned, but what man ever understands a woman?" he asked philosophically.

"Why would you want to?" she returned in the same vein. She opened the door and jumped to the ground.

They went into the lodge and upstairs to the private dining room. Her arm burned where he held her, guiding her through the throng of merchants to a table. They joined Whitney Deveraux and Rafe Barrett, plus several others. She recognized her neighbor.

"Well," Mr. Tall commented, "looks like there's a twosome here. Those wedding bells going to be ringing soon?"

"One never knows," Shane replied smoothly.

Tina gritted her teeth and smiled perfunctorily. She and her involvement with Shane would always be a subject of speculation in Riverton. Gossip could drag on for years in a small town. She knew that from personal experience.

She'd stay for a year—just to show people she couldn't be run off—then she'd sell out and leave, she decided. That would give her time to finish the book and seek a new direction.

With that decision made, she sat back and listened to the flow of conversation about her, feeling isolated, an island that nothing could touch. Life was better this way, she'd found.

Once, when Shane sent her a curious glance, she smiled in her old manner—defiant, a tad mocking, revealing nothing.

"Keeping up with the latest in medicine is the hardest," Dr. Payne admitted. "It's difficult for a regular physician to evaluate new procedures. Some are no better than the old methods. Some are worse. There are fads in medicine just as there are in everything else."

"I see." Tina brushed a strand of hair away from her face. She was tired. She'd been up almost all night while the harried doctor had handled two emergencies, one involving surgery at three that morning. He'd let her observe the operation.

Today was the last day she would follow the family doctor on his myriad rounds. She had to get the final copy ready tomorrow for the paper on Friday.

She had successfully written up the sheriff's "day" last week, and Dolly was ecstatic over the comments from local citizens on the story. This week Tina was doing the doctor, since the mayor was out of town at a convention.

Dr. Payne put the patient's folder on his desk and sat back with his fingers linked behind his head. He looked weary, as if his soul were burdened by the hurts of others.

"The Macklin case," he murmured.

Her heart speeded up. "How is Jonathan?"

He shook his head. "Not good. He's on chemotherapy. The specialist wants him transferred from the local hospital to Seattle while they try to find a bone-marrow donor."

"A donor?" she repeated. "What about his family? I thought there had to be a strong genetic link."

"That's where we looked first, but none of his immediate kin has the same blood factors."

"Was Shane tested?"

"Yes, but he's A negative. Jonathan is O negative—the universal donor—which means he can accept blood only from other O negatives." The doctor rubbed his eyes, then yawned.

Little bolts of current shot along her nerves as Tina digested the news. She was also O negative, having neither the A, B, nor the Rh factor in her blood. She and Jonathan were the same. There was a possibility, a strong possibility, that she and the child were compatible.

"I'm O negative," she said.

The doctor dropped his hands to the arms of the chair and looked at her with interest. "There's a slim chance," he mused aloud. "You might be a match. Would you volunteer to be a donor if you were?"

"Yes," she said without hesitation.

"It can be painful," he warned. "Any intrusive procedure, any time a person goes under anesthesia, has a potential—"

"It doesn't matter," she interrupted. "A child's life is at stake. Even if he weren't..." She stopped before she revealed her connection to Jonathan. "Children have hard lives in many ways," she said when Dr. Payne gave her a thoughtful scrutiny. "If I can help one child to a happier future, then I want to do it."

"We'll have to move fast," he told her. "Jonathan's illness is of a particularly virulent form. When could you be ready if you pass the test?"

"I'm ready now."

"All your... affairs in order?"

She smiled at the delicate phrasing. "Yes. I have no dependents, no responsibility to anyone but myself. I'll let my parents know, of course. My will is already made, if that's what you're asking," she assured him with a wry smile.

He smiled, too. "Well, let's set up a schedule."

Tina wrote her feature articles during the next few weeks. She helped get the paper out each Friday. The rest of the time she walked for miles, too restless to stay still while waiting for the results of the many tests being done on her and Jonathan.

Monday, a month after the tests began, they would know the results. Dr. Payne had called to tell her that last Friday.

The doctor had told her the procedure was simple for Jonathan. He would receive an injection of cells. The marrow cells would migrate to his own bone marrow, where they belonged, and start making good cells for Jonathan. If all went well, he would be cured.

Simple, she thought. As simple as life and death. She waited by the telephone Monday morning. When it rang, she jumped, almost afraid to pick it up, afraid she wasn't a match....

"Hello?"

"You're it," Dr. Payne said in an elated voice. "An almost perfect match. It couldn't be closer if you were his twin."

Relief rushed through her. "Thank God," she breathed. "When do we do the transplant?"

"Can you report in to the hospital Thursday?"

"Yes."

She made the arrangements with the doctor, then picked up her purse and headed downtown. She had to talk to Clint and Dolly. She had an idea she thought she could handle in the short week. Whitney Deveraux's bed-and-breakfast would make an interesting article.

After she explained her plan, the newspaper couple agreed wholeheartedly. "Here's another feature," Dolly exclaimed. "You donating bone marrow to Jonathan, saving him twice—"

"No, please, I'd rather the news not get out," Tina protested. "It's a private thing."

"Now, now. Don't be so modest. It isn't often we get one heroine, much less two... or rather, one who's a heroine twice." She cast an appealing eye at her husband. "Help me out."

"Dolly's right. This isn't news that you're going to be able to hide. All the wire services will pick it up. Give us an exclusive and that will save you from the rest." Clint grinned.

Tina knew when to give in gracefully. "Okay, but can't I wait until we know whether the transplant is a success?"

"The TV people will want it on the news tomorrow night. It might be better if you have an official spokesman to feed them details, such as the surgeon. Or Shane. He could handle it," Dolly suggested.

Shane paced the narrow corridor in front of the double swinging doors where he wasn't allowed to enter, not even as sheriff. Only doctors, nurses and hospital staff could go into the inner sanctum of the operating wing. Today was the big day.

They had found a donor for Jonathan. An anonymous donor.

It worried him that he didn't know who the person was. He'd wanted to run a thorough check to make sure the donor wasn't a drug addict or something like that.

Old Doc Payne had laughed and assured him that wasn't the case. The physician, who'd been doctor to both Shane and Ty since they'd been born, had screened the person, he'd told Shane. He'd said he knew her personally.

Her. A female. Shane wondered who it was and how the doctor had found her on such short notice. He had a gut feeling....

A nearby door opened and his sister-in-law came out into the hallway. "Let's get some coffee," she said irritably.

The strain of hospital life was showing on her, Shane noted. Ronda didn't handle crises well. In fact, she'd been a bitch, at times demanding more sympathy than she deserved. After all, it was the child who was ill.

They walked down the hall toward the coffee machine set up in a small room next to the nurses' station. The surgeon and Dr. Payne stood in the doorway of the room. They were talking to someone he couldn't see.

"We'll keep you overnight for observation. The marrow is taken from the hip. You'll be sore for a few days. You understand the risks?" the surgeon asked.

"Yes, Dr. Payne spelled them out," a familiar voice said.

"What the hell is going on?" Shane demanded.

The two doctors turned and looked at him in surprise. Beyond them, he saw a small, dark-haired woman.

"No," Ronda said, pushing past him. "Not her. I won't allow it." She grabbed Dr. Payne's sleeve and shook it furiously. "Is she the donor for Jonathan? She can't be! We have to find someone else, someone more suitable."

Shane put a hand on Ronda's shoulder. "Easy," he cautioned. He felt as stunned as his sister-in-law. However, he wasn't angry, only perplexed. "Is she the donor?" he asked.

Dr. Payne nodded. The surgeon looked annoyed.

"How?" Shane asked, unable to accept the fact that the woman who haunted his nights was again coming to his nephew's rescue. "I mean, is she really that close?"

"She was tested for six blood-antigen factors. She and Jonathan are compatible on all of them," Dr. Payne explained.

"No," Ronda insisted. "I don't believe you."

A page sounded. The surgeon walked off a few paces. "I'm due in surgery. I'd appreciate it if you'd solve this problem and let me know the outcome. I'll be ready for Miss Henderson right after lunch." He walked toward the swinging doors.

Ronda turned on the other woman. "You're not wanted here. No one wants you. My father didn't want you or your mother when you were born. No one wants you now. We'll find someone else."

Shane felt as if the blood had drained from his body. He knew the circumstances of Tina's birth. He'd checked her out eleven years ago when she'd had Ty in her clutches.

Now the truth hit him. Tina was the illegitimate daughter of John Franklin Snyder. Half sister to Ronda. Aunt to Jonathan.

Looking at her still form, her white face, he realized she knew. He thought of all the things he'd said to her, accused her of, and felt a sickening wrench of guilt inside.

When Ronda made a move toward Tina, he grabbed her arms, not sure of her intent. Tina turned whiter, if possible.

"I'll be in the waiting room when you're ready for me," she said quietly to the doctor as she walked past them, disappearing into a room down the corridor.

Shane noticed several nurses staring at them. This would be all over town before nightfall.

"The match is perfect," Dr. Payne said coldly. "Your son's life depends on Miss Henderson. I'd suggest you treat her with more respect. She doesn't have to do this. She volunteered."

He, too, walked off and left them. Shane pushed Ronda into the coffee room. "How long have you known Tina was your sister?" he asked, fury mounting in him.

"She isn't," Ronda cried. "The detective lied to my father, saying he'd found the long-lost child. I destroyed the report. No one could have known. But Aunt Anne found out—" She broke off her hysterical tirade and stared at him.

The hatred in Ronda's voice chilled Shane. Things fell into place. He realized Ronda had known of Tina, of her father's desire to find his lost daughter, and had destroyed the evidence. Anne had somehow found out and befriended the girl.

Tina ... Anne's niece. Ronda's half sister. Jonathan's aunt.

The perfect match for the child's needs. The perfect match for anyone....

"You got everything from your father," he said slowly. "She got nothing, because of you."

Ronda threw herself against his chest, her tears wetting his shirtfront. "I had to do it. I couldn't have her here. It would have been a disgrace. He wanted to give half ... *half!* ... of everything to a—a bastard."

Shane felt an acute dislike for her, this selfish, conniving woman who put her jealousy and hatred ahead of her son's life. He pushed her away. "Control yourself," he snapped. "You have a sick child. Try to think of him for once."

"Well, well," Ty said, "hasn't it been written—that you can fool all the people some of the time, and some of the people all the time, but..." He let the words trail off.

Shane met his brother's eyes. They exchanged a glance so full of understanding it nearly made him weep. He'd blamed Ty for a lot of things that might not have been his fault, at least not entirely. It took two to make a marriage.

He swallowed hard as he thought of his own failures. He'd blamed Tina for things that hadn't been her fault. He'd cast her in the same mold as his stepmother that summer they'd met, and, in spite of evidence to the contrary, he'd kept her there upon her return to the area, afraid to believe the prompting of his heart.

A hard pain hit him in the middle of his chest. He had to talk to her. "Excuse me," he said as he hurried down the hall.

She was gone.

He searched the corridors and the main lobby, but Tina wasn't in any of them. He returned to the nurses' station. He found out she had been admitted and was in her room. She'd requested that no visitors be permitted.

"It's important that she doesn't get upset, Shane," the head nurse told him sternly. "She has surgery at one."

"Will you let me know the moment she's back in her room?"

The woman softened toward him. "Of course."

He returned to the waiting room. The noon hour crept by. Ty joined him while Ronda sat with Jonathan. Another hour crept past. It was almost two o'clock when an alarm sounded over the hospital paging system.

He and Ty leapt to their feet and stood in the doorway while several doctors and nurses ran for the double doors and disappeared inside. The surgeon they'd met earlier came down the hall, stripping out of his white coat as he went. A nurse met him at the swinging doors and started filling him in. They, too, disappeared.

"It might not be her," Ty said, laying a hand in brief comfort on his brother's shoulder.

"Yeah," Shane agreed, but he knew something was wrong.

"You're in love with her," Ty continued after a moment.

There was nothing to say to this.

"She loves you, too. She did from the first. I asked her to elope, but she turned me down. After she saw you—"

"I hurt her," Shane said, doubling his fist and bringing it down quietly against the wall. "I doubted her. Every time there was a chance for us, I blew it by doubting her."

"So?" Ty challenged. "When has a Macklin ever let a little setback stop him? You'll just have to convince her that you've seen the light." His smile was tinged with bitterness and resignation. "I wish I had it so good. You know there's going to be a divorce, don't you?"

Shane nodded. "I'm sorry, Ty, for not understanding sooner. I thought, because Ronda came from money and had money of her own, that she...well, I was wrong."

Ty shrugged. "They're going to do the transfer later today if everything checks out okay. I think I'll go to lunch, then relieve Ronda with Jonathan."

After his brother left, Shane paced the hall from the waiting room to the swinging doors. He glared at the No Admittance sign.

He knew something was wrong with Tina, knew it gut deep, the way a bird knows to fly south, the way a whale knows to migrate to its mating grounds. When he saw the surgeon come out in wrinkled green surgical clothes, he rushed to him.

"How is she?"

"You are?" the man asked.

"Her fiancé," Shane replied in no-nonsense tones. A giggle behind him made him turn his head. Milly Smith, one of the nurses, had evidently heard his declaration. She gave him a big smile.

"She had a reaction to an injection, but she's resting now. She'll be fine."

"Can I see her?" He heard the desperation in his voice, but there was no help for it. He was desperate.

The doctor thought it over. "Yes. She'll be moved to Room 307 in about ten minutes."

Shane hurried to the room. He saw it was ready for her, the bed made, the water jug filled and her clothing neatly tucked into the closet. He hung his jacket and hat there. Then he waited.

* * *

Tina woke for the second time feeling like she'd been run over by a truck. No one had mentioned this terrible, aching soreness. Nausea swept over her, making her weak. She clamped a hand over her mouth and retched helplessly.

A basin appeared under her chin as if by magic. A soothing hand slipped behind her neck as she pushed upright.

She got a fleeting glimpse of Shane before she was wrenchingly sick. She fought illness and embarrassment in equal parts until the episode was over. Lying exhausted against the pillow, she flinched as a cool cloth was drawn over her face. She realized she wasn't in the recovery room this time, but in her room again.

"Rinse your mouth," a deep baritone suggested.

She sipped through a straw that touched her lips, then spat into the basin, which had been emptied.

"Would you like to try some soda?" Shane asked.

She shook her head. If she kept her eyes closed, maybe he would go away. Maybe this whole thing was a bad dream.

The cloth brushed gently over her face again, then stayed on her eyes. She lifted it so she could look at him.

As usual, he was incredibly handsome in gray flannel slacks and a red chamois shirt with a white T-shirt under it. His hair fell over his forehead in a thick, tawny wave.

"I told them I didn't want visitors," she said.

"I'm not a visitor," he murmured. He smoothed her hair back from her face.

She was weak and helpless, and she hated it. She was going to cry in front of him again, and she couldn't bear it.

"Go away," she said, not sounding firm at all.

"Never."

She put the damp cloth back over her eyes so she wouldn't have to look at him…so he wouldn't see her cry. She breathed slowly and deeply until she was in control once more.

"Well, look at the lovebirds," a cheery voice exclaimed. A nurse bustled into the room, placing vases of flowers on the table and windowsill. "Look at these red roses! Aren't they the prettiest things you ever saw?"

She stuck a thermometer in Tina's mouth and took her pulse. Then she raised the bed so that Tina was sitting almost upright. "I have some broth heating for you. It'll make your tummy feel better. Are you nauseated?"

"She threw up," Shane answered.

Tina tossed him a glare. "I'd like to be alone," she told the friendly nurse, who looked capable of evicting Shane from the room.

"Don't worry about how you look. Shane thinks you're beautiful," Milly teased. "Here, you should read your cards. People from all over are sending cards and flowers to you and Jonathan. Clint Adams was on TV news at noon telling all about it. Here's the card from the roses."

Tina smiled faintly. Clint had appointed himself official spokesman, it seemed. She opened the envelope Milly had thrust into her hand. There were only two lines, both in a bold hand she instinctively knew was Shane's.

"Roses are red … I'll tell you the rest in person," the note said.

She tried to make sense of it. There were lots of endings to the old Valentine verse. "Roses are red, violets are blue," she said aloud. "Get out of town, before I arrest you?"

It took an effort, but she managed to smile, a wry, mocking smile meant to throw Shane off balance.

The tiny indentation that she didn't dare call a dimple deepened in his cheek. He nodded.

"What's my crime?" she demanded, insouciant to the end.

"Breaking and entering," he said in the strangest voice she'd ever heard from him. "Stealing."

She had to look at him then. When she did, her breath nearly stopped. He looked so solemn, so serious...so sad?

"Jonathan?" she said in alarm.

"Shh, he's fine." He smoothed the hair from her temple. "Rest now. I'll see what I can find out."

She waited restlessly for his return. Milly brought the broth and stayed until Tina drank it down, then left.

Tina couldn't keep her gaze from straying to the tall vase of red roses. Red roses meant "I love you" in the language of flowers.

Her heart beat so hard it caused an ache in her chest. She pressed a hand to it and waited for Shane.

Ty came back with his older brother. He came to the bed and gathered her into his arms. He kissed her on the mouth, a closed-mouth kiss, but one full of tenderness and warmth.

"Ahem," Shane finally said.

Ty raised his head. "Don't get jealous," he advised his brother. "This is probably the last time I'll ever get to hold her. You know how I feel, don't you?" he asked Tina.

She nodded and patted his lean jaw with deep affection.

"Words aren't enough to thank you for my son's life," he continued. "The doctor is pretty sure it's going to work. Jonathan isn't showing one adverse sign, not even a rise in temperature. It's like the bone marrow came from himself. Or a close relative." He paused. "Are you his aunt?"

"I . . . yes."

She and Ty talked while Shane stood by and listened. Under Ty's prodding, she told them the whole story, or what she knew of it from Anne's letters. She faltered when it came to disclosing that Ronda had destroyed the first report from the detective. She didn't want to tell Ty that.

"It's okay," he assured her. "I know about it. Ronda and I had a little talk while you were in surgery. The truth will out, as someone once said. In fact, it's all over town. Everyone in the hospital heard the little scene in the hall."

"Everyone knows about me—who my father was?"

He nodded. "Don't let it bother you," he advised. "None of it was your fault."

Tina sighed. A curtain of darkness settled over her soul. "I'll leave," she said. "It'll all blow over—"

"No," Shane cut in. "You won't leave."

He gave her such a fierce look, she forgot to tell him that he couldn't tell her what to do and instead wondered why he seemed so miserable.

Shane stayed with her the rest of the day. Clint came in to take some pictures of her smiling bravely from her hospital bed. He loved the fact that she'd had a reaction and nearly died . . . but didn't.

"What a story!" he said. "Dolly is thrilled."

"I didn't nearly die," she contradicted.

"You could have," Shane told her in a low growl.

As if he blamed her for staging the reaction just to alarm everyone. She gave him a hard glance, then ignored him.

That night, when she fell asleep, he was still there.

The real problem started the next morning. When it came time for her to go home, Shane was there. So were several reporters and cameras. She resigned herself to being gracious.

Until they were in the car and on the way. When he passed the turnoff to her house, she protested. "I want to go home," she said.

"You are," he said calmly, ignoring her anger as he turned into his driveway. "Mrs. Perkins is back. She'll take care of you until you're feeling better."

"I hate you," she said, her voice quavery.

"I know." He stopped the car and looked at her quietly. "I know."

Chapter Fourteen

Mrs. Perkins was angry with her.

Tina watched the housekeeper move about the bedroom, dusting the furniture and picking up the newspapers on the floor.

The mess wasn't hers, but Shane's. He'd had breakfast with her each morning for the four days she'd been imprisoned there.

Mrs. Perkins disapproved of Tina's coolness to the mighty Macklin. She also thought Tina was an ingrate for wanting to go to her own home.

When the other woman left the room, Tina grimaced and forced herself out of bed. Her body still felt like it had been run over by a truck.

She showered and dried off, then wrapped the towel around her and returned to the bedroom—a guest room this time.

Memories of that other visit stuck in her mind. She vividly recalled sleeping next to Shane, her body tucked close to his. Worse, she remembered every caress they'd shared during that time.

Dropping the towel, she pulled on her clothing. It still hurt her hip when she bent forward or put any weight on her right leg.

A knock sounded on the door, then Shane entered. He looked her over in a quick survey that left her feeling warm and filled with yearning. "You seem to be better," he said.

She licked her lips nervously. Her hands trembled as she buttoned the blouse she'd worn to the hospital and hadn't had on since. "I am." She took her courage in her hands. "I'd like to go home...today...now."

Lifting her chin, she looked at him resolutely.

He nodded.

Her mouth dropped open in surprise.

A smile touched the corners of his mouth, then was gone. She watched him curiously. Since leaving the hospital, he'd been very quiet, sort of...sad. There seemed to be a mocking bitterness in him, directed at himself or life or something, but not at her.

She didn't understand him at all.

"Jonathan sent you a message," Shane told her. "He says he feels much better already and is glad that you're his aunt."

She nodded. "Dr. Payne called earlier. He says it looks good so far. I'm glad for Jonathan. I hope...do you think Ronda would let me see him once in a while?"

"Ty will. He's going for joint custody."

She couldn't think of anything else to say. "Well, I'm ready," she said brightly, picking up her purse and retrieving her jacket from the closet. She glanced at him.

"Shane, what's wrong?" she asked. "Is there something you're not telling me?"

His smile was definitely sardonic. "I don't think it's anything you'd want to hear."

She sat in one of the comfortable chairs by the window, placed her purse and coat on the table and invited, "Try me."

He walked toward her slowly. Fear crawled through her. She couldn't begin to imagine what awful thing he was going to tell her.

He dropped to the floor and sat at her feet, startling her into drawing back. "Don't worry. I'm not going to touch you."

She leaned toward him. "What's wrong?"

"Me. I'm what's wrong."

"I don't understand." She couldn't bear for him to look so sad and sort of lost... and vulnerable. Something terrible must have happened to shake his confidence this way.

"I met a girl once," he murmured, almost as if talking to himself. "She was brave...and honest...and good. Only I didn't know it at the time. I got her confused with another woman, who had made my life miserable for a couple of years."

"Your stepmother," Tina guessed.

He nodded. "I was wrong about you eleven years ago. I was wrong about you when you returned. I looked at you and saw someone after the main chance. I couldn't figure out how you'd wheedled the house and jewelry from a sharp old gal like Anne. I was wrong," he ended. He looked at her.

Something that had been closed and hard within her softened at his admission. "I... that's all right. It doesn't matter now."

"Doesn't it?"

She couldn't bear the brief glimpse of misery she saw in his eyes before he sighed and shut it away. "Not to me," she said quickly. "Actually, I had a happy life, taken as a whole. I think I was luckier than Ronda. My parents loved each other. And they loved me. They still do."

"Everyone who knows you comes to love you," he said softly.

"Not everyone."

"Oh, yes, everyone. Including me. Only I was too busy being the Mighty Macklin to see it. It made me furious when you called me that. I thought I had to protect my family from you and keep Ty's marriage from falling apart." He shook his head. "Stupid, that's what it was."

"Shane..." She didn't know what to say. She wasn't sure what he was telling her.

"So I deserve your hatred. But I wish you felt the flip side of that coin." He paused and looked at her, letting her see inside him, into his soul.

She explored the depths of him. She felt the powerful forces of his emotions as he let her delve further and further into his heart. She felt dizzy, faint....

Fleeting impressions of hope bubbled within her. Yet she was afraid. She'd been wrong about them too often in the past.

"Shane?" She didn't know what she was asking.

He took her hand. Suddenly, he was pressing against her knees, opening a space for him between her thighs. His mouth was close to hers. He pressed her hand to his chest. She could feel the rapid beating of his heart.

"Shane?"

"Yes," he said. "Yes, to whatever you're asking. If you want to know if I love you... I do. If you want to know if I want you to stay with me, to live with me, to marry me... I do."

Tina wasn't sure if she could believe her ears.

Shane closed his eyes briefly, then looked directly into er eyes. "Ty thinks you love me. If you do, then tell me. need the words. I can't take anything for granted where ou're concerned."

She was enchanted. Any moment now, the fairy would vave her magic wand and Tina would wake up, the fairy ale over....

He sighed and let go of her hand. "It's too late. I've detroyed anything we might have had—"

"No!" She caught his hand and, following his lead, ressed it against her heart. "No. I—I..."

The words were incredibly hard to say.

"I love you," he coaxed. "Say it. Please." He looked so esperate.

"I—I love you."

Before she could blink or smile or anything, she was aught up in a bear hug that nearly shut off her breath. Iext, kisses rained over her face like a summer storm. Fially, she was lifted and planted firmly in his lap while he ook her place in the chair.

"God, I never thought I'd hear those words from you," e whispered raggedly. He kissed her, passionately, pos-essively, as if he'd never let her go.

When he let her up for air, she stared at him.

"I love you," he told her. "I think I have for years. I iink Anne knew. She kept me informed of your where-bouts and let me read your letters. I wouldn't let myself elieve in your kindness and affection for an old lady. I old myself you were probably trying to get something out f her."

Tina gave him a reproving glance.

"I know. I was wrong, so wrong." He hugged her close, aking her wince. "I'm sorry, darling. I want you so

damned much, but I'll try to be patient until you're com
pletely well. When can we be married?''

''Well, I need to tell my folks. And have you mee
them,'' she said, still dazed. ''I...why can't we make lov
now?''

''Do you want to?'' His eyes blazed with desire.

''Oh, yes.''

He looked at her for a long minute, then lifted her int
his arms. She wrapped her arms around his neck. The ligh
of love shone in his eyes. His step was light and confi
dent. She smiled and snuggled against him.

This time...this time there would be no parting.

''Happy birthday to you, happy birthday to you...''

Tina smiled as the children sang the song to six-year-ol
Jonathan, who was taking a deep breath in preparation fo
blowing out his candles. He gave a huge *whoos*
and...made it.

Everyone cheered.

Across the lawn, her eyes met Ty's. He winked at he
and made motions in the air with his hands, then pointe
to her. She grinned and nodded.

He had outlined a pregnant female's figure, asking if sh
were expecting. She had replied in the affirmative. She'
seen Dr. Payne yesterday to have her suspicions con
firmed. Now her favorite brother-in-law—as he'd entitle
himself—laughed, clasped both hands in a victory signal
then loped off to bring Jonathan's surprise birthday pres
ent from the shed.

Shane wrapped an arm around Tina's waist and held he
close. She leaned her head against him. He'd been ecstati
at the news and had made the most incredibly tender lov
to her.

''Tired?'' he asked.

"A little."

"We'll take a nap after the surprise is over."

Ty returned while Mrs. Perkins was cutting the cake and dishing up the ice cream. He led a brown-and-white spotted pony by a halter.

"My horse!" Jonathan screeched at the top of his lungs.

He was doing well in spirit and body, she thought. There were no signs of the leukemia a year and a half after the injection of the marrow cells. He lived with Ty and attended the local school. His mother lived in New York and traveled extensively with her new, very rich husband. Jonathan spent vacations with her for short periods. It seemed his new stepfather had little patience with children. The little boy took the arrangements well.

"Look, Aunt Tina, look!" he called. "I told you! I told you I'd get a horse when I was six!"

"I remember. He's a beauty." She watched as Ty lifted his son into the saddle. Jonathan took the reins and clicked his tongue, not at all afraid. The Macklin confidence.

She laid a hand over her abdomen, thinking of the child she carried.

Shane's hand covered hers. "Life is good," he said, surprising her with the husky emotion in his voice. "Life is good."

"Yes," she said. "It is."

* * * * *

Dark secrets, dangerous desire...

Lovers DARK AND DANGEROUS

Three spine-tingling tales from the dark side of love.

This October, enter the world of shadowy romance as Silhouette presents the third in their annual tradition of thrilling love stories and chilling story lines. Written by three of Silhouette's top names:

LINDSAY McKENNA
LEE KARR
RACHEL LEE

Haunting a store near you this October.

MILLION DOLLAR SWEEPSTAKES (III)

No purchase necessary. To enter, follow the directions published. Method of entry may vary. For eligibility, entries must be received no later than March 31, 1996. No liability is assumed for printing errors, lost, late or misdirected entries. Odds of winning are determined by the number of eligible entries distributed and received. Prizewinners will be determined no later than June 30, 1996.

Sweepstakes open to residents of the U.S. (except Puerto Rico), Canada, Europe and Taiwan who are 18 years of age or older. All applicable laws and regulations apply. Sweepstakes offer void wherever prohibited by law. Values of all prizes are in U.S. currency. This sweepstakes is presented by Torstar Corp., its subsidiaries and affiliates, in conjunction with book, merchandise and/or product offerings. For a copy of the Official Rules send a self-addressed, stamped envelope (WA residents need not affix return postage) to: MILLION DOLLAR SWEEPSTAKES (III) Rules, P.O. Box 4573, Blair, NE 68009, USA.

EXTRA BONUS PRIZE DRAWING

No purchase necessary. The Extra Bonus Prize will be awarded in a random drawing to be conducted no later than 5/30/96 from among all entries received. To qualify, entries must be received by 3/31/96 and comply with published directions. Drawing open to residents of the U.S. (except Puerto Rico), Canada, Europe and Taiwan who are 18 years of age or older. All applicable laws and regulations apply; offer void wherever prohibited by law. Odds of winning are dependent upon number of eligibile entries received. Prize is valued in U.S. currency. The offer is presented by Torstar Corp., its subsidiaries and affiliates in conjunction with book, merchandise and/or product offering. For a copy of the Official Rules governing this sweepstakes, send a self-addressed, stamped envelope (WA residents need not affix return postage) to: Extra Bonus Prize Drawing Rules, P.O. Box 4590, Blair, NE 68009, USA.

SWP-S994

Jilted!

Left at the altar, but not for long.

Why are these six couples
who have sworn off love
suddenly hearing wedding bells?

Find out in these scintillating books
by your favorite authors,
coming this November!

#889 **THE ACCIDENTAL BRIDEGROOM**
by Ann Major
(Man of the Month)

#890 **TWO HEARTS, SLIGHTLY USED**
by Dixie Browning

#891 **THE BRIDE SAYS NO**
by Cait London

#892 **SORRY, THE BRIDE HAS ESCAPED**
by Raye Morgan

#893 **A GROOM FOR RED RIDING HOOD**
by Jennifer Greene

#894 **BRIDAL BLUES**
by Cathie Linz

Come join the festivities when six handsome
hunks finally walk down the aisle...

only from

SILHOUETTE®
Desire®

JILT

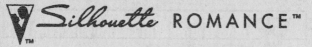

Silhouette ROMANCE™

First comes marriage.... Will love follow?
Find out this September when Silhouette Romance presents

Join six couples who marry for convenient reasons, and still find happily-ever-afters. Look for these wonderful books by some of your favorite authors:

#1030 *Timely Matrimony* by Kasey Michaels

#1031 *McCullough's Bride* by Anne Peters

#1032 *One of a Kind Marriage* by Cathie Linz

#1033 *Oh, Baby!* by Lauryn Chandler

#1034 *Temporary Groom* by Jayne Addison

#1035 *Wife in Name Only* by Carolyn Zane